Anne Gracie
Gallant Waif
"Superbly written. One [scene] had me in tears. As good a story about the healing of two wounded souls as I have ever read."
All About Romance

Gayle Wilson
Lady Sarah's Son
"...a moving tale of love overcoming great obstacles, of promises kept and trust restored."
Romantic Times

Nicola Cornick
The Rake's Bride
"...vivid detail...rollicking tug-of-war...subtle humour...."
Publishers Weekly

Anne Gracie was born in Australia but spent her youth on the move, living in Scotland, Malaysia, Greece and different parts of Australia before escaping her parents and settling down. Anne Gracie's debut novel, *Gallant Waif*, was a finalist in the Romance Writers of America's Best First Book competition. She has published two further novels for Mills & Boon Historical Romance™. Anne lives in Melbourne, in a small wooden house which she will one day renovate. You can contact Anne Gracie via her website at www.annegracie.com. She would love to hear from you.

Gayle Wilson is an award-winning author of both historical fiction and romantic suspense. She is a former teacher of English and world history. Gayle still lives in Alabama, where she was born, with her husband and an ever-growing menagerie of beloved pets. She has one son. Gayle loves to hear from her readers. Write to her at P.O. Box 3277 Hueytown, AL 35023, USA or via her website at http://suspense.net/gayle-wilson

Nicola Cornick became fascinated by history when she was a child and spent hours poring over historical novels and watching costume drama. She still does! She has worked in a variety of jobs, from serving refreshments on a steam train to arranging university graduation ceremonies. When she is not writing she enjoys walking in the English countryside, taking her husband, dog and even her cats with her. Nicola can be contacted by e-mail at ncornick@madasafish.com and via her website at www.nicolacornick.co.uk

Regency BRIDES

Anne Gracie
Gayle Wilson
Nicola Cornick

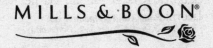

MILLS & BOON®

*First published in Great Britain 2002 by
Harlequin Mills & Boon Limited,
Eton House, 18-24 Paradise Road,
Richmond, Surrey, TW9 1SR*

REGENCY BRIDES © Harlequin Books S.A. 2002

The publisher acknowledges the copyright holders of the individual works as follows:

The Virtuous Widow © Anne Gracie 2002
My Darling Echo © Mona Gay Thomas 2000
The Rake's Bride © Nicola Cornick 2002

ISBN 0 263 83655 X

24-1002

*Printed and bound in Spain
by Litografia Rosés S.A., Barcelona*

CONTENTS

Author Note

Imagine you are an isolated young widow, with no money for the traditional Regency Christmas feasting, no friends to celebrate with you and no family except a small, beloved daughter. A daughter whose greatest wish is for a father.

Imagine now that you are a man coming into this home with no memories, no money and no name. A special encounter at a special time of year. A time for new beginnings, for the rebirth of hopes and dreams, for joy in the midst of bitter winter cold. Surely the most beautiful time of year for a wedding...

I hope you enjoy this story.

Look out for a further Regency tale from Anne Gracie, *Gallant Waif*, in a special collection, ***The Regency Rakes***, October 2002.

The Virtuous Widow
by
Anne Gracie

For my parents, Jack and Betty Dunn, who met and fell in love on a flight of stairs many years ago, and who have remained very much in love ever since.

Chapter One

Northumberland, England, December, 1816

"Is my wishing candle still burning, Mama?"

Ellie kissed her small daughter tenderly. "Yes, darling. It hasn't gone out. Now, stop your worrying and go to sleep. The candle is downstairs in the window where you put it."

"Shining out into the darkness so Papa will see it and know where we are."

Ellie hesitated. Her voice was husky as she replied, "Yes, my darling. Papa will know that we are here, safe and warm."

Amy snuggled down under the threadbare blankets and the faded patchwork quilt that covered them. "And in the morning he will be with us for breakfast."

A lump caught in Ellie's throat. "No, darling. Papa will not be there. You *know* that."

Amy frowned. "But tomorrow is my birthday and you said Papa would come."

Tears blurred her eyes as Ellie passed a gentle work-worn hand over her daughter's soft cheek. "No, darling, that was last year. And you know why Papa did not come then."

There was a long silence. "Because I didn't put a candle in the window last year?"

Ellie was horrified. "Oh, no! No, my darling, it had nothing to do with you, I promise you." She gathered the little girl into her arms and hugged her for a long moment, stroking the child's glossy curls, waiting until the lump had gone from her throat and she could speak again. "Darling, your papa died, that's why he never came home."

"Because he couldn't see the way, because I didn't put a candle out for him."

The misery in her daughter's voice pierced Ellie's heart to the core. "No, sweetheart, It wasn't the candle. Papa's death was nobody's fault." It wasn't true. Hart's death had been by his own hand, but gambling and suicide was too ugly a tale for a child.

"Now stop this at once," said Ellie as firmly as she could. "Tomorrow is your birthday and you will be a big girl of four. And do you know what? Because you've been such a good girl and such a help to Mama, there will be a lovely surprise waiting for you in the morning. But only if you go to sleep immediately."

"A surprise? What surprise?" asked the little girl eagerly.

"It wouldn't be a surprise if I told you. Now go to sleep." She began to hum a lullaby, to soothe the anxieties from her daughter's mind.

"I know what the surprise is," murmured her daughter sleepily. "Papa will be here for breakfast."

Ellie sighed. "No, Amy, he won't. Papa has been dead for more than a year. You know he is, so why do you persist with this?"

"It's a special candle, Mama. The lady said so. A wishing candle. It will bring Papa, you'll see." She smiled and snuggled down under the bedclothes, curling up like a little cat.

Ellie frowned. That wretched gypsy woman with her false tales! Unbeknown to her mother, Amy had traded half a dozen eggs and some milk for a thick red candle. A wishing candle, indeed! More like a rather expensive Christmas candle. And a hurtful candle, if the old woman had put the notion in Amy's head that it could bring her father back.

Amy's few memories of her father were idealised fairy tales. The truth was too painful for a little girl. Hart had never been an attentive father or husband. Sir Hartley Carmichael, Baronet, had wanted a son— an heir. A small, spirited girl with tumbled dark curls and bright blue eyes held no interest for him. Was quite useless, in fact, and he'd said so on many occasions—in front of Amy herself.

Ellie looked at her sleeping daughter and her heart

filled. There was nothing more precious in the world than this child of hers. She picked up the candle and went into her own room. Shivering in the bitter December cold, she hurriedly slipped into her thick, flannel nightgown and climbed into bed.

She was about to blow the candle out when she recalled the one burning in the downstairs window. Candles were expensive. She couldn't afford to let one burn down to a stub for no purpose. No practical purpose, that is. She recalled her daughter's face, freshly washed for bed and luminous with hope as she placed the candle in the window. A lump filled Ellie's throat. She got out of bed, slipped her shoes back on and flung a shawl around her for warmth. She could not afford the happy dreams that came so easily to children.

She was halfway down the steep, narrow staircase, when suddenly a loud thump rattled the door of her cottage. She froze and waited. Bitter cold crept around her, insidious drafts of freezing air nibbling at her bare legs. She scarcely noticed.

The thump came again. It sounded like a fist hitting the door. Ellie did not move. She hardly dared to breathe. There was a swirl of air behind her and a small, frightened voice behind her whispered, "Is it the squire?"

"No, darling, it isn't. Go back to bed," said Ellie in a low, calm voice.

A small warm paw slipped into her hand, gripping it tightly. "Your hand's cold, Mama." The thump came again, twice this time. Ellie felt her daughter jump in fright.

"It *is* the squire," Amy whispered.

"No, it's not," Ellie said firmly. "He always shouts when I don't open the door to him. Doesn't he?" She felt her daughter's tight grip on her hand relax slightly as the truth of her words sank in. "Wait here, darling, and I shall see who it is."

She crept down another six steps, to where she could see the front door, the sturdy wooden bar she'd put across it looking reassuringly strong. Ellie had soon learned that the cottage keys counted for little against her landlord.

Light flickered and danced intermittently across the dark room from Amy's wishing candle.

Someone banged again, not as loud as before. A deep voice called, "Help!"

"It must be Papa," squeaked Amy suddenly, from close behind her. "He's seen my candle and he's come at last." She slipped past Ellie and raced towards the door.

"No, Amy. Wait!" Ellie followed her, almost falling down the stairs in her rush to prevent her daughter from letting in who-knew-what.

"But it's Papa, Mama. It's Papa," said Amy, trying to lift the heavy bar.

"Hush!" Ellie snatched her daughter to her. "It isn't Papa, Amy. Papa is dead."

Their cottage was isolated, situated a little off the main road and hidden behind a birch spinney. But further along the road was the Angel, an isolated inn which attracted the most disreputable customers. Ellie had twice been followed home... With that den of villains down the road, there was no way she would open her door to a stranger at night.

The deep voice called again, "Help." It sounded weaker this time. He hit the door a couple of times, almost half-heartedly. Or as if he was running out of strength, Ellie thought suddenly. She bit her lip, holding her daughter against her. It might be a ruse to trick her.

"Who is it?" she called. There was no reply, just the sound of something falling. Then silence. Ellie waited for a moment, hopping from one foot to the other in indecision. Then she made up her mind. "Stand on the stairs, darling," she ordered Amy. "If it's a bad man, run to your room and put the bar across your door, as I showed you—understand?"

Amy nodded, her heart-shaped little face pale and frightened. Ellie picked up the heaviest pan she had. She turned the key and lifted the bar. Raising the pan, she took a deep breath and flung open the door.

A flurry of sleet blew in, causing her to shiver. She peered out into the darkness. Nobody. Not a sound. Still holding the pan high, she took a tentative step forward to look properly and encountered something large and cold huddled on her doorstep.

It was a man, lying very, very still. She bent and touched his face. Cold. Insensible. Her fingers touched something wet, warm and sticky. Blood. He was bleeding from the head. There was life still in him, but not if she left him outside in the freezing weather for much longer. Dropping the pan she grabbed him by the shoulders and tugged. He was very heavy.

"Is he dead, Mama?" Amy had crept back down the stairs.

"No, darling, but he's hurt. We need to bring him inside to get warm. Run and fetch the rug from in front of the fire, there's a good girl."

Amy scampered off and returned in a moment dragging the square, threadbare cloth. Ellie placed it as close as she could to the man's prone body, then pushed and pushed until finally he rolled over onto the rug. Then she pulled with all her might. Amy pulled too. Inch by inch the man slid into the cottage. Ellie subsided on the floor, gasping.

She barred the door again and lit a lantern. Their unexpected guest wore no jacket or coat—only a shirt and breeches. And no shoes, just a pair of filthy, muddied stockings. And yet it was December, and outside there was sleet and ice.

Blood flowed copiously from a nasty gash at the back of his head. Hit from behind; a cowardly blow. He'd been stripped of his belongings, even his coat and boots, and left to die in the bitter cold. Ellie knew what it felt like to lose everything. She laid a hand on his chest, suddenly possessive. She could not help his being robbed, but she would *not* let him die.

His shirt was sopping wet and freezing to the touch,

the flesh beneath it ominously cold. Quickly she made a pad of clean cloth and bound it around his forehead as tight as she dared to staunch the blood.

"We'll have to get these wet clothes off him," she told Amy. "Else he'll catch his death of cold. Can you bring me some more towels from the cupboard under the stairs?" The child ran off as Ellie stripped the man's shirt, undershirt and wet, filthy stockings off.

He had been severely beaten. His flesh was abraded and beginning to show bruises. There were several livid, dark red, curved marks as if he'd been kicked and one clear imprint of a boot heel on his right shoulder. She felt his ribs carefully and gave a prayer of thanks that they seemed to have been spared. His head injury was the worst, she thought. He would live, she thought, as long as he didn't catch a chill and sicken of the cold.

Carefully, she rubbed a rough-textured towel over the broad planes of his chest and stomach and down his arms. Her mouth dried. She had only ever seen one man's naked torso before. But this man was not like her husband.

Hart's chest had been narrow and bony, white and hairless, his stomach soft, his arms pale, smooth and elegant. This man's chest was broad and hard, but not bony. Thick bands of muscles lay relaxed now in his unconscious state, but firm and solid, nevertheless. A light dusting of soft, curly dark hair formed a wedge over the golden skin, arrowing into a faint line of hair trailing down his stomach and disappearing into his breeches. She tried not to notice it as she scrubbed him with the towel, forcing warmth and life back into his chilled skin.

He was surprisingly clean, she thought. His flesh did not have that sour odour she associated with Hart's flesh. This man smelt of nothing—perhaps a faint smell of soap, and of fresh sweat and…was it leather? Horses? Whatever it was, Ellie decided, it was no hardship to be so close to him.

Despite his muscles, he was thin. She could count each of his ribs. And his stomach above the waistband of his breeches was flat, even slightly concave. His skin carried numerous small scars, not recent injuries. A man who had spent his life fighting, perhaps. She glanced at his hands. They were not the soft white hands of a gentleman. They were strong and brown and battered, the knuckles skinned and swollen. He was probably a farm labourer or something like that. That would explain his muscles and his thinness. He was not a rich man, that was certain. His clothes, though once of good quality, were old and well worn. The shirt had been inexpertly patched a number of times. As had his breeches.

His breeches. They clung cold and sodden to his form. They would have to come off. She swallowed as she reached for his waistband, then hesitated, as her daughter arrived with a bundle of towels. ''Good girl. Now run upstairs, my love, and fetch me a blanket from my bed and also the warm brick that's in it.''

Amy trotted off and Ellie took a deep breath. She was not unacquainted with the male form, she told herself firmly, as she unbuttoned the stranger's drenched breeches. She had been married. But this man was not her husband. He was much bigger, for a start.

She grasped the breeches and tugged them over his hips, rolling him from side to side as she worked them downwards. The heavy wet fabric clung stubbornly to his chilled flesh. Finally she had them off him. Panting, she sat back on her heels. He was naked. She stared, unable to look away.

''Is Papa all right?'' Amy came down the stairs, carefully lugging a bundled-up blanket.

Hastily, Ellie tucked a towel over the stranger's groin. ''He's *not* your papa.''

Amy gave her an odd look, then raced back upstairs. Ellie dragged the man as close as she could to the fire. When Amy returned with the brick, Ellie placed it in the hearth. She heated some soup, then strained it through a piece of muslin into the teapot.

''Soup in the *teapot?*'' Amy giggled at something so silly.

Ellie smiled, relieved that her daughter found something to laugh at. ''This is going to take some time, so it's back to bed for you, young lady.''

''Oh, but, Mama—''

''The man will still be here in the morning,'' Ellie

said firmly. "We already have one sick person here—I don't want you to catch a chill as well. So, miss, off to bed at once." She kissed her daughter and pushed her gently towards the door. Reluctantly, Amy went. Ellie hid a smile. Her curious little puss would stay up all night if she could.

She cleaned his head wound thoroughly, then laid a pad of hot, steaming herbs on it, to draw out any remaining impurities. He groaned and tried to move his head.

"Hush." She smoothed a hand over his skin, keeping the hot poultice steady with her hand. "It stings a little, but it's doing you good." He subsided, but Ellie felt tension in his body as if part of him was awake. Defensive. She soothed him gently, murmuring, "Rest quietly. Nobody will harm you here." Slowly his big body relaxed.

His eyelids flickered, then his eyes slowly opened. Ellie bent over him earnestly, still supporting his head in her hand. "How do you feel?" she asked softly.

The stranger said nothing, just stared at her out of blue, blue eyes.

How did he feel? Like his head was about to split open. He blinked at her, trying to focus on her face. Pretty face, he thought vaguely. Soft, smooth skin. His eyes followed the fall of shining dark hair from her smooth creamy brow, down to a tumble of soft curls around her shoulders.

Who was she? And where the devil were they? With an effort he glanced away from her for a second, taking in the room. Small…a cottage? Had he been billeted in some nearby cottage? They did that sometimes with the wounded. Left them to the dubious care of some peasant woman while the fighting moved on… He frowned, trying to recall. Had they won the battle or lost it? Or was it still raging? He listened. No, there was no sound of guns.

His gaze returned to the woman. The cottage told him nothing. But the woman… He couldn't take his eyes off her. Soft, worried eyes. Soft worried mouth. Pretty mouth. Worried? Or frightened? He had no idea.

He tried to move and heard himself groan. His head was killing him. Like someone had taken an axe to it. How had that happened? Was he bleeding? He tried to feel his head. And found he could not move. Trapped, dammit! He could not move his hands and legs. Someone had tied him up. He'd been taken prisoner. He began to struggle.

"Hush," the woman said soothingly. She began to loosen the bindings around his arms as she spoke. "It's all right. I just wrapped you tight in my blanket because you were all wet and I feared you would take a chill."

He blinked up at her. His head throbbed unbearably. The rest of his body ached as well, but his head was the worst. Dizziness and confusion washed over him.

And then it hit him. She had spoken in English. Not Portuguese, or Spanish or French. English—not foreigners' English, either—proper English. His sort of English. So where were they? He tried to speak, to ask her. He felt his mouth move, but it was as if someone had cut out his tongue. Or severed it from his brain. He felt his lips moving, but no words came out. He fixed his gaze on her face and tried to muster the energy to ask her the question. Questions. They crowded his splitting head.

The woman sat down on the floor beside him again and smoothed his hair gently back from his forehead. It felt so good, he closed his eyes for a moment to savour it.

"I don't have any brandy," she said apologetically. "All I have is hot soup. Now, drink a little. It will give you strength and warmth."

Warmth? Did he need warmth? He realised that he was shivering. She lifted his head up and though he knew she was being as gentle as she could be, his brain thundered and swirled and he felt consciousness slipping from him. But then she tucked him against her shoulder and held him there, still and secure and somehow…cared for. He gripped her thigh and clung stubbornly to his senses and gradually felt the black swirling subside.

He recoiled as something clunked against his teeth. "It is only the teapot," she murmured in his ear. "It contains warm broth. Now, drink. It will help."

He wanted to tell her that he was a man, that he would drink it himself, out of a cup, not a teapot, like some helpless infant, but the words would not come.

She tipped the teapot up and he had to swallow or have it spill down him. He swallowed. It was good broth. Warm. Tasty. It warmed his insides. And she felt so soft and good, her breasts against him, her arm around him, holding him upright against her. Weakly, he closed his eyes and allowed himself to be fed like a baby.

He drank the broth slowly, in small mouthfuls. The woman's breath was warm against his face. She seemed to know how much to give him and when he needed to wait between mouthfuls. He could smell her hair. He wanted to turn his head and bury his face in it. He drank the broth instead. The fire crackled in the grate. Outside the wind whistled and howled, rattling at the doors and windows. It was chilly inside the cottage, and the floor underneath him was hard and cold, but oddly, he felt warm and cosy and at peace.

He finished the broth and half-sat, half-lay against her, allowing her to wipe his mouth, like a child. They sat for a moment or two, in companionable silence, with the wind swirling outside the cottage and the questions swirling inside his head.

Beneath the blanket he was stark naked, he suddenly realised. He stared at her, another question on his unmoving lips. Who was she, to strip him of his clothes?

As if she knew what he wanted, she murmured gently in his ear, "You arrived at my cottage almost an hour ago. I don't know what happened to you before that. You were half-dressed and sopping wet. Frozen from the sleet and the rain. I don't know how long you'd been outside, or how you managed to find the cottage, but you collapsed at the door—"

"Is Papa awake now?" a little voice said, like the piping of a bird.

Papa? He opened his eyes and saw a vivid little face staring at him with bright, inquisitive eyes. A child. A little girl.

"Go back to bed this instant, Amy," said the woman sharply.

He winced and jerked his head and the blackness swirled again. When he reopened his eyes, he wasn't sure how much time had passed. He was no longer leaning against the woman's shoulder and the little face of the child was gone. And he was shivering. Hard.

The woman bent over him, her eyes dark with worry. "I'm sorry," she murmured. "I didn't mean to bump you like that. My daughter gave me a fright, that was all. Are you all right?" A faint frown crumpled the smoothness of her brow. "The bleeding has stopped and I have bandaged your head."

He barely took in her words. All he could think of was that his head hurt like the devil and she was worried. He lifted a hand and stroked down her cheek slowly with the back of his fingers. It was like touching fine, cool, soft satin.

She sighed. And then she pulled back. "I'm afraid you will freeze if I leave you down here on the stone floor. Even with the fire going all night—and I don't have the fuel for that—the stone floor will draw all the warmth from your body.''

He could only stare at her and try to control the shivering.

''The only place to keep you warm is in bed.'' She blushed and did not meet his eye. ''There…there is only one bed.''

He frowned, trying to absorb what she was telling him, but unable to understand why it would distress her. He still couldn't recall who she was—the blow had knocked all sense from his head—but the child had called him 'Papa.' He tried to think, but the effort only made the pain worse.

''It is upstairs. The bed. I cannot carry you up there.''

His confusion cleared. She was worried about his ability to get up the stairs. He nodded and gritted his teeth over the subsequent waves of swirling blackness. He could do that much for her. He would climb her stairs. He did not like to see her worried. He held out his hand to her and braced himself to stand. He wished he could remember her name.

Ellie took his arm and heaved until he was upright—shaky and looking appallingly pale, but standing and still conscious. She tucked the blanket tight under his armpits and knotted it over his shoulder, like a toga. She hoped it was warm enough. His feet and his long brawny calves were bare and probably cold, but it was better than having him trip. Or naked.

She wedged her shoulder under his armpit and steered him towards the stairs. The first step was in a narrow doorway with a very low lintel, for the cottage had not been designed for such tall men as he.

"Bend your head," she told him. Obediently, he bent, but lost his balance and lurched forward. Ellie clung to him, pulling him back against the doorway, to keep him upright. Fearful that he would straighten and hit his injury on the low beam, she cupped one hand protectively around his head and drew it down against her own forehead for safety. He leaned on her, half-unconscious, breathing heavily, one arm around her, one hand clutching the wooden stair-rail, his face against hers. White lines of pain bracketed his mouth.

There were only fourteen steep and narrow stairs, but it took a superhuman effort to get him up them. He seemed barely conscious, except for the grim frown of concentration on his face and the slow determined putting of one foot in front of the other. He gripped the stair-rail with fists of stone and hauled himself up, pausing at each step achieved, reeling with faintness. Ellie held him tightly, supporting him with all the strength she could muster. He was a big man; if he collapsed, she could not stop him falling. And if he fell, he might never regain consciousness.

There was little conversation between them, only the grim, silent battle. One painful step at a time. From time to time, she would murmur encouragement—"we are past the halfway mark," "only four steps left"—but she had no idea if he understood. The only sound he made was a grunt of exertion, or the raw harsh panting of a man in pain, at the end of his tether. He hung on to consciousness by willpower alone. She had never seen such stubbornness, or such courage.

At last they reached the top of the stairs. Straight ahead of them was the tiny room where Amy's bed was tucked—no more than a narrow cupboard it was, really, but cosy enough and warm for her daughter. On the right was Ellie's bedroom.

"Bend your head again." This time she was ready when he lurched forward and stumbled into her room. She managed to steer him to the small curtained-off alcove where her bed stood. He sprawled across it with a groan and lay there, unmoving. She collapsed beside him, gasping for breath, weak with relief. Her breath clouded visibly in the icy air. She had to get him covered, while he was still warm from the exertion of the climb.

She had no nightshirt for him to wear. He was too broad in the shoulders and chest for any of her clothing and she had long ago sold anything of Hart's that remained. The few thin blankets she had did not look warm enough to keep an unconscious man from catching a chill. The thickest, warmest coverings were on Amy's bed.

She wrapped him in a sheet and tugged the covers over him. She took all the clothes she possessed and spread them out over the bed—dresses, shawls, a faded pelisse, a threadbare cloak—any layer of cloth which would help keep out the cold. She fetched the hot brick and set it at his feet. Then she stood back. She could do no more. She was shivering herself, she realised. And her feet were frozen. She normally got into bed to keep warm.

But tonight there was a strange man in her bed.

Amy's bed was only a narrow bench, as long and as wide as a child. No room for Ellie there. Downstairs, the fire was dying. Ellie sat on the wooden stool, drew her knees against her chest and wrapped her shawl even tighter around herself in an illusion of warmth. She had used up all her extra clothes to make the bed warm for the stranger. She stared across at him. He lay there, warm, relaxed, comfortable while she hugged herself against the cold. He had collapsed. He was insensible. He wouldn't know she was there.

She crept to the edge of the bed on frozen toes and looked at him. He lay on his back, his breathing deep and regular. In the frail light of the candle the bandage glimmered white against his tanned skin and the thick, dark, tousled hair. There was a shadow of dark bristle on his lean, angular jaw. He seemed so big and dark and menacing in her bed. He took up much more of it than she did. And what if he woke?

She couldn't do this. She crept back to her stool. The chill settled. Drafts whispered up at her, insinuating themselves against her skin, nibbling at her like rats. Her chattering teeth echoed a crazed counterpoint to his deep, even breaths.

She had no choice. It was her bed, after all. It

would do nobody any good if she froze to death out here. What mattered propriety when it came to her very health? She ran downstairs again and fetched her frying pan. She took a deep breath, wrapped the sheet more tightly around herself and stepped into the sleeping alcove, frying pan in hand. Feeling as if she were burning her bridges, she closed the curtains which kept the cold drafts out. In the tiny, enclosed space, she felt even more alone with the stranger than ever…

Outside, pellets of hail beat against her window.

Carefully, stealthily, Ellie tucked the pan under the edge of the mattress, comfortingly to hand, then crept under the bedclothes. He wasn't just in her bed, he took up most of the space. And almost all of the bedclothes. Without warning, she found herself lying hard against him, full length, his big body touching hers from shoulder to ankle. Threadbare sheets were all that lay between them. Ellie went rigid with anxiety. She poked him. "Hsst! Are you awake?" Her hand hovered, ready to snatch up the pan.

He didn't move; he just lay there, breathing slowly and evenly as he had for the last fifteen minutes. She tried to move away from him, but his weight had caused the mattress to sag. Her body could not help but roll downhill towards him. Against him. It was a most unsettling sensation. She wriggled a little, trying to reduce the contact between them. Her frozen toes slipped from their sheet and touched his long legs…and she sighed with pleasure. He was warm, like a furnace.

Fever? She put out a hand in the darkness and felt his forehead. It seemed cool enough. But that could be the effect of the cold night air. She slipped a hand under the bedclothes and felt his chest. The skin was warm and dry, the muscles beneath it firm. He didn't feel feverish at all. He felt…nice.

She snatched her hand away and tucked herself back in her own cocoon of bedclothes. She closed her eyes firmly, trying to shut out the awareness of the man in her bed. Of course, she would not get a wink of sleep—she was braced against the possibility that he was awake, shamming unconsciousness, but at least she would be warm.

She had never actually slept with a man before. Hart had not cared to stay with her longer than necessary. After coitus he had immediately left her, and once she had quickened with child he had never returned to her bed. So the very sensation of having a man sleep beside her was most…unsettling.

She could smell him, smell the very masculine smell of his body, the scent of the herbal poultice she had made for his injury. His big, hard body seemed to fill the bed. It lifted the bedclothes so that there was a gap between him and her smaller frame, a gap for cold drafts to creep into. She wriggled closer, to close the gap a little, still lying rigid, apart from him, straining against the dip in the mattress.

Slowly, insidiously, his body heat warmed her and

gradually her defences relaxed. The combination of his reassuring stillness and the regularity of his deep breathing eased her anxious mind until finally she slept.

And as she slept, her body curled against his, closing the gap seamlessly. Her cold toes slipped from their cool linen cocoon and rested on the hard warmth of his long bare calves. And her hand crept out and snuggled itself between the layers that wrapped him, until it was resting on that warm, firm, broad masculine chest...

Weak winter sun woke her, lighting the small, spare room, setting a golden glow through the faded curtains that covered her sleeping alcove. Feeling cosy, relaxed and contented, Ellie yawned sleepily and stretched...and found herself snuggled hard against a man's ribs, her feet curled around his leg, her arm across his prone body.

She shot out of bed like a stone from a catapult and stood there shivering in the sudden cold, staring at the stranger, blinking as it all came back to her. She snatched some of her clothes and hurried downstairs to get the fire going again.

The man slept on through the day. Apart from him sleeping like the dead, Ellie could find nothing wrong with him. She checked his head wound several times. It was no longer bleeding and showed no sign of infection. His breathing was deep and even. He wasn't feverish and he didn't toss and turn. He muttered occasionally, and each time, Amy came running to tell.

Amy was fascinated by him. Ellie had managed to stop her daughter referring to the stranger as Papa, but she couldn't seem to keep her away from his bedside. The weather was too bitter for her to play outside and the size of the cottage meant that if Amy wasn't with Ellie downstairs, she was upstairs watching the man.

It was harmless, Ellie told herself. And rather sweet. While Amy played with her dolls upstairs, she told him long, rambling stories and sang him songs, a little off-key. She told him of her special red wishing candle, that had brought him home. The child seemed quite unperturbed that he never responded to her prattle, that he just slept on.

It would be a different story when he woke. If he ever did wake…

She probably should have fetched Dr. Geddes. But she disliked him intensely. Dr. Geddes dressed fashionably, yet his tools of trade were filthy. He would bleed the man, give him a horrid-tasting potion of his own invention and charge a large fee. Ellie had little money and even less faith in him. Besides, Dr. Geddes was a friend of the squire…

She folded the shirt, now clean and dry, and set it with his buckskin breeches on the chest in her room. Both garments had once been of good quality, but had seen hard wear and tear. There was nothing incongruous about a poor labourer wearing such clothes, however. In the last year she had been amazed to learn of the thriving trade in used clothing—second-, third-, even fourth-hand clothing. Even things she'd thought at the time were total rags she knew now could have been sold for a few pennies, or a farthing.

She'd sold everything too cheaply, she realised in retrospect. Her jewellery, her furniture, treasured possessions, Amy's clothes, her beautiful dolls' house, with its exquisitely made furnishings, the tiny, perfect dolls with their lovely clothes and charming miniature knick-knacks—she could have sold them to far more purpose now. She had been ignorant, then, of the true value of things.

Still, they were neither starving nor frozen, and her daughter derived just as much pleasure from her current dolls' house, made from an old cheese box, with home-made dolls and furnishings made from odds and ends.

Ellie examined the stranger's other belongings. There were precious few—just the clothes he stood up in. His stockings were thick and coarse but walking on the bare ground in them had made holes, which she had yet to darn. She had found no other belongings to give a clue to his identity, only one item found wadded in his breeches pocket, a delicate cambric handkerchief, stiff with dried blood. An incongruous thing for such a man to be carrying. It did not go with the rest of him, his strong hands and his bruised knuckles.

She recalled the way those big, battered knuckles

had slipped so gently across her cheek and sighed. Such a small, unthinking gesture…it had unravelled all her resolve to keep him at a distance.

He was a stranger, she told herself sternly. A brawler and possibly a thief as well. She hoped he had not stolen the handkerchief. It was bad enough having a strange man sleeping in her bed, let alone a thief.

Rat-tat-tat! Ellie jumped at the sound.

Amy's eyes were big with fright. "Someone at the door, Mama," she whispered.

"Miz Carmichael?" a thick voice shouted.

"It's all right, darling. It's only Ned. Just wait here." Ellie put aside her mending and went to answer the door. She hesitated, then turned to her daughter. "You mustn't tell Ned, or anyone else, about the man upstairs, all right? It's a secret, darling."

Her daughter gazed at her with solemn blue eyes and nodded. "'Coz of the squire," she said, and went back to playing with her dolls' house.

Ellie closed her eyes in silent anguish, wishing she could have protected her daughter from such grim realities. But there was nothing she could do about it. She opened the door.

"Brought your milk and the curds you wanted, Miz Carmichael," said the man at the door and added, "Thought you might like these 'uns, too." He handed her a brace of hares. "Make a nice stew, they will.

No need to tell the squire, eh?'' He winked and made to move off.

"Ned, you shouldn't have!" Ellie was horrified, and yet she couldn't help clutching the dead animals to her. It was a long time since she and Amy had eaten any meat, and yet Ned could hang or be transported for poaching. "I wouldn't for the world get you into troub—"

Ned chuckled. "Lord love ye, missus, don't ye worry about me—I bin takin' care o' Squire's extra livestock all me life, and me father and granfer before me."

"But—"

The grizzled man waved a hand dismissively. "A gift for little missie's birthday."

There was nothing Ellie could say. To argue would be to diminish Ned's gift, and she could never do that. "Then I thank you, Ned. Amy and I will very much enjoy them." She smiled and gestured back into the cottage. "Would you care to come in, then, and have a cup of soup? I have some hot on the fire."

"Oh, no, no, thank ye, missus. I'd not presume." He shuffled his feet awkwardly, touched his forehead and stomped off into the forest before she could say another word.

Ellie watched him go, touched by the man's awkwardness, his pride and the risky, generous gift. The hares hung heavy in her arms. They would be a feast. And the sooner they were in the pot, the safer it would be for all concerned. She had planned to make curd cakes for Amy's birthday surprise. Now they would both enjoy a good, thick meaty stew as well—it would almost be a proper birthday celebration. And if the man upstairs ever woke up, she would have something substantial to feed him, too.

She smiled to herself as she struggled to strip the skin from the first hare. She'd thought him a thief because of the handkerchief. Who was she to point her finger, Ellie Carmichael, proud possessor of two fat illegal hares…?

He had slept like the dead now, for a night and a day. Ellie stared at his shape and wished she could do something. She wanted him awake. She wanted him up and out of her bed. She wanted him gone. It was unsettling, having him there, asleep in her bedclothes. It was not so difficult to get used to it during the day, to assume he was harmless, to allow her daughter to sit beside him, treating an unconscious man—a complete stranger—as if he was one of her playthings. During the day he didn't seem so intimidating. Now…

She hugged her wrapper tighter around her, trying to summon the courage to climb into the bed beside him once more. In the shadows of the night he seemed to grow bigger, darker, more menacing, the virile-looking body sprawled relaxed in her bed more threatening.

But he hadn't stirred for a night and a day. Another night of sharing would do no harm, surely. Besides, she didn't have any choice... No, she'd made a choice, her conscience corrected her. She could have called for help. He would have been taken "on the parish." But he wouldn't have received proper care—not with the poor clothing he wore. An injured gentleman, yes, the doctor or even the squire would see to his care. But there were too many poor and injured men in England since the war against Napoleon had been won. They'd returned as brief heroes. Now, months later, as they searched for work or begged in the streets, they'd come to be regarded as a blight on the land. It wouldn't matter if one more died.

There were too many indigent widows and little girls, too.

She could not abandon him. Somehow, with no exchange of words between them, she had made herself responsible for this man—stranger or not, thief or not. He was helpless and in need. Ellie knew what it felt like to be helpless and in need. And she would help him.

Without further debate, Ellie wrapped herself in her separate sheet—she hadn't lost all sense of propriety—and slipped into the bed beside him. She sighed with pleasure. He was better than a hot brick on a cold winter's night.

This time there was little sense of strangeness. She was used to his masculine smell, she even found it appealing. The sag of the bed felt right, and she didn't struggle too hard against it. After all, if there was too much of a gap between them, icy drafts would get in.

But recalling the immodest position she had woken in, she determinedly turned her back to him. It was not so intimate, having one's back against a stranger, she thought sleepily, as she snuggled her backside against his hip.

And once again, in the warmth of his body heat and the calm steady rhythm of his deep, even breathing, Ellie forgot her fears of the stranger and went to sleep. And her toes reached out and curled contentedly against his calves…

Ellie came awake slowly to a delicious sense of…pleasure. She had been having the most delectable dream. She kept her eyes closed, prolonging the delightful sensation of being…loved. Hart was caressing her in the way she had always dreamed of… His big, warm hands smoothing, kneading, loving her skin. She felt beautiful, loved, desired in a way she had never before felt. Warm, sleepy, smiling, she stretched and moved sensually, squirming pleasurably in the grip of the marvellous dream. Her skin felt alive as his hands moved over, across, around, between…sending delicious shivers through her body, shivers which had nothing to do with the cold and everything to do with…desire.

Hands slipped up her thighs and caressed her hips and she moved restlessly, her legs trembling. She felt a big, warm hand cup one breast, felt her flesh move silkily against the rougher skin of his hand. Her breasts seemed to swell under the caress and when she felt warm breath against her naked skin she clenched her eyes shut and felt her body arch with pleasure. A hot mouth closed over her breast and his tongue rubbed gently back and forth across her turgid nipple. She shuddered uncontrollably, waves of pleasure and excitement juddering through her with a force she had never experienced. He sucked, hard, and she almost came off the bed in shock as hot spears of ecstasy drove though her body. She could barely think, only feel. Her hands gripped his shoulders and gloried in the feel of his power and the smooth, naked skin under her palms.

Still creating those glorious sensations at her breast, she felt a large, calloused hand smooth down over her belly, caressing, smoothing, exciting... Her legs fell apart, trembling with need.

His mouth came down over hers, softly, tenderly, possessively, nipping gently at her lips. ''Open,'' he murmured huskily, and their mouths merged as his tongue tasted her, learned her, possessed her, and she tasted him and learned him in response.

And froze...

It wasn't Hart! Ellie jerked her head back and opened her eyes. *It wasn't Hart!*

He smiled at her early morning bewilderment. ''Morning, love.''

It was the stranger! It hadn't been a harmless, delicious dream of her husband. She had been lying with a stranger! Allowing him intimacies even her husband had never taken. Her breast still throbbed with want.

And his hand was still creating the most incredible sensations between her—

With a small scream, Ellie shoved him away from her and shot out of bed. There was a thud as his head connected with a bedpost and he swore. She stood shivering in the middle of the room, staring at him, outraged, dragging her nightgown down over her flushed and trembling nakedness.

"Who are you? How—how dare you! Get out—get out of my bed!"

"You didn't need to shove so hard," he grumbled. "My head was bad enough when I woke. Now it feels like—"

"I don't care what your head feels like! I said, get out!" Ellie almost screeched it.

He blinked at her in puzzlement, rubbing his head absently. "What's the matter, love?"

"As if you don't know, you—you ravisher! Get out of my bed!"

He frowned in vague confusion, then shrugged, climbed out and walked towards her. Stark naked. Acres of naked masculine skin, bared to her shocked gaze. With not a shred of shame.

"Stop! Get back!" She felt her whole body blushing in response.

He gave her a very male look, as if to say, make up your mind, but he stopped his movement towards her and sat back down on the bed, rubbing his head. Still naked. Making no attempt to cover himself. Even though he was still shamefully, powerfully aroused.

As, even more shamefully, was she. Her knees trembled, so she sat on the stool, half-turned away from the beautiful, shocking sight of him. "Cover yourself!" Ellie snapped.

She heard a slither of fabric, and turning back to face him, she felt herself blush again. He had picked up one of her stockings and draped it carefully across himself. Across the part which had most shocked her. The rest of him sat there in shameless naked glory. His body was glorious, too. She tried not to notice how much.

His blue, blue eyes were twinkling roguishly. "Is that better, love?"

"Don't call me that!" she snapped. "And cover yourself properly. My daughter could come in at any moment."

At her words he glanced towards the door and drew one of the blankets around his shoulders, covering his chest and torso and…the rest. It didn't seem to make him any less naked. His long legs, bare, brawny and boldly masculine, were braced apart on the edge of the bed. She tried not to think about what the blanket concealed.

"You'll have to leave," Ellie said firmly. "I shall go downstairs and make you some breakfast while you dress yourself. And then you will have to leave."

He frowned. "Where do you want me to go?"

Ellie stared in astonishment. "Where do *I* want you to go? Go wherever you want. It's nothing to do with me."

"Are you so angry with me, then?" His voice was soft, deep and filled with concern.

Ellie recalled the shocking things he had done to her. It seemed even worse that she had enjoyed them so much. "Of course I am angry. What did you expect when you attacked me in that appalling way?"

His brow furrowed. "Attacked?" His brow cleared after a minute and he looked incredulous. "You mean just now, in bed? But you were enjoying it as much as I was."

Ellie went scarlet. "Oh, you are shameless! I want you out of my house this instant!" As she spoke, his stomach rumbled. "As soon as you have eaten," she amended gruffly, feeling foolish. It was ridiculous to care whether he was hungry or not. She had taken in a stranger and cared for him for several days and how had he repaid her? With near-ravishment, that's how! The scoundrel! She wanted him out!

There was a short silence. "Did we have a quarrel, love?"

"Quarrel!" Ellie said wrathfully. "I'll give you quarrel! And I *told* you not to call me that!"

"Call you what?" He frowned. "Love?"

Ellie flushed and nodded curtly.

He rubbed his head and then said in an embarrassed voice. "I'm sorry if it makes you cross, but the truth is, I have the devil of a head on me and cannot seem to recall your name."

"It is Ellie. Mrs. Ellie Carmichael," she added for emphasis. Better he think she was married, not a widow. He might leave faster if he thought she expected a husband home any minute. It was Lady Carmichael, in truth, but it seemed ludicrous for a pauper to be titled.

"Ellie," he said softly. "I like it…Carmichael, eh?" He frowned, as if suddenly confused. "Then—"

"What you think of my name is immaterial to me." Ellie tossed him his clothes. "Have the goodness to dress yourself at once and leave this house!"

"Why do you want me to leave?"

Ellie narrowed her eyes at him. "Because this is my home and I say who can stay here! And you, sir, have outstayed your welcome!"

He looked at her seriously. "And have I no rights?"

She gasped at his audacity. "*Rights!* And what rights, pray, do you think you may have here, sirrah!" Did he think a few stolen caresses gave him rights? She was no doxy!

He hesitated, looking oddly uncertain. "Is this property not in my name?"

"*Your* name? Why should it be?" Ellie glared at him, but could not help feeling suddenly frightened at this talk of rights. What if the squire had sold the cottage without telling her? He had threatened to do so, often enough. Nor would she be surprised to learn he would imply that Ellie was part of the sale. The squire was a vindictive man.

"Women do not commonly own property. It is generally held in the husband's name."

The squire *had* sold the cottage. And this man had bought it for his wife and himself. And had been set upon by thieves while on his way to inspect his new property. Fear wrapped itself around Ellie's throat but she drew herself up proudly. "I am not for sale. My daughter and I will leave this place as soon as possible. You will give us a week or two, I presume, out of simple decency."

"Dammit, woman, you don't have to go anywhere!" he roared. "What sort of man do you think I am?"

"I have not the slightest idea," said Ellie frostily. "Nor do I care. But I am *not* for sale!"

"Who the devil suggested you were, for heaven's sake!" he said, exasperated, and clutched his head again. "Blast this head of mine. What the deuce is the matter with it?"

"Someone hit you," said Ellie. He gave her a look, which she ignored. "I do not know what the squire told you, but I am a virtuous woman and I will not be bought! Not by the squire, not by you or any other man, no matter what straits of desperation you try to bring me to." Her voice quavered a little and broke.

There was a long silence in the upstairs room. The wind whistled around the eaves, rattling the window panes. Ellie sat on the hard stool, her shawl wrapped around her defensively, staring defiantly across the room at him. She swallowed. She had no idea of what she might be forced to do to keep Amy safe, but she had not reached that point. Yet.

He stared back at her, an unreadable expression on his face. Finally he spoke. ''I have no idea what this conversation is about... I think whoever hit me over the head—was it you?''

She shook her head.

''That's a relief, then,'' he said wryly. ''But whoever it was made a good job of it. My brain is quite scrambled. I have no idea what you are talking of. I cannot think straight at all. And my head feels as if it's about to split open.'' He stood and made to take a step, then swayed and went suddenly pale.

Without thinking she jumped up and hurried to help. ''Put your head down between your knees.'' She pushed him gently into position. ''It will help the dizziness.''

After a few moments he recovered enough to lie back on the bed. He was still as pale as paper. Ellie tucked blankets around him, all thought of throwing him out forgotten. Whether he owned the cottage or not, whether he thought her a doxy or not, she could not push a sick man out into such weather. She could, however, send for his relatives.

''Who are you?'' she said when he was settled against the pillows. ''What's your name?''

He looked blank for a moment, then his eyes narrowed. ''You tell me,'' he said slowly. ''I told you my brain was all scrambled.''

"Don't be silly. Who are you?" She leaned forward intently, awaiting his reply.

He stared at her, his blue eyes dark and intense against his stark white pallor. There was a long silence as his gaze bored into her. And then he answered.

"I am your husband."

Chapter Two

Ellie stirred the porridge angrily. The cheek of him! *I am your husband.* Why would he say such an outlandish thing? To her, of all people! He'd sounded quite sure of it, too, even a little surprised, as if wondering why she had asked him. And then he'd lain back on the bed as if too exhausted to speak any further.

She spooned the thick oatmeal porridge into two bowls and set one before Amy.

"Sugar?" the little girl asked hopefully.

"Sorry, darling. There's no sugar left." Ellie poured milk on to her daughter's bowl, and watched her daughter make islands and oceans out of porridge and milk. Gone were the days of silver dishes on the sideboard, containing every imaginable delicacy.

She picked up the other bowl. "I'll take this to the man upstairs." She took a deep breath and mounted the stairs. *I am your husband.* Indeed!

He was awake when she entered the room, his blue eyes sombre.

"How is your head?" She kept her tone brusque, impersonal.

He grimaced.

"I have brought you some porridge. Can you sit up?" She made no move to help him. She would have no truck with his nonsense. He had disturbed her quite enough as it was.

He sat up slowly. She could see from the sharp white lines around his mouth that he was in pain. She said nothing, set the bowl down with something of a snap and helped him to arrange the pillows behind him. She tried to remain indifferent, but it was not possible to avoid touching him. Each time her hand came in contact with his skin, or brushed across his warm, naked torso, she felt it, clear through to the soles of her feet. And in less acceptable regions.

He knew it, too, the devil! He'd looked up at her in such an intimate, knowing way! How dare he embarrass her any further! She ripped a blanket off the bed and flung it around his naked back and chest, then she thrust the bowl and spoon at him. "Eat."

"Yes, Mrs. Carmichael," he said in a tone of crushed obedience.

She glanced at him in suspicion. His blue, blue eyes caressed her boldly. She glared at him, then began to tidy the room briskly.

"You're gorgeous when you're angry," he said in

a deep, low voice and as her breath hissed in fury, he applied himself in a leisurely manner to the porridge.

By the time she went up again to fetch his empty bowl, her wrath had dissipated. She was now more puzzled than angry. His behaviour made little sense. Why lie to her, when she was the one person in the world who would know it was a lie? And though he was teasing her now, he hadn't been teasing when he'd claimed to be her husband. It was all very odd. She decided to ask him, straight out.

"What is your name—no nonsense now. I want the truth, if you please." She took his bowl and stood looking down at him.

There was a long pause. Finally he said, "I don't know."

He said it with no inflexion at all. Ellie stared at him, and suddenly she knew he was telling the truth. "You mean you cannot remember who you are?"

"No."

Ellie was stunned. She sat down beside him on the edge of the bed, quite forgetting her resolve to keep her distance. She had heard tales of people who had lost their memories, but she had never thought to meet one. "You cannot remember *anything* about yourself?"

"No. All morning I have tried and tried, but I cannot think straight. I have no idea what my name is, nor anything about my family, or what I do for a living, or even how I came to be here." He smiled, a little sheepishly. "So you will have to tell me everything."

"But I don't know myself!"

He patted her knee and she skittered away. "No, not how I came to be hurt, but the rest. My name and all the rest."

"If you cannot remember anything, then why did you say you were my husband?"

He frowned at the accusing note in her voice and said teasingly, "Am I not your husband, then?"

"You *know* you are not."

He blinked at her in amazement. "You cannot mean it! But I thought—"

Ellie shook her head.

He considered her words for a moment and his frown grew. "But if Amy is my daughter…"

"She is no such thing!" Ellie gasped, and jumped up, horrified. "I just said you were not my husband. How dare you suggest—?"

"Then why does she call me Papa?"

"You mean—? Oh…" She sank back down on the bed. "That explains a good deal." She turned to him and said slowly, "Amy's papa, my husband, Hartley Carmichael, died a year ago. She was just a little girl and she doesn't quite remember him…" It was too difficult to explain, she realised. She finished lamely, "You have blue eyes, like her papa. And her."

"That doesn't explain how you and I came to be sharing a b—"

She knew what he was thinking and interrupted, "I

never saw you before in my life until two nights ago when you arrived at my door, bleeding and frozen half-solid.''

''What!''

She stood up and added in a wooden little voice, ''There is only one bed big enough for an adult. It was a bitter night, one of the coldest I can recall. You were hurt and in danger of freezing to death. I could not leave you on the floor.'' She was unable to meet his eyes. ''And as I did not want to freeze to death myself, I shared my bed with a stranger.''

She flushed, recalling how the stranger had found her in his bed this morning. She had responded wantonly to his caresses. She did not blame him for thinking her a fallen woman. Her voice shook. She did not expect him to believe her, but forced herself to add, ''You are the only man I have ever shared a bed with. Except for my husband, of course.''

She could stay in the room no longer, with those eyes boring into her. She couldn't meet their icy blaze, couldn't bear to see the look in them. She snatched up the bowl and ran downstairs.

He watched her go, his head splitting, his mind a whirl. They were strangers? Then why would he feel this ease in her company, this sense of belonging? She didn't feel like a stranger. He'd never felt so right, so much at home as he had in bed that morning, bringing Ellie to sweet, sensual wakefulness…as if she were a part of him.

Unanswered questions gnawed at his vitals like

rats. What the devil was his name? It seemed to be floating somewhere just beyond him...hovering there, on the tip of his tongue...but each time he tried for it, it drifted out of reach. He tried some names, hoping one would leap out at him, bringing the rest of his identity tumbling with him. Abraham...Allan...Adam... Was he an Adam, perhaps? He tasted it on his tongue. Familiar, yet also strange.

Bruce...David...Daniel... Was he trapped in the lion's den? He smiled and wriggled lower in the bed. His Ellie could be a little lioness when roused... She'd certainly roused him. Edward...Gilbert...James... He pulled the bedclothes around him. He could smell Ellie on them. He inhaled deeply and felt his body respond instantly. Walter...William... He dozed.

"Hello, Papa." A little voice pulled him back from the brink of sleep. He opened his eyes. A pair of big blue eyes regarded him seriously across an old cheese box.

"Hello, Amy." He sat up, drawing the sheets up with him, across his chest.

"Does your head hurt a lot?"

The headache had dwindled to a dull thump. "No, it feels a lot better, thank you."

"Mama says you don't know who you are."

He grimaced ruefully. "That's right. I can't even remember my name. I don't suppose you know my name, do you?" He tensed when the child unexpectedly nodded her head. Had Ellie not told him the truth after all? He'd had a feeling she was hiding something.

The little girl carefully put the cheese box on to the bed and then climbed up after it. She sat cross-legged and regarded him solemnly. "I think your name might be…" Her big blue eyes skimmed his chin, the top of his chest and along his arms.

He had not the faintest notion of what she found so interesting.

"Your name is…" She leaned forward and hesitantly touched his jaw and giggled. She sat back, her eyes full of mischief and said, "I think your name is…Mr. Bruin."

"Mr. Bruin?" He frowned. Bruin meant bear. "Mr. Bear?"

"Yes, because you are big and even your face is hairy." The little girl chortled in glee. "Just like a bear!"

He had to laugh at her neat trick. So, he looked like a big hairy bear to a little girl, did he? He ran a hand over his jaw. Maybe she was right. He did need a shave.

"If you think I'm a bear, then why did you call me Papa?"

She glanced guilty at the doorway. "Mama says I'm not s'posed to call you that. You won't tell, will you?"

"No, I won't tell." Again he wondered what Mama was trying to hide.

She beamed at him.

"But if your mama does not like you to call me Papa, maybe you could call me Mr. Bruin instead." It was better than having no name at all.

Her face screwed in thought, then she nodded. "Yes, that will be a good game. And you can call me Princess Amy. Do you like dolls, Mr. Bruin? I hope you don't eat them."

He resigned himself to being a little girl's playmate for the afternoon. It was better than cudgelling his aching brain for information which would not come, he supposed.

"Oh, no," he said firmly. "We bears never eat dolls."

She looked at him suspiciously. "Bears might eat *my* dolls—my dolls are very special dolls. The type which are delicious to bears."

He heaved a huge regretful sigh. "Oh, very well, you have caught me there. I solemnly promise never to eat Princess Amy's Very Special Dolls."

"Good." She snuggled closer to him, pulled the box on to his knees and began to introduce her dolls to him.

The cheese box was a home-made dolls' house, he realised. Everything in it was made by clumsy small fingers or her mother's neat touch. And some of her dolls were made of acorns, with cradles and all sorts of miniature items made of acorn caps and walnut shells.

He smiled to himself. Delicious to bears, indeed.

She was a delightful child. Her eyes were such a bright blue...almost the exact same colour as his. It was a most discomforting thought. He hoped Ellie had not lied about Amy's parentage. If he had created this charming child with Ellie...and left her to grow up without his name, in what looked to him a lot like poverty...then he didn't much like himself.

All thoughts led to the same question—who the devil was he? And was he already married?

"He was so badly hurt he now cannot remember a thing," explained Ellie to the one person who could be trusted not to tell the squire of her unexpected houseguest.

"It's an absolute disgrace!" The vicar paced the floor in agitation. "That gang of robbers is getting bolder and bolder and will the squire do a thing about it? No—he is much too indolent to bother! He ought to close down the Angel. I'm sure that den of iniquity is their headquarters. Can your fellow identify any of the miscreants?"

"No, he doesn't even know his own name, let alone anything that happened."

The elderly vicar pursed his lips thoughtfully. "And there was nothing on his person to indicate his identity?"

Ellie shook her head. "Nothing. Whoever robbed him had stripped him of even his coat and shoes. I thought you may have heard something."

"No. No one has made enquiries. Er…he is not causing you any, er, difficulty?"

"No, he has been a gentleman the entire time…" Except for where his hands had roamed this morning, she thought, fighting the blush. The vicar had no idea of the sleeping arrangements at her cottage, otherwise he wouldn't have countenanced it for a moment.

The vicar frowned suddenly and glanced around. "Where is little Miss Amy?"

"I left her at the cottage. It is very bitter out and she had a bad cold which she has only just recovered from. It…it was only for a few minutes…" Her voice trailed off.

"You left her alone with this stranger?" He sounded incredulous.

Ellie felt suddenly foolish. Criminally foolish. "I didn't think…I don't *feel* as though he would hurt Amy—or me." She bit her lip in distress. "But… you're right. He could be a murderer, for all I know."

The vicar said doubtfully. "I'm sure there's nothing to worry about. If you'd had doubts about this fellow, you'd have brought Amy with you. You have good instincts."

With every comforting word, Ellie's doubts grew. As did her anxiety.

He nodded. "You are having second thoughts. Leave this matter in my hands. If a man has gone missing, we shall eventually hear something. Go home, my dear. See to your child."

"Oh, yes. Yes, I will. Thank you for the loan of these items, Vicar." She lifted the small packet in her hand. "I shall return them shortly."

Ellie ran most of the way home, her fears growing by the minute. How could she have let her…her feelings, outweigh her common sense! Leaving Amy behind, just because it was cold and damp outside! Taking a man's word for it that he recalled nothing. Assuming that simply because she liked him—liked him far too much, in fact—that he was therefore trustworthy. For all she knew, he could be the veriest villain!

It was all very well for the vicar to talk of her instincts being sound, but he didn't know of the mess she had made of her life. She trusted her instincts and her feelings as far as she could throw them. Which was not at all! Dear Lord, she had left her daughter with a complete stranger! If anything happened to Amy, she couldn't bear it.

She raced to the cottage and flung open the door. The downstairs room was empty. No sign of her daughter. She heard voices above her. She could not make out what was being said. Then she heard a small anxious squeak.

"No, no! Stop that!" Amy shrieked.

Ellie raced up the steep stairs, taking them two at a time, almost tripping on her skirts as she did. She hurtled into the room and stood there, gasping for breath, staring at the sight which greeted her.

The murderer she had left her daughter with was

sitting in her bed where she had left him. He had found his shirt, thank goodness, and wore it now, covering that broad, disturbing chest. He was also wearing one of her shawls and her best bonnet, albeit crookedly, its ribbons tied in a clumsy bow across his stubble-roughened jaw. His arms were full of dolls. Across his lap, over the bedclothes, a tea towel had been laid and on it, a diminutive tea party was set out, with pretend food and drink in acorn-cap bowls.

He met Ellie's gaze rather sheepishly, his blue eyes twinkling in wry humour.

"Oh, Mama, Mr. Bruin keeps moving and spilling my dolls' picnic. Look!" Amy crossly displayed several tipped-over bowls. "Bad Mr. Bruin!" the little girl said severely.

"I'm sorry, Princess Amy, but I did warn you that we bears are great clumsy beasts and not fit company for a picnic with ladies," responded Ellie's murderer apologetically.

Ellie burst into tears.

There was a shocked silence. "Mama, what is it? What's the matter?" Amy scrambled off the bed and threw her arms around her mother's legs tightly.

Ellie sat down on the stool, pulled Amy into her arms and hugged her tightly, tucking the child into her body, rocking her. The sobs kept coming. Hard, painful, from deep in her chest. She couldn't stop them.

She heard movement from the direction of the bed, but the weeping had taken hold of her. She could do nothing but hold her daughter and let the tears come. She knew it was weak, knew it was spineless of her, that she was supposed to be strong and look after Amy…Amy, who was now sobbing in fright because she had never seen her mother cry before…

But Ellie could not control the harsh sobs. They came from somewhere deep inside her, wrenching painfully out of her body, almost choking her. She had never cried like this before. It was terrifying.

In a vague way, she sensed him standing beside her. She thought she felt a few awkward pats on her shoulder and back, but she couldn't be sure. Suddenly she felt powerful arms scoop her up. He lifted both her and Amy and carried them back to the bed and sat down, holding them on his lap, in the circle of his arms, hard against his big, warm chest. Ellie tried to resist, but feebly and after a moment or two, something inside her, some barrier, just…dissolved and she relaxed against him, letting herself be held in a way she had never in her life been held. The sobs came even harder then.

He asked no questions, just held them, nuzzling Ellie's hair with his jaw and cheek, making soothing sounds. Amy stopped crying almost immediately. After a moment, Ellie heard him whisper to her daughter to go and wash her face, that Mama would be all right soon, that she was just tired. She felt her daughter slip out of her grasp. Amy leaned against his knee and waited anxiously, patting and stroking her mother's heaving shoulders.

Ellie forced herself to smile in a way she hoped would reassure the little girl. She tried desperately to get control of her emotions, but she couldn't yet speak—she was breathing in jerky gasps, gulping and snuffling in an ugly fashion. Sobs welled up intermittently; dry, painful shuddery eruptions. She heard Amy tiptoe downstairs.

Finally, the last of the frightful, frightening outburst passed. Ellie was exhausted, with as much energy as a wet rag—and feeling about as attractive.

"I...I'm sorry about that," she said gruffly. "I...I don't know what came over me."

"Hush, now. It doesn't matter." His arms were warm and steady around her. He smoothed a damp curl back from her face.

"I'm not usually such a dreadful watering pot, really I'm not."

"I know." His voice was deep and soft in her ear.

"It was just...I suddenly got the idea—I mean, I thought..." How could she tell him what she'd thought? What could she say? *I thought you were going to hurt my daughter and when I found you hadn't, I burst into tears all over you instead. How ridiculous was that?* He would think she belonged in Bedlam. She wasn't sure herself that she didn't belong there!

"I've never cried like that in my life. Not even when my husband died."

"Then you were well overdue for it. Don't refine too much on it," he said in a matter-of-fact voice.

"No doubt you were at the end of your tether and things had built up inside you until there was no bearing it. When that happens, you have to let it out somehow."

She made a small gesture of repudiation of his words and he went on, "Women cry, men usually get into a fight, or—" she felt the smile in his voice "—take to the bedchamber. But I have seen men weep and weep, just like you did when things have got too much to bear. There is no shame in it."

There was a small silence. "Have you wept like that?"

She felt him tense. He said nothing for a long moment and then shook his head. "No, blast it! I still cannot recall. I thought I had it for a minute." He sighed and she felt his warm breath in her hair. "It is so frustrating, as if it's all there, waiting. Like something half glimpsed in the corner of my eye and when I turn my head to look at it directly, it is gone…"

She laid her hand on his. "It will come soon, I am certain of it."

"That's as may be. Now, do you want to talk about it?"

"About what?"

He turned her in his arms so that she could see his face properly. "Don't prevaricate. What was it that so upset you? Tell me. I might not be able to remember anything, but I'll help you in any way I can. Did someone try to hurt you?'' His voice was deep and sincere.

Ellie couldn't bring herself to confess the ugly suspicion that had crept over her at the vicarage. She looked at him, trying to think of how she could explain...

Her face must have shown more than she realised.

"It's me, isn't it?'' he said softly. "I'm your problem.''

She said nothing for a moment, but he knew it anyway. His hands dropped away and suddenly she felt cold. He gently lifted her off his lap and placed her on the bed beside him.

"No, no,'' she said hurriedly. "It's—there are so many problems and difficulties, but I don't want to burden—''

"Just tell me this—I...I need to know it.'' His voice was a little hoarse. "Do you *truly* not know me, or do you know me and...and fear me for some reason?''

There was a short silence, then he reached down beneath the mattress and drew out the frying pan she had placed there on the first night.

Ellie reddened. She didn't know where to look.

"I found it this morning, as I was getting dressed. This was for me, wasn't it? In case I attacked you in the night.''

Ellie nodded, embarrassed.

"And when you came rushing in here just now, having run a mile or more...I was the reason. You were worried about Amy, weren't you? About leaving her alone with me. And when you found her safe and...untouched, you burst into tears of relief..."

Ellie was miserably silent.

His fist curled into a knot of tension at her unspoken confirmation of his theory. "I cannot blame you for it. We neither of us have any notion of the sort of man I am. I do not *believe* I would harm a child...but until I get my memory back, I cannot *know* what sort of man I am...or have been." Frustration and distress were evident in his voice.

Ellie tried to think of what to say. He was a good man, she felt it in her bones. But he was right. They didn't know anything about him.

"I suppose I made the situation worse, grabbing you like that," he said bitterly. "I didn't know what to do. I just needed to hold you... I see now it was presumptuous of me."

Ellie wanted to cry out, No! She wanted to tell him that he had done exactly the right thing, that she had derived such comfort from being held that it was too embarrassing to admit. She couldn't explain how in his embrace she had discovered the release of being weak for once...even for a short while. All her life she had had to be the strong one.

She wanted to tell him how wonderful it had been to be held by a strong man as if she were precious, as if he cherished her...despite her weakness.

But she could not expose such vulnerability to him. Men exploited a woman's vulnerability. And God help her, she was coming to care for him—much more than was reasonable—a nameless stranger she had known two nights and two days, and most of that with him insensible. She could not let him know that about her.

"And for this morning…in bed…I also apologise."

Ellie's face flamed. She scrambled to her feet. "There's nothing to apologise for," she said huskily. "We were both half-asleep and you cannot be held responsible for…for what you did. You did not know what you were—"

"Yes, I did," he interrupted her in a deep voice. "I knew exactly what I was doing. And I give you fair warning, Mrs. Carmichael. While my memory is impaired, your virtue is safe with me. But the moment I discover who I am, and whether I am married or not…"

She waited for him to finish his sentence and, when he did not, looked up at him anxiously.

He smiled at her in a possessive, wolfish manner and said with soft deliberation. "If I am not married, then be warned, Mrs. Ellie Carmichael…I plan to have you naked in bed with me again, doing all of those things we were doing and more." It was a vow.

Ellie's face was scarlet, but she managed to say with some composure. "I think I may have some say in that matter, sir."

"You liked it well enough this morning…"

"You have no idea what I thought!" she snapped.

"And we will discuss this foolishness no further! Now, I have brought some slippers for you. The vicar's feet are too small to borrow his boots, but the slippers will do at a pinch. And there is a razor, too."

He ran a rueful hand over his jaw. "So you don't like my bristles, eh? Your daughter didn't, but I thought you may have rather enjoyed the...stimulation." He grinned at her, a thoroughly wicked twinkle in those impossibly blue eyes.

"Enough!" said Ellie briskly, thinking her whole body must have turned scarlet by now. "I shall fetch hot water for you to shave and then we shall dine. There is hare stew in the pot."

"Yes, the smell has been tantalising me for some time." His eyes were warm upon her. "There are so many tantalising things in this cottage, a hungry fellow like me has no chance..." His eyes told her exactly what he meant by "hungry." And it wasn't about stew.

She fled.

"Mama sent me up with her looking glass," announced Amy from the doorway. "She says you will need it to shave."

He grinned. A few minutes earlier, Mama had poked her head in the room, dumped a pot of hot water just inside the doorway and disappeared again, muttering things about having work to do. He probably shouldn't have taken off his shirt, but he was damned if he was going to shave in the only shirt he apparently owned.

Amy handed him the small, square looking glass and he took it gingerly, suddenly unnerved by the prospect of his own reflection. Would he recognise himself?

He lifted the glass slowly and grimaced. No wonder she didn't trust him an inch! He was a bloody pirate! All that was missing was the gold earring and the eyepatch! His skin was dark—tanned by weather, he decided, comparing it with other parts of his body. So he lived a lot out of doors. Gentlemen didn't do that. Pirates, however…

His eyes were blue, but then he knew that earlier from the little girl watching him so solemnly. No wonder she'd thought him a bear, though—he didn't just need a shave, he needed a haircut as well. Under the bandage, his hair was thick and dark and unruly. His brows were thick and black and frowning like the devil. His nose was long and—he turned his head slightly—not quite straight. He'd broken his nose at some time. And his skin carried several small scars as well as the remains of recent bruises. All in all, not a pretty sight. He'd found old scars on his body, too. He'd been in more than his share of fights.

A fine fellow for a woman to take in and care for— a brawling, hairy, black-bearded pirate! He wouldn't have blamed anyone for leaving such a villainous creature out in the cold, let alone an unprotected woman with a small daughter. He reached for the hot water and soap. At least he could take care of the beard.

"Will you hold the looking glass for me, please, Princess?"

Eagerly Amy took it and watched, fascinated, as he soaped up his skin and then carefully shaved the soap and beard off.

"Better?" he asked when he'd finished.

She reached out and passed a small soft palm over the newly shaven skin. "Nice," she said consideringly, "but I liked Mr. Bruin's prickles, too."

He chuckled. "Prickly bears don't belong in cottages. Now, I'm going to finish washing, so you pop downstairs, Princess, and help your mother. I'll be down shortly."

Ellie's throat went dry. She tried to swallow as he bent his head under the low beam and came down the last few steps. He suddenly looked so...different. Freshly shaved, he had removed the bandage and combed his hair neatly back with water. His skin glowed with health, his eyes were bright and lit with a lurking devilish gleam. His clean white shirt seemed to shine against his tanned skin; the sleeves were rolled back almost to his elbow. The shirt was tucked into buckskin breeches, not quite skin-tight, but nevertheless...

It was foolish, she told herself severely. They must have been tight when he arrived, too—in fact, tighter, because he was drenched. It was knowing the body beneath the buckskins, knowing it had been pressed against her, naked, only this morning, which was creating this unwanted heat in the pit of her stomach.

"Sit down. The table is set." She gestured and turned back to the fire to lift off the heavy pot of bubbling stew.

A brawny arm wrapped itself around her waist, while with his other hand, he whisked the cloth pad from her hand and used it to lift the black cast-iron pot off its hook.

"I can do that," she muttered, wriggling out of his light clasp.

"I know. But I've caused you enough work. While I'm here, I'll lighten your load as much as possible." He carried the pot carefully to the table.

While I'm here... The words echoed in her head. Yes, as soon as he recovered his memory, he would be off, no doubt, back to his wife and children. All twelve of them, she thought glumly.

They ate in silence. He ate neatly and without fuss. He passed her the bread and the salt and refilled her cup of water without being asked. Ellie pondered as she ate. His manners and his accent suggested he was gently bred, but his body bore the signs of one who had led a very physically challenging existence. He was also familiar with the workings of a cottage hearth; he deftly swapped the stewing pot with the large water kettle, rebuilt the fire in a manner which revealed he knew not to squander her precious fuel and generally showed himself to be at home in her

meagre surroundings—as no gentleman would be. A
servant might acquire table manners and an accent,
but he showed none of the servility of a man who
had been in service. On the contrary, he was rather
arrogant in the way he simply did what he wished,
whether she wanted to be helped or not.

He fixed a loose shutter. The banging had driven
her mad most of the year, but somehow, his fixing
it—without saying a word to her—annoyed her. He
went outside into the cold, despite his lack of coat,
and chopped her a huge pile of wood, stacking it under the eaves at the back door which was much more
convenient than where she had stored her wood before. He swung the axe with ease and familiarity. And
his muscles rippled beneath the loose, soft shirt in a
way that dried her mouth. Her eyes clung to his form
like ivy to a rock…until she remembered to go on
with what she had been doing. She should have been
grateful for his help. She was grateful…only…

Any minute now he would remember his name and
that he had a wife who had a right to command these
services from him! And twelve children. How dare he
make himself indispensable…making her and Amy
feel like they were part of a family… It wasn't fair.

In the afternoon she'd seen Amy standing outside
looking up, her little face pale and stiff with fear. Ellie
had rushed out to see what was happening, only to
rival her daughter in fear as she watched the wretched
man clambering about on her steep roof, replacing

and adjusting slates as if he hadn't a care in the world. She stood there, twisting a tea-towel helplessly in her hands, watching. Several times his foot slipped and her heart leapt right out of her chest and lodged as a hard lump in her throat as she realised he was fixing her leaking roof. He must have noticed the pot she placed in the corner of her room to catch the drips.

She hadn't breathed a scrap of air the whole time he was up there, and how he'd got up there without a ladder she didn't even want to think about! But when he'd come down finally in a rush which left her gasping in fright, and then he'd stood there, with that…that *look* in his eye, as if she should be pleased he'd risked his fool neck for such a trivial matter, well!

She'd wanted to throttle him there and then. Or jump on him and kiss him senseless.

But of course, she couldn't do any of that, because he wasn't hers to kiss or throttle and he probably never would be. She couldn't even yell at him, because how could she possibly yell at him for helping her? For scaring her silly? For making her realise that she loved him? The wretch!

She loved him.

The triumphant grin died slowly from his face and a light came into his eyes that made Ellie wonder whether she had said the words aloud. He stared at her, burning with intensity, his blue eyes blazing at whatever he read in her face. He strode towards her purposefully. She knew he was going to gather her up in his arms and kiss her like he had in the morning, in that way that melted her very bones.

But she could not, oh, she could not. For if she let him love her she could not bear it if she had to let him go... She held a shaking hand up to stop him and he came to a halt a scant pace away. His eyes devoured her, his chest heaving. Her eyes clung to him, even as her hands warded him off. They stood there, unmoving.

"Mr. Bruin!" said a cross little voice.

He ignored it, staring at Ellie, eating her up with his eyes.

"Mr. Bruin!" Amy tugged furiously at his buckskin breeches.

With a visible effort, he finally tore his gaze from Ellie and squatted down in front of her daughter. "What is it, Princess?"

"You are *not* allowed to climb up on the roof without askin' Mama! It's very dangerous. You could've fallen down and broken your head again. You're a bad bear!" Her voice quivered as she added, "And you frightened me and Mama terrible bad."

His voice softened. "Did I, Princess? I'm very sorry, then." And he gathered the little girl into his arms and hugged her gently. His eyes met Ellie's across the little girl's head, filled with contrition and some nameless emotion.

Ellie's eyes misted. What was she to do with a man like this? How could any woman not love him? She turned back to the cottage. He probably had half a dozen adoring wives.

Ellie was jumpy. The night was closing in on her. They sat by the fire in companionable silence. She was mending, he was whittling at a stick. Amy had gone to bed some time before. It was long past Ellie's bedtime too, but she had been putting off the moment. They would share a bed again soon. There was no choice. Of course, they had shared a bed for the last two nights, but he had been mostly unconscious. Mostly…

She kept trying not to think about the feeling of waking up in his embrace. She could not allow it to happen again. It was unseemly behaviour in a respectable widow and she would have no part of it. Besides, she feared if she allowed him to touch her like that again, there could be no stopping. She had already fallen more than halfway in love with him. If she gave herself to him she knew she would be letting him into her heart as well as her body…

She'd lost almost everything in her life as it was, but she had survived the loss. If she let herself love him and then lost him, it might be the loss she could not bear. For Amy's sake, if not for her own, she had to keep herself strong. She could not afford to break her heart. She would not *let* him break her heart.

She cleared her throat. "Mr. Bruin." She had taken to using Amy's name for him.

He looked up. "Mrs. Carmichael?" A slow smile

crinkled across his face, white teeth gleaming wolf-ishly in the firelight. He had that look in his eye again. She felt her pulse flutter.

"It is about the sleeping arrangements," she said in an attempt to sound brisk and matter of fact. It came out as something of a squeak.

"Yes?" His voice deepened.

"I am a virtuous widow," she began.

He raised an eyebrow.

"I am—" she repeated indignantly.

"It's all right, love," he said. "I am not doubting your virtue."

"Don't call me lo—"

He held up his hand pacifically. "Mrs. Carmichael…Ellie…your virtue is safe with me. On my honour as a gentleman, I will do nothing to cause you distress."

Ellie looked troubled. It was all very well for him to make a noble-sounding promise, but how did either of them know he *was* a gentleman? And what did causing her distress mean? His leaving would cause her distress, but would he stay, once he recovered his wits? She doubted it. Why would a handsome man in the peak of health and fitness want to stay in a small cottage in the middle of nowhere with a poverty-stricken widow and a small girl?

"There is no choice but to…" she swallowed con-vulsively "…share a bed, but that is as far as it goes. I will wrap myself entirely in a sheet and you shall do the same. And thus we may share a bed and blankets, but remain chaste. Are you agreed?'' Her voice squeaked again.

He bowed ironically. ''I am agreed. Now, shall I go up and disrobe while you do the same down here with the fire?''

Ellie felt herself go hot. ''Very well.'' She fetched down her thickest nightgown and, the moment she heard his footstep overhead, began to unbutton her dress. She undressed in the firelight, glancing once or twice at the window, at the black, opaque night outside, feeling exposed. Wrapping her thickest shawl around her, she took a candle and hurried upstairs. On the threshold she paused.

''Did you find your sheet?'' she whispered. ''I put it on the bed for you.''

A deep chuckle answered her. The sound shivered through her bones deliciously.

''Did you?'' she repeated, lifting the candle to peer into the sleeping alcove.

''Yes, love. I gave my word, remember. I'm as chaste as a bug in a rug.'' His bare upper chest and shoulders glowed dark against the white sheet. His eyes were deep shadows of mystery, and his white teeth gleamed briefly. He didn't look chaste. He looked handsome and powerful and altogether far too appealing for a virtuous widow's peace of mind.

She swallowed and turning her back, sat down to remove her shoes and stockings. Then she picked up her own sheet and wrapped herself tightly in it, feeling his eyes watching her every movement. Finally she blew out the candle, set it on the floor next to the bed, took a deep breath and slipped in beside him.

She lay stiffly on her back, huddled beneath the blankets in the cocoon of her sheet, trying not to touch him. All she could hear was the wind in the trees and the breathing of the man beside her. It was worse than the first time she had slept with him. Then she'd feared him as a stranger. Now the danger he represented was not the sort that a frying pan could fix.

Before, he had been a stranger to her, nothing more than a wounded, beautiful body. Now she knew how his eyes could dance, what he tasted like, how his hands felt moving over her skin, caressing her as if she was beautiful to him, precious. Before her marriage, men had only wanted her for her inheritance. Now she had nothing to offer a man except herself. And yet this man in her bed wanted her. And when he touched her she felt…cherished.

It was dangerously seductive. He had already found his way under her skin, if not her skirts. Now, all she had was a thin cotton sheet to protect her virtue—and her heart. She lay rigid, hardly daring to breathe.

"Oh, for heaven's sake!" With a surge of bed-clothes he turned, flipped her on her side and pulled her into the curve of his body.

"Stop it! You promised—"

"And I do not break my promises! This is as chaste as I can manage it. Now stop fussing, Ellie. There is a sheet wrapped around each of us—it is perfectly decorous. But I cannot possibly sleep while you lie there as stiff as a board…'' He chuckled awkwardly. ''That's my problem, too, if you want to know.''

Ellie buried her hot cheek in her cool pillow. No, she didn't want to know that. It was bad enough that she could feel his problem, even through the sheets. The feel of him set off all sorts of reactions in her own body.

''I'm sorry, I shouldn't have said that. Now, stop worrying, love, and go to sleep. We'll both rest better like this, you know it.''

Ellie did not know it, but she allowed herself to remain in the curve of his body, enjoying the warmth of him and the feeling of strength and protection which emanated from him. It was a strange and seductive sensation, this feeling of being…cherished.

They lay in silence for a long time, listening to the wind in the trees. And finally, Ellie slept.

He lay in the dark, holding Ellie against the length of his body. Even through the sheets wound around them, he could feel her soft curves, curled trustfully against him. Her feet had kicked free of their cotton shroud and tucked themselves between his calves, like two cold little stones. He smiled in the dark. He was happy to be her personal hot brick.

She sighed in her sleep and snuggled closer to him. He buried his face in the nape of her neck. He laid his mouth on her skin and tasted her gently with his tongue. Her scent was unique, like fresh harvested wheat…like bread dough, before it was baked…and hay as it was scythed. Fresh and good. He felt as if the fragrance of her skin had become a part of him.

Who the devil was he? It was unbearable to be so helpless, to be imprisoned in the dark, unable to make decisions about his life. How the hell could he plan any sort of a future when his past was a blank slate?

And what if his memory failed to return? Would he be forever hamstrung by self-ignorance? And if his memory didn't come back, how long could he stay here with Ellie? He couldn't ask her to support him. Yet he couldn't continue to live with her—a few days in winter they might get away with, but much more and her reputation would be compromised. And Ellie was a woman who valued her reputation. He inhaled the scent of her. He must not damage her. Must not let her be hurt by his situation. But how?

Questions continued to rattle fruitlessly in his head, until at last he fell asleep.

When he awoke Ellie was wrapped around him. They were lying face to face. Or rather her face to his chest. She was using him as a pillow. Warm little puffs of air warmed his chest as she breathed. Her hair, loosened from its braid, flowed in waves over his skin. One of her hands was curled around his neck, the other was draped across his chest. The sheets they had been wrapped so chastely in were now bundled ineffectively around their middles, leaving them uncovered above and below. There was nothing chaste about their current positions.

The warm soft weight of her against his naked skin was irresistibly appealing. He stifled a moan. He was rock hard and aching from wanting her. Her legs were twined around his, one leg over his hip. She was open to him. One small movement and he could be inside her. He had never wanted anything so much. She was his woman, his heartmate and she was soft, sleepy and open to him.

He swallowed hard. He wanted so badly, needed so much, to be inside her. His entire body throbbed with the need. He fought it. He had given his word. She trusted him. He might be a nameless pirate, but he had given his word and she'd believed him.

He would not take her, but that didn't mean he had to be a saint. He ran his hand down her body. The sheets were bunched around her middle, riding up over her thighs. He ran his hand along the leg she'd thrown across his hip, caressed her sweetly rounded backside, hesitated, then stroked the silken skin of her belly and thighs. She was warm, sweet and more than ready for him. A hard shudder rocked his body. He closed his eyes, willing the need back down.

He must have awoken her. Eyes still closed, she stretched languidly and the need rocked through him, almost shattering his fragile self-control. She moved her legs against his and he tried unsuccessfully to close his mind against the delicious friction of her soft skin rubbing against his.

Sleepily, she opened her eyes and looked at him, blinking drowsily. Still barely awake, she smiled at him. Her skin was flushed a soft pink, her lips were parted and damp and smiling in welcome. His hand moved again, caressing her intimately and her eyes widened in shock, even as her body arched towards him. He had not broken his word, but he was perilously close to it. He removed his hand.

She moved back in sudden caution, only to find her legs were gripping him.

"Oh!" she exclaimed and tried to untangle herself from him. He watched her sweet embarrassment as she discovered her sheet and nightgown pushed up to her middle, and the extremely intimate position they were in. She struggled to pull the sheet and nightgown down and in the process her hand brushed against his arousal.

She froze as she realised what she'd done and he gritted his teeth, willing control. Her face flamed adorably and she avoided his eyes in sudden shyness. It was odd for a married woman with a child to be so shy, but he had no time to explore that question. His focus was on the battle between his body and his mind. His body wanted nothing more than to make love to her. His mind also wanted it, heart and soul.

But for a man who had no memories, one single extremely inconvenient memory remained: *"your virtue is safe with me. On my honour as a gentleman, I will do nothing to cause you distress…"*

Again, she tugged surreptitiously at the hem of her nightgown, and again, she brushed up against him. Another encounter and he would not be answerable for the consequences. He reached down and lifted her hands away from the danger zone.

"Don't worry about it, Ellie. These things happen," he said softly. "I haven't forgotten my promise. Good morning," he added, and kissed her.

Recalling her earlier shyness, he planned to make it a gentle, tender, unthreatening kiss, but as her mouth opened under his and he tasted her sweet, tart, sleepy mouth, he was lost.

Their second kiss was more passionate.

He kissed her a third time and felt at the end of it that his body was about to explode. He raised his head, like a drowning man going down for the last time, and said softly, "Three is my limit, Mrs. Carmichael."

She blinked at him, her eyes wide and dazed looking, her lips slightly swollen from his kisses. She gazed into his eyes, as if reading his soul. He wondered what she saw in him but was distracted when her eyes dropped.

"Three?" she whispered vaguely. Staring hungrily at his mouth, she licked her lips.

He groaned. She didn't understand. He was poised on the brink. If she didn't get out of bed now, he would be lost. "Three kisses. If I kiss you again, I fear I will forget my promise to you." She frowned, so he reminded her. "My promise that your virtue would be safe with me," and added ironically, "*on my honour as a gentleman.* If you are not out of this bed in one minute, I will not be answerable for the consequences.''

It took a moment for her to comprehend what he was saying and he had to smile. She was even more befuddled by passion than he was. But once his meaning percolated to her brain, she gasped and scrambled hurriedly out of the bed. She stood there on the bare floor, staring, her chest heaving as if she had run a race. His own breathing was just as ragged.

''I...I am sorry,'' she said in a low voice and, snatching her clothes from the hook behind the door, left the room.

A moment later she was back, in the doorway, clutching her clothes against her chest, looking uncomfortable. ''I...I wish...we could have...you know.'' She blushed rosily. ''I'm sorry.'' She turned to go then paused and turned back, resolutely. ''It was the loveliest awakening I have ever had, thank you,'' she said in a gruff little voice and hurried down the stairs.

He lay back in the bed, his body throbbing with unsatisfied need, a wry smile on his face. *''It was the loveliest awakening I have ever had, thank you.''* It took courage for Mrs. ''I-am-a-Virtuous-Widow'' to admit that; courage and a kind of shy, sensual honesty that made him want to leap down the stairs after her and drag her back to bed. It would be an awakening in more ways than one, he suspected.

It would be wise to spend the day in making a straw pallet for him to sleep on during the coming night...but he had no intention of being wise. Tonight he would retract his gentlemanly promise. It didn't matter that he didn't know who he was. Whoever he was, he would make it right for her.

Tonight she would be his.

Chapter Three

Ellie swept out the ash and charcoal from last night's fire and began to set a new one, her hands moving mechanically, her mind reliving the wondrously delicious sensations she had experienced at his hands a few moments earlier. His hands... She felt herself blush, again, thinking of where his hands had been, so big and capable...touching her with such tenderness...and creating such sensations. She had never felt anything so...so...

It made her want to weep again, at the beauty of it...and the frustration.

The wood shavings which remained from his whittling smouldered, then smoked. She blew on them gently and flames licked at the wood. He'd built a fire inside her, a fire which still smouldered within her. She watched curl after curl of wood smoulder, then burst into brilliant flame. A moment of splendour, then each one crumbled into grey ash. Was that what it would be like to be possessed by him? One moment of glory, followed by a lifetime of regret? Or would it build into a more permanent fire, one with deep hot coals?

She filled the big black kettle with water and swung it on to the lowest hook. Hastily, because he might come down at any minute, she washed herself with soap and cold water and dressed before the fire. The kettle soon began to steam and she set the porridge to cook, stirring it rhythmically, her mind dreamily recalling the sensation of waking up in his arms.

Rat-tat-tat!

Ellie jumped. Someone at the door at this hour of the morning? Her eye fell on the hare skins hung up to dry on a hook near the door. Of course. Ned with the milk. She flung open the door, a smile of welcome on her face.

It froze there. "Sq...Squire Hammet."

A large burly man dressed more to suit a London afternoon promenade than a rural Northumberland morning pushed past her. His gaze raked her intimately.

Ellie shrivelled inside and braced herself. "To what do I owe this unexpected visit?"

"You've had a man here, missy!" The squire's angry gaze probed the small room.

"Why do you say that?" Ellie prayed that the floorboards overhead would not squeak.

"A man was seen on your roof yesterday." The

squire thrust his red face at her. The scent of expensive pomade emanated from him, as did the faint scent of soiled linen. Like his friend, her late husband, the squire favoured expensive clothing, but disdained bathing.

Ellie turned away, trying to hide her fear and disgust. "There was a man here yesterday. He fixed the leaking roof for me."

"It's my blasted cottage! I say who fixes the roof or not! So, you have a secret fancy man do you, Miss-Prim-and-Proper?" His face was mottled with anger. "Too high and mighty to give the time of day to me, who lent you this house out of the kindness of my heart, and now I find you've let some filthy peasant come sniffing around your skirts."

"You are disgusting!"

"Who was it, dammit—I want to know the fellow's name!"

Ellie turned angrily. "I have no idea of his name or anything about him. He merely fixed my roof for me and I gave him some food in return! I've been asking you to fix those broken slates for months now and you have done nothing!"

"Only because you have refused your part of the bargain." Small, hot eyes ran over her body lasciviously.

Ellie shuddered and forced herself to ignore it. "There was no bargain. There never will be. I pay rent on this cottage and that is the end of it."

"Pah, a peppercorn rent!"

"The rent you offered me on the day of Hart's funeral! If it was lower than usual, I did not know it at the time. I thought you were being kind because you were my husband's friend. I should have known better," she finished bitterly and turned to stir the porridge.

"You should have indeed. There's no such thing as something for nothing." The squire's voice thickened and Ellie jumped as thick, meaty hands slid around her, groping for her breasts.

"Take your hands off me!" She jerked her elbow into his stomach, hard and he gasped and released her. She whirled and pushed him hard. Off balance, he staggered back and banged his head on the shelf behind him.

She flung open the door and stood there, holding it. "You are not welcome in this cottage, sir. If I've told you once, I've told you a hundred times, I am— and shall be—no man's mistress. And even if I was so inclined, I would *never* be yours, Squire Hammet!"

The squire stood there, breathing heavily and rubbed his head. "You little vixen! I'll punish you for that, see if I don't. His eyes ran over her again. "I don't mean to leave here unsatisfied again. I had a good eyeful of you this morning and I liked what I saw."

Ellie felt ill. She never got dressed downstairs, usu-

ally. Of all the days to do it, when Squire Hammet
was outside the window, watching. She glanced at the
fire, to where her cast-iron poker was propped. If only
she could get hold of it…

"No, you don't, vixen." The squire put his big
burly body between her and the poker.

Ellie was beside the open door. She could run away
into the forest and hide, but she couldn't leave Amy
in the house.

The squire seemed to read her mind. "Where's that
brat of yours?" He glanced around the room and his
eyes came to rest on the cheese-box dolls' house.
"You would not want her to…have an accident,
would you?" With no warning his shiny boots
stamped down on the child's toy, smashing it to bits.
He kicked the shattered remains into the fire.

Ellie gasped with fright and rage. She watched the
flames devour a little girl's dream world. Amy was
upstairs, still asleep, she hoped. She did not want her
daughter to witness what would come next. She
would kill the squire before she let him touch her.

"Mama, Mama!" In bare feet and nightgown, Amy
came hurtling down the stairs. She flew across the
room to her mother, but in a flash the squire reached
out and grabbed the child by the arm. Amy shrieked
with fear and pain.

"Let go of her!" screamed Ellie.

Amy squirmed in the squire's grasp, then, unable
to break free, the little girl suddenly turned and fas-

tened her teeth in the hand of the man who held her. The squire let out a bellow of rage and Amy wriggled out of his grasp and fled.

Ellie darted forward and grabbed the poker. She lifted it, but before she could bring it down on the man's elegantly curled and pomaded head, a strong hand grabbed the squire by the collar, whirled him around and flung him across the room.

It was Mr. Bruin, dressed in nothing but a shirt and breeches, thick, dark stubble covering his jaw, blue eyes blazing with fury.

"Get out!" he said. "And if I ever find you bothering this lady again—"

"Lady!" the squire spat. "Some lady! You've obviously spent the night in her bed, but don't assume it's anything special! Half the men in the county have been under those skirts—and she's not fussy about class—in fact, she enjoys a bit of the rough—"

A big, powerful fist cut off the rest of the sentence. "Enjoy a bit of the rough, yourself, do you, Squire?" said Mr. Bruin softly, punctuating each word with a punch.

The squire was a big man, thicker and more solid in build than Mr. Bruin, but he was no match for Ellie's barefoot avenger. She winced at the sound of flesh punishing flesh, even as part of her was cheering.

"Now get out, you piece of carrion!"

The squire wheezed, sagged and scuttled out the

door, looking much smaller than when he had arrived.
His nose was bleeding and from the crack she'd
heard, it was probably broken. His face bore numerous marks from the fight and his eyes were swollen
half-closed. They would probably be black by the afternoon.

Mr. Bruin, on the other hand, was unmarked and
not even winded.

"I'll have you for this!" the squire swore from a
safe distance. "I'm the magistrate around here. I'll
have you transported, you ruffian!"

"I'm sure the court will enjoy hearing how a lone
virtuous widow and child were forced to defend themselves with a poker from the unwanted attentions of
a prancing, pomaded, middle-aged Lothario. Yes, I
can just see you admitting to the world you were
bested by a woman, a poker and a little girl," said
Ellie's defender in a deep, amused voice.

The squire swore vilely.

"Need another lesson in manners, do you, louse?"
Mr. Bruin bunched his fists. "Or shall I leave you to
the tender mercies of Mrs. Carmichael and her
poker?"

Ellie watched as the squire fled, still cursing and
muttering threats. He had made her life almost unbearable before: after this humiliation he would make
it impossible. She would have to leave this place, but
she didn't regret it one iota.

"That saw him off!" she said with satisfaction.

"You've dealt with this before," he said slowly.

She nodded. "He was one of my husband's closest friends, you know. When the magnitude of Hart's indebtedness became known, he offered me help." She laughed, bitterly. "I was an heiress when Hart married me. I was a pauperess when he died. I knew nothing—then—about the cost of living. None of our friends wanted to know me, so when the squire offered to help his dear friend's widow and child...I believed him. It seemed all perfectly above board." She shrugged. "I was stupid."

"A little naïve, perhaps," he corrected her, his gaze intense.

"Stupid," she repeated in a flat voice. "He said he'd keep an eye on me." She shuddered. "I didn't realise exactly what he meant by that."

"And that's why you feared for Amy that day when you left her with me. You thought you'd been 'stupid' again. Trusted another wrong 'un."

She nodded. They fell silent. It was too silent, she suddenly realised. *"Amy!"* Had she been hurt in the scuffle? Ellie raced into the cottage.

Her daughter was squatting before the fire, earnestly stirring the porridge. "It nearly burned, Mama," she said, "an' it was too heavy to lift and you said I wasn't to touch the fire things, so I just kept stirring it. Was that right?" She gave them an odd, guilty look.

Relieved, Ellie hugged her daughter. "Yes, darling,

it was very right. Mr. Bruin has saved us and you have saved our breakfast.''

He chuckled. ''Nonsense, you were both well on the way to saving yourselves. Princess, I never would have expected it of you!'' His laughter died as Amy's gaze dropped in shame.

''It's wicked to bite people, isn't it, Mama?'' she whispered.

''Oh, my darling,'' Ellie's eyes misted. ''You're not wicked at all. I thought you were very brave and clever to do what you did.''

''You mean you're not vexed with me, Mama?''

''No, indeed.''

''And it's all right to bite the squire again?''

Before Ellie could reply, she and Amy were swept into Mr. Bruin's arms and whirled around the room in a mad, impromptu waltz. ''Yes, indeed, Princess,'' he said. ''You may bite the nasty old squire as often as you want. And your mama may hit him with a poker. And then when my two little Amazons are finished with him, I will toss him out the door.''

Laughing, he set them down, then knelt down and said, ''Princess Amy, you are one of the bravest, cleverest young ladies I know. Not only did you bite the evil Squiredragon and rescue yourself, you saved the porridge from burning! I would fain be your knight.''

The little girl laughed delightedly, seized a wooden spoon and tapped him lightly on each shoulder. ''Arise, Sir Bruin!''

Ellie laughed, even as her eyes filled. His nonsense had transformed the ugly incident into a bold adventure. He understood children so well... Too well for a bachelor?

"Are knights and princesses interested in porridge?" She forced a light-hearted note.

"Oh, yes, indee—"

Rat-tat-tat!

Everyone froze for a moment as the knock echoed through the small cottage.

"The squire," whispered Amy. "He's come back to put us in prison!"

"Blast him for his impudence! I'll see to this!" He strode to the door and flung it open. "What the devil do you—?"

He stopped. A small, spare, neatly dressed man stood at the door.

"Gawd be praised, Capt'n!" said the man, beaming up at him. "When your horse came home without you, we all thought you was dead! Only I know'd better. I told 'em you was a survivor."

There was a sudden silence in the small cottage. The stranger's words seemed to echo. Ellie wondered whether anyone else could hear her heart thudding the way she could.

It was over, then, their brief idyll. He had been found.

"Capt'n? What's the matter?" The small man frowned at the tall, silent man in the doorway and then glanced behind him, to where Ellie and Amy stood, watchful and apprehensive. His bright bird-like gaze ran over Ellie and the little girl and his eyes narrowed.

The man he called Capt'n finally spoke. "Since I gather you know who I am, you'd better come in out of the cold."

The small man's head snapped back at that. "Know who you are? Are you bammin' me, Capt'n? Course I know who you are!"

"Come in, then."

He ushered the stranger inside and closed the door. He turned and met Ellie's gaze briefly. She couldn't read his expression. He began to offer a chair, then stopped in mid-movement. It was as if he was suddenly unsure of anything, she thought. Ellie filled the gap.

"Please, have a seat," she said to the stranger. "We were about to break our fast. It is only porridge and some milk, but you are very welcome to join us."

The man didn't respond. He continued to stare at "the Capt'n" with a puzzled expression.

"It's all right, the porridge isn't burnt," a little voice assured him. "I stopped it from getting burnt, didn't I, Mama?"

It broke the ice. Ellie couldn't help but smile and the stranger glanced down at Amy, smiled and said to Ellie, "I thank you for the offer, ma'am—and little miss—but I ate earlier. I wouldn't mind a drink to whet me whistle, though.''

Ellie grimaced. ''I'm sorry. There is only milk or water.''

''Adam's ale will do me nicely, ma'am.''

As Ellie fetched him a cup of water she glanced surreptitiously at Mr. Bruin. He was standing stiff and silent, a frown on his face. His body was braced, as if for a blow.

''Eat your porridge while it's hot,'' she said quietly. He sat down at the table and began to spoon porridge into his mouth.

They ate in silence, unanswered questions hovering over them, like the spectre at the feast. Even Amy was silent and anxious. The stranger watched the tableau, his eyes narrowed, going from one to the other, taking in everything.

Finally the porridge was finished, though Ellie doubted if anyone had enjoyed it. She began to collect the bowls, but Mr. Bruin stopped her with a gesture. He was nervous, Ellie knew. She sat down beside him again and took his hand.

The stranger noticed. She felt his disapproval and a sliver of ice slipped into her heart. It meant something, that look. It meant he thought she had no right to be holding this man's hand, this dear, battered hand, beloved in such a short time. He knew who her Mr. Bruin truly was. She hung on to the hand tighter, knowing it might be the last time.

She felt him squeeze her hard in response. He was as worried as she was. Amy came around the table and leaned against him. He put an arm around the little girl. Ellie felt a half-hysterical bubble of emotion rise in her throat. It was as if the three of them were a family, ranged defensively against the stranger, when, in fact, the opposite was true. This small spare man had come to take their beloved Mr. Bruin back to his true family.

"So, you say you know me. Then who am I?"

The stranger stared disbelievingly back at him.

Ellie explained in a flat voice, "He arrived here having been robbed and injured. His head was bleeding profusely and he slept like the dead for a night and a day. When he awoke, he had no recollection of anything—who he was, where he lived—nothing."

"Head injury, eh? That explains a lot."

At Ellie's look, he explained, "I've seen it before ma'am, in the army. Man gets hit on the head and loses it all for a time. Knew one bloke what never recovered all the memories, but most of 'em does." He turned. "You'll be all right, Capt'n Ambrose. Soon as I get you home, it'll all come back to you."

"Captain Ambrose? It doesn't sound the least bit familiar. What is my full name?"

"Capt'n Daniel Matthew Bramford Ambrose, late of the 5th Regiment."

Daniel. Ellie thought. It suited him.

"And you are?" said Daniel.

The small man leapt to his feet and saluted. "Sergeant William Aloysius Tomkins, sir!" He waited a moment, then shrugged and sat down again. "Thought it might bring something back, sir. I was your sergeant for nigh on seven years. You call me Tomkins when you're with the nobs and Tommy when we're on our own."

Daniel smiled faintly. "So, I am…I was a soldier…"

The sergeant grinned. "Indeed you was, Capt'n, for the last seven years—all but a month or two—and a mighty good one, at that. Best man in a scrap anyone could ask for."

Daniel glanced down at his big battle-scarred hands and glanced up at Ellie, a rueful look in his eyes. She thought he'd been a fighter and he was, just not the sort of fighter she'd imagined. He wasn't a gutter brawler—he was possibly a hero.

Ellie found herself fighting a battle between wanting to hear more about him—and wanting to know nothing more, for with every word the sergeant spoke, her Mr. Bruin and the fragile dreams she'd built around him drifted further away from her…

"Where do I live?"

"Until recently, all over the Peninsula, fighting Boney, sir, but when your brother died a few months back, you sold out and came home. To Rothbury. Ring a bell, sir?"

Ellie knew it. It was a town about a half-day's travel to the north-west of her.

Daniel shook his head.

"No? Oh, well, it'll come, don't you worry." The sergeant paused, then said deliberately, "You have family responsibilities at Rothbury, Capt'n."

Family responsibilities. Ellie felt the sliver of ice slide deeper in her heart.

"Family responsibilities?" Daniel said at last. He was squeezing Ellie's hand so tightly it was painful, but she couldn't bear to have him let go of her. It would happen all too soon.

"I have a wife, then?"

Say no, say no, say no! Ellie prayed silently. She could not breathe.

The stranger took an age to answer. He glanced at Ellie, then at Amy and then back at Daniel. And then said in the most ordinary of voices, "Yes, Capt'n, of course you have a wife. And a fine, beautiful lady she is, too."

Ellie could not breathe. Something was blocking her throat. *Of course he had a wife.* She had known it from the start. Stupid, stupid Ellie, to have let herself fall in love in a matter of days with a mysterious stranger.

He was strong and rugged and handsome, he was honourable, he was protective of women, he loved children. Of course he had a wife. He was altogether lovable.

And of course, his wife would be a fine, beautiful lady and probably sweet-natured and intelligent as well. She certainly wouldn't be a poverty-stricken, shabbily dressed widow. Stupid, stupid Ellie, thinking she had found love at last. Foolish, woolly-headed widgeon for forgetting that even when she had been a carefree young lady, passably pretty and very well dressed, she hadn't found love. She had needed her late father's money to buy her a husband. And not a very good one at that.

She'd long ago learned that fate was not her friend. She'd just forgotten the lesson.

The sergeant continued, "And, of course, your, um…Mrs. Ambrose has been terribly distressed by your disappearance."

Daniel nodded vaguely. He was still gripping her hand so hard Ellie knew it would come up in a bruise later. Even so, she hung on to his hand for all she was worth. If a bruise was all she was going to have of him, then a bruise was what she would have. She could take that to bed with her instead. That and her dreams and memories. And regrets.

Regrets.

How she wished he hadn't been such a gentleman this morning.

"Mr. Bruin, you're squeezin' me too hard," complained Amy.

"Sorry, Princess," he murmured and gave her a

gentle hug. "You run and play with your dolls while your mother and I talk to Sergeant Tomkins, here."

"I can't. The squire smashed them up and kicked them in the fire." Amy touched him, hesitantly. "Are you going to leave Mama and me, Mr. Bruin?" Her voice quavered.

That was Ellie's signal. Amy needed her mother to be strong. She wasn't going to fall apart. She wasn't going to be ruled by her instincts, those instincts which shrieked inside her to weep and cling and rage at fate, the instincts which had made her fall in love with a married man. He wasn't her Mr. Bruin; he was a Mr. Daniel Ambrose, with a loving wife awaiting his return. She had pride. She had her daughter to think of. She refused to disgrace herself.

Ellie wrenched her hand out of Daniel's, jumped to her feet and said brightly. "Yes, darling, isn't that wonderful for Mr. Bruin? Although he isn't Mr. Bruin any more, he's Mr. Ambrose. And Sergeant Tomkins is his friend and has come to take him home to his family, who is waiting for him and who love him very much and miss him terribly. Isn't that exciting? Now come and help Mama wash these dishes and let the gentlemen talk." She gathered up the bowls, knowing she was babbling, smiling so hard she thought her face would split.

But Amy didn't move. She fixed big blue eyes on Daniel and asked in a tragic little voice, "Have you already got a little girl of your own, Mr. Bruin?"

He stroked her curly head with a big, gentle hand. His voice was deep and husky and it seemed to catch in his throat as he said, ''I don't know, Princess. Have I got a little girl, Sergeant? Or any children at all?''

The sergeant tugged at the neatly tied stock around his stiff collar. He cleared his throat. ''Er...not yet, sir. Though...er, hrrumph, your mother has...er, expectations of...of being made a grandmother...soon. She speaks of it often.''

Oh mercy, his wife must be expecting a child. Ellie closed her eyes and swished the bowls and water frantically, appearing busy. ''Oh! So you are anticipating a happy event! How splendid! No wonder your wife is so anxious about you, Mr. Ambrose. A woman is always more emotional at that...delicate time. What delightful anticipation for your mother. To be a grandmother must be marvellous. A child has a special relationship with a grandmother. If she has one, that is. Amy never had a grandmother. They both died before she was born.''

Foolish, babbling Ellie. She forced herself to take a deep breath and added brightly, ''It's so amazingly lucky that Sergeant Tomkins managed to find you in such an out-of-the-way place. How did you find him, Sergeant? Tell us the whole story.''

The sergeant regarded her thoughtfully for a moment and then explained to Daniel, ''You'd decided to go to Newcastle to order some new clothes, them that you'd come home from the wars with bein' unfit

for company, so your mother said, an' nothing in the
house to fit you, your late brother bein' a smaller man
than you, sir.''

That explained the worn and shabby clothes,
thought Ellie sadly as she rubbed apathetically at the
dishes. They'd been to war with him.

''You'd decided to stay for a few weeks, to get out
of your m—'' The sergeant stopped and cleared his
throat. ''You were feeling a little restless at Rothbury,
sir. So you sent me on ahead to find lodgings and set
up a few appointments. But when you didn't arrive
in the lodgings I got worried—you being a man what
keeps to your word, sir.''

Oh, yes, he kept to his word, thought Ellie regret-
fully, thinking of those few glorious moments when
she'd woken in his arms. And he'd told her to go. On
his honour.

''So then when they sent word that your horse had
been found but no sign of you, I came a'lookin'. I
asked in every village between here and town, lookin'
in every ditch and gully and clump of trees, headin'
for Rothbury. And then I saw a pair of boots, sir, on
sale in the market place, and I thinks to myself, I've
seen them boots before.''

There was a pause and the sergeant said a little
throatily. ''I don't mind saying the sight of them
boots gave me a right nasty turn, Capt'n, because I
figured the only way you'd give up your boots was
if you was dead.''

He loved Daniel, too, thought Ellie sadly. And he'd grieved when he thought him dead.

"So then I went to the church, to see if the minister had buried anyone lately. He told me you were alive and in the care of a local widow..." He glanced at Ellie and then back at Daniel. "I bought back your boots. And there's a change of clothes for you, sir, in the bag there."

An awkward silence fell in the cottage.

"Ah, right," Daniel finally said. "Good thinking, Sergeant."

Ellie forced herself to say it. To get it over with. "So, Mr. Daniel Ambrose, you'd better put on your boots and change your clothes. With any luck this mild weather will hold and you will be home to your wife by this evening." She smiled, a wide, desperate smile that stretched her lips and made her jaw ache. Could a smile shatter a person? She hoped not.

"Oh, Ellie," he said softly and put out a hand.

She wanted to grab it, to cling and never let him go, but she turned away instead. "Hurry up, then." She felt her eyes fill and blinked furiously to keep them from spilling down her cheeks. "You don't want to keep the sergeant waiting. Your wi—" Her voice cracked. "Your family is waiting to hear the news that you are alive."

Daniel watched her turn away. He felt ill. *He had a wife!* Dammit! How could he have forgotten that? The sergeant seemed to think this wife loved him, too.

Had he loved her, this unknown beautiful lady who was expecting his child?

And if he had, how could he go on loving her, now that he had found Ellie?

Because he didn't believe it was possible to love anyone more than he loved Ellie. He might not remember any details of his life, but right at this moment he knew, deep within himself, in his bones and his blood, that he loved Ellie with every shred of his being.

Had he loved another woman in this same way, with this intensity of feeling, before he was hit on the head by footpads?

This wife meant nothing to him now. Would Ellie mean nothing to him once his memory was regained? The thought terrified him. He didn't want his memories. He wanted Ellie.

He looked at her. She turned away, her mouth stretched in a travesty of a smile, her eyes brimming with tears. She was trying so hard to be brave and cheerful, not to make him feel bad. Oh Ellie, Ellie… How was it possible to love someone so much in such a short time? How was it possible to lose so much with one blow?

And how was he ever going to leave her?

The sergeant handed him his boots.

Ellie watched Daniel trudge up the stairs to her bedroom for the last time. Her hands were busy wiping the table down, but her mind was with him, imagining every move he made. The way he pulled off his shirt, the look and feel of the broad, hard chest underneath, his beautiful sculpted shoulders, the way he bent his head when—

"Here y'are, Mrs. Carmichael. This should cover everything."

Ellie blinked. The sergeant was holding something out to her. Without thinking she extended her hand and took it. Then she glanced down. It was a small leather pouch. It was heavy and the contents clinked. "What is this?"

"Payment."

"Payment? For what?"

"For looking after Capt'n Ambrose, of course. What else?"

It was as if he had slapped her. She gathered her dignity together and laid the pouch gently on the table. "No, thank you."

The sergeant frowned. "Ain't it enough?"

Ellie stared at the man incredulously. Her heart was breaking and he thought she wanted to haggle over a few coins? "No payment is necessary, Sergeant."

The sergeant jutted his chin mulishly. "Capt'n Ambrose always pays his shot."

Ellie just looked at him. He shifted, uneasy under her gaze.

"Ellie, could you help me with this for a moment?" Daniel called from upstairs.

"Coming," she called. "Put your money away, Sergeant Tomkins," she said wearily. "It's not wanted here."

The moment she entered the upstairs room he pulled her into his arms. He hugged her hard against his body and she could feel his need and his pain. "I don't want to leave you," he groaned and covered her mouth with his, tasting her hungrily, devouring her.

It was nothing like the gentle, teasing, warmly passionate kisses of the morning. This was need, pure and simple. Heat. Desperation. Fear and desire. Urgency.

Ellie returned every kiss, each caress in equal urgency, knowing she might never see him again. Oh, why had they not made love this morning? Her foolish scruples seemed meaningless, now she was faced with the probability of a life without Daniel.

She shook with the force of the knowledge.

He took her head in his hands, his palms framing her face. His eyes burned into her soul. "Ellie, I *promise* you, this isn't the end. I'll sort something out." His voice was ragged. "I'll try to come back and see—"

Ellie shook her head. "No, Daniel. It must be a clean break. I could not bear to live on crumbs." She kissed him fiercely. "I want all of you. Crumbs would be the worst form of torture. As it is, I will have my memories. Only I wish we had…you know…this morning.''

"Made love," he corrected her, in a low, husky voice. "Not *you know*. You mean you wish we had made love.''

Tears spilled down her cheeks and she said in a broken voice, "No, Daniel, even without the…the consummation, we have already made…created love. Can you not feel it all around us? I hope we made enough, for it's going to have to last me the rest of my life…''

"Oh, Ellie, my sweet, lovely Ellie.'' He groaned and held her tighter, "How can I bear to leave you?''

"You must, Daniel. You have a wife. There is no choice for either of us.''

"Ready, Capt'n?'' called the sergeant from downstairs. "Need a hand with anything?''

"Blast him,'' muttered Daniel. He clung to her, burying his face in her hair, inhaling the scent of her, the scent of life, of love. He wished they had celebrated their love physically, for it would add a dimension he thought she was unaware of. But she was right; even without that consummation, they had already created so much love.

He desperately hoped it was enough to survive the return of his memories.

Finally, reluctantly, they pulled apart and went downstairs. Ellie felt the sergeant's shrewd gaze run over her, and knew that she looked like a woman who had just kissed and been well kissed in return. She raised her chin. She did not care what he thought of her.

The sergeant had brought two horses. They were saddled. Ready. Waiting.

"What about the squire?" said Daniel in a rough undervoice. "I canno—"

Ellie put her hands over his lips. "Hush. Don't worry about it. I've been dealing with him for months. Nothing has changed." His mouth twisted under her fingers. He touched them with his tongue and she pulled them away, unable to take much more.

"Mr. Bruin, Mr. Bruin, you're not goin', are you?"

Daniel picked up the distressed little girl and hugged her. "I have to, Princess. Now, be a good girl and look after your mother for me, won't you?" He kissed her goodbye.

Amy wept and clung to his neck. "No, no, Mr. Bruin, you have to stay. The wishing candle brought you…"

His face rigid with the effort of staying in control, Daniel unhooked the small, desperate hands and passed Amy over to her mother.

"I *will* sort something out, I promise you," he said in a low, ragged voice.

"Don't make promises you cannot keep."

"I always keep my promises. Always." His eyes were damp. They clung to her, but he didn't kiss or touch Ellie again. She was relieved. Neither of them could have borne it.

The best way to perform drastic surgery was fast. He turned and strode to the horses, mounting his in one fluid movement. He turned in the saddle, looked across the clearing at Ellie and her daughter with burning blue eyes and said, *"Always."* And he galloped away.

Always, thought Ellie miserably. Did he mean he always kept his promises? Or that he would always love her? Whichever it was, it didn't matter. He was gone. She had the rest of the day to get through somehow, a sunset to await, a daughter to feed and tuck into bed and watch over until she fell asleep. Only then could she seek her own bed and find the release she needed.

The release she needed. Tears and sleep. Not the release she craved...

She carried Amy into the cottage. Making a drink for them both, she found the small pouch of money the sergeant had offered her hidden away behind the milk jug. She looked inside it. Twenty pounds. A fortune, enough to keep her and Amy fed for a long time yet.

Capt'n Ambrose always pays his shot. The sergeant had prevailed yet again.

Somehow, she got through the rest of the day.

When it came time to go up to bed, Amy trotted ahead of her mother, up the stairs.

"Mama." Amy turned, her freshly washed little

face lit up. "Look what I found on my bed." She held up a tiny wooden doll, carved, a little clumsily, out of birchwood. "It's got blue eyes, just like me. An' Mr. Bruin, too." Amy's eyes shone.

A thick lump formed in Ellie's throat. Daniel's whittling. She'd thought he'd been simply killing time, making wood shavings, but he'd made her daughter a doll.

"It's lovely, darling. I'll make her some clothes tomorrow."

"Not her. This is a boy doll," said Amy firmly. "I'll call him Daniel, after Mr. Bruin."

"L...lovely." Ellie managed a smile, though she feared it wobbled a bit.

Later, when Amy was asleep, and the cold descended around her so that she could delay the moment no more, Ellie stepped reluctantly into her own room. Her eyes were drawn inevitably to the sleeping alcove, to the bed.

And then, finally, the tears came, for of course there was nothing there. Not even a small wooden doll. There was never going to be a Daniel there for her again.

He was gone.

Chapter Four

"No, darling, I cannot make you a new dolls' house yet. Not until we find a new house of our own. Houses for people come before houses for dolls."

Amy nodded. "The squire doesn't like us any more, does he, Mama?"

"No, darling he doesn't. Now help Mama pack by bringing all your clothes down here. I'm going to bundle them all up in a sheet, so we can put them on Ned's cart."

"Don't worry, Mama. If the squire comes back again, Daniel will hit him for us again, won't you Daniel?" Amy gestured fiercely with her small wooden Daniel.

"Nobody is hitting anybody," snapped Ellie. "Now fetch your things down here at once."

Ellie bit her lip as, chastened, Amy did her bidding. She had no idea where they were going to live. The vicar had offered them a room in the vicarage until after Christmas, but then his pupils would return for their lessons and there would be no room. But she was sure she would find something soon.

She had to.

Rat-tat-tat!

She froze. The squire had been back twice already since Daniel had left. Ellie remembered her daughter's words and her temper suddenly flared. She didn't need a Daniel to protect her; a wooden Daniel would do no good and the real Daniel…well, the real Daniel was back where he belonged, with his loving wife who was expecting their child. Daniel would be there to protect that woman and that child, not the woman and child he had stumbled across in a storm, brought by the light of a gypsy candle.

His memory would no doubt have returned by now. He probably didn't even remember Ellie. Whereas, she…she remembered everything. Too much, in fact. She couldn't forget a thing. He was there, in her mind and her heart, every time she slipped into a cold and empty bed. And she woke with the thought of Daniel every morning, missing his warm caresses, the low rumble of his voice… Bitter regret choked her as she recalled how she had fended him off. If only they had made love…just once.

It wasn't only in bed that he haunted her. He was there, in every corner of her cottage, in the stories her daughter prattled, in the doll he'd made for her. Ellie stoked the fire, morning, noon and night, with wood that Daniel had chopped, and her mouth still dried as she remembered the way his shoulder muscles bunched and flowed with each fall of the axe.

He was there each time it rained and her roof didn't leak. Her heart still caught in her throat when she recalled the way he'd come down off the roof in such a rush, giving her such a fright. The moment she realised she loved him…

It had rained most days since Daniel had left.

The knocker banged again. Ellie forced the bitter lump from her throat. She lifted the poker, strode to the door and flung it open, weapon brandished belligerently.

There was no one there. The rain had stopped and a heavy mist had fallen. It swirled and ebbed, making the cottage surroundings eerily fluid. Poker held high, Ellie stepped out on to the wet ground.

''Hello, Ellie.'' The deep voice seeped into her frozen bones like heat.

She whirled around, stared, could say nothing. The fog eddied around a tall silhouette, wrapped in a dark cloak, but the cloak was no disguise to Ellie. She knew every plane of that body, had been living with it in her mind and her heart for weeks.

''What are you doing here, Daniel?'' she managed to croak.

He moved towards her. ''I've come for you, Ellie. I want you with me.''

Pain streaked through Ellie. The words she had so wanted, but now it was all wrong. She held up the poker, as if to ward him off, and shook her head. "No, Daniel. I can't. I won't. I have Amy to think of."

He stood stock-still, shocked, his brow furrowed. "But of course I want Amy as well."

Ellie shook her head, more frantically. "No, I can't do that. I won't. Go back home, Daniel. No matter what my feelings for you are, I won't come with you. I won't ruin Amy's life that way."

There was a long silence. Behind her Ellie could hear the slow plop, plop of water dripping off the roof…the roof he had fixed for her.

"And what *are* your feelings for me?"

Ellie's face crumpled with anguish. "You know what they are," she whispered.

He shook his head. His eyes blazed with intensity. "No, I thought I did, but now…I'm only sure of my own feelings." He took a deep breath and said in a voice vibrating with emotion, "I love you, Ellie. I have my memory back and I know I have never loved anyone and will never love anyone again as much as I love you. You are my heart, Ellie."

Tears blurred Ellie's vision at his words. All she'd ever dreamed of was in those few words… *You are my heart, Ellie.* But it was too late.

"Go back to your wife, Daniel," she said miserably and turned away.

There was a short, fraught silence. Then Daniel swore. Then he laughed. "I'd forgotten that."

Ellie turned. "Forgotten your wife?" she said, shocked.

Daniel's blue eyes blazed into her. "I don't have a wife. I've never had a wife. It was all a stupid misunderstanding." He laid his hand over his heart and declared, "I am a single man, in possession of all my wits and I'm able to support a wife in relative comfort. I love you most desperately, Mrs. Ellie Carmichael, and I've come to ask you to be my wife."

There was a long silence. Ellie just stared. The raised poker wavered. A strong masculine hand took it gently out of her slackened grasp.

"Well, Ellie-love, aren't you going to answer me?"

Ellie couldn't see him for tears, but she could feel him and she flung herself into his arms and kissed him fiercely. "Oh, Daniel, Daniel, yes, of course I'll marry you! I love you so much it hurts!"

"The sergeant lied," Daniel explained some time later, an arm around both Ellie and Amy. "The silly clunch thought he was rescuing me from a designing hussy. He'd started to wonder if he'd made a mistake—apparently you just about gave him frostbite when he offered you money—but he thought it would be better to get me out of your clutches and recover my memory before I made any decisions."

He grinned and kissed Ellie again. "So, having regained my memory, I've brought myself straight back to your clutches. And what very nice clutches they are, too, my dear," he leered in a growly voice and both Ellie and Amy giggled.

"So you remember everything, now?"

"Indeed I do. The moment I arrived back at Rothbury, it all came back to me. Most peculiar how the mind works—or doesn't, as the case may be. Rothbury is a house as well as a village," he explained. "I was born there."

"And, er, what do you do there?" Ellie enquired delicately.

"I oversee the farm. I've found a position for you, too. You will be in charge of the house. After we're married, of course." He looked at her. "You're sure, Ellie? Knowing nothing about me, you'll marry me and come and keep house with me?"

She smiled mistily and nodded happily. "Oh, yes, please. I could think of nothing more wonderful. I would be a good housekeeper, I think. In fact, I did try to find a position like that after Hart died and we found there was no money left, but having no references…and also a daughter…" She hesitated. "You know I bring nothing to this marriage."

He looked affronted. "You bring yourself, don't you? You're all I want, love. Just you. Oh, and a small bonus called Princess Amy."

"Oh, Daniel…" She kissed him again. It was that or weep all over him.

He had brought a special licence. "I've arranged everything, my love. The vicar has agreed to marry us this afternoon—no need to wait for the banns to be called. Then Tommy—Sergeant Tomkins to you—will take Amy to stay the night at the vicarage."

"But why—''

He looked at her and his blue eyes were suddenly burning with intensity. "We have a wedding night ahead of us, love…and this is a small cottage. Amy is better off at the vicarage. Don't worry, she already has Tommy eating out of her hand. He loves a bossy woman! And the vicar is delighted, too. He loves Christmas weddings.''

Christmas. They were only a few days away from Christmas. She'd been trying to forget about it, expecting this to be her worst Christmas ever. But now…

Daniel continued, "We'll stay one night here and then I'll take you home to Rothbury. I thought it would be nice if we celebrated Christmas there, with my poor old mother.''

Ellie smiled. "Oh, yes, that would be lovely. But…a wedding, today…I have noth—'' She glanced down at the shabby dress she wore. "I don't suppose my old blue dress—''

"You look beautiful in anything, my love, but I brought you a dress…and some other things.'' He gestured to a portmanteau, which the sergeant had carried in earlier.

Hesitantly Ellie opened the lid. Inside, wrapped in tissue, was a beautiful heavy cream satin dress. She lifted it out and held it against herself. The dress was exquisite, long-sleeved and high-waisted, embroidered over the bodice and around the hem in the most delicate and lovely green-and-gold silk embroidery. It was utterly beautiful... Totally unsuitable for a house-keeper, of course, but did she care?

"Is it all right?"

She turned, clutching the dress to her breasts and whispered, "It's beautiful, Daniel."

"The colour is all right, is it?"

She smiled. "It's lovely, though I'm not exactly a maiden, Daniel."

"You are to me," he said. "Anyway, that wasn't why I chose it. It reminded me of when I first saw you—you were dressed in that white night-thingum-my."

Ellie thought of her much-patched, thick flannel nightgown and laughed. "Only a man could see any similarity between my shapeless old nightgown and this beautiful thing." She laid the dress carefully over the chair and flew across the room to hug and kiss him.

"A man in love," he corrected her. "And that night-gown did have shape—your shape, and a delectable shape it is too." He ran his hands over her lovingly and kissed her deeply. Ellie kissed him back, shivering with pleasurable anticipation.

"Enough of that, my love. We'll be churched be-fore long. We can wait until tonight."

"I don't know if I can," she whispered.

He laughed, lifted her in his arms and swung her around exuberantly, then kissed her again and pushed her towards the table. "There's more stuff in the port-manteau."

She looked and drew out a lovely green merino pelisse, trimmed with white fur at the collar and cuffs and a pair of pretty white boots which even looked to be the right size. Beneath it was a miniature pelisse identical to the first, but in blue. With it was a dainty little blue dress with a charming lace collar. And the sweetest pair of tiny fur-lined red kid boots, perfect winter wear for a little girl. Ellie's eyes misted. He'd brought a wedding outfit for Amy, too. And of the finest quality. She wondered how he could afford it, but it didn't matter.

She smiled a wobbly smile and hugged him. How did she ever deserve such a dear, kind thoughtful man? "Thank you, Daniel. I don't know how—"

"Come on, love, let's get you to that church, or we'll be anticipating our vows. The sergeant shall escort you and Amy. I shall meet you there, as is proper." He pulled out a fob-watch and consulted it. "Shall we say one hour?"

"One hour!" gasped Ellie. "Two, at least. Amy and I need to wash our hair and—"

"Very well, two hours it is," he said briskly and kissed her mouth, a swift, hard, possessive promise of a kiss. "And not a moment longer, mind! I have waited long enough!"

Freshly prepared for Christmas, the church looked beautiful. Small and built of sombre grey stone, it glowed inside as the soft winter sunshine pierced the stained-glass windows, flooding the inside with rain-

bows of delicate colour and making the brass and
silver gleam. It smelt of beeswax and fresh-cut pine-
wood. Greenery decorated the softly shining oak pews
and the two huge brass urns on either side of the altar
were laden with branches of holly and ivy and pine.
Braziers had been lit, taking the chill from the air,
throwing out a cosy glow.

Ellie and Amy, dressed in their new finery, stood
at the door. The sergeant, looking smart and neat in
what Ellie guessed was a new coat, had gone to inform Daniel and the vicar of their arrival. Ellie, suddenly nervous, clutched Amy's hand. Was she doing
the right thing? She had only known Daniel a matter
of days, after all.

She loved him. But she had loved once before...and
had been badly mistaken. She had never felt for Hart
half the feelings she had for Daniel. Did that mean she
had made the right choice this time...or double the mistake? She shivered, feeling suddenly cold. Amy's little
hand was warm in hers. A tiny white fur muff dangled
from her daughter's wrist. A gift from Daniel...

"Are you ready, love?" The deep voice came from
her right. Ellie jumped. Daniel was standing there,
with a look in his eyes that drove all the last-minute
jitters from her mind.

"Oh, yes. I'm ready," she said, and with a full
heart laid her hand on his arm.

"Then lead the way, Sergeant and Amy."

Gravely the sergeant offered his arm to the small
girl. Like a little princess, Amy walked solemnly be-

side him down the aisle. As they reached the altar, Amy's attention was distracted. "Look, Mama, the vicar has a dolls' house, too," she whispered.

Ellie followed her daughter's gesture and her hand tightened on Daniel's arm. To the right of the aisle at the front of the church sat a Christmas diorama on a small wooden table. A stable, thatched with straw, was surrounded by carved wooden sheep and cows and a donkey. Over the building a painted wooden star gleamed. Inside the stable stood a woman in a blue painted robe, a woman with a serene expression and kind eyes. Beside her stood a tall dark-haired man smiling down at a child not his own, with love in his eyes and his heart.

Like the man at Ellie's side.

Amy stared at the diorama in fascination. She was too small to remember it from the previous Christmas. "The vicar's dolls' house has a family, too—a mama and a papa and a baby, just like us, only I'm not a baby any more."

Ellie glanced up at the tall man by her side, looking at Amy as if he'd just received the most wonderful of gifts. She said huskily, "That's right, darling. It's a very special family. That's Mary and that's Joseph and that's little Baby Jesus."

"It's lovely." Amy was entranced.

Daniel's arm tightened around Ellie and he drew her forward as the vicar began.

"Dearly beloved..."

* * *

Daniel and Ellie returned to the cottage alone, their footsteps crunching on the cold ground, anticipation their only companion. Daniel lit a fire downstairs, then went upstairs to light another one in the bedroom, while Ellie laid out some supper. They ate almost in silence, eating slowly, barely touching the wine and the game pie that Daniel had brought.

He laid down his knife and fork and said with a wry smile, "I can't think of a word to say or take in a mouthful of food, love, for wanting you. Shall we go upstairs?"

Tremulously she nodded.

They walked up the stairs with arms wrapped tight around each other. Ellie recalled that first frightful battle to get him up the stairs, his dogged courage as he took each step, and felt a fresh surge of love. How far they had come in such a short time...

When they reached the bedroom, she hesitated, suddenly realising she should have gone up ahead of him and changed into her nightgown. She glanced at the curtains across the sleeping alcove and wondered if she should go behind them to change. It would be a little awkward. There was not much room.

She glanced up at Daniel and the questions in her mind dissipated like smoke as his mouth came down over hers in a tender kiss. She leaned into him, returning the kiss with all her heart. Her hands curled into his hair, loving the feel of hard bone beneath crisp short waves. She could feel the place where he had been injured, where she had cut his hair away.

Daniel felt her trembling against him. He wanted her so much, wanted to dive on to the bed with her and make her his in one bold passionate glorious movement. She was his! His beloved. The woman of his heart. Ellie. Pressing small moist kisses over his face. So soft, so warm, so giving. He felt proud, primitive, possessive.

But she was trembling. And it was not simply desire.

He recalled her shock when he'd touched her intimately, all those mornings ago, her surprise and bemusement at the pleasure his hands had given her. He deepened the kiss, feeling a jolt like lightning surge through him at her enthusiastic, yet endearingly inexpert return of his caresses. She was a married woman, a mother, and a widow, his little Ellie, but of the pleasures between a man and woman she seemed almost as ignorant as any new bride.

Daniel reined in his desires and set himself to introduce his love to the joys between a man and woman. He rained her soft, smooth skin with kisses, running his hands over her, soothing her anxieties wordlessly, caressing her, warming, knowing her.

The cream of the silk gown looked heavy and lifeless against the vibrant delicacy of Ellie's skin. He unbuttoned the gown, pearl button by pearl button, revealing more and more of her soft, silken skin. He slipped the gown off her shoulders and she flushed shyly under his gaze, all the way down to her pink-tipped breasts. It was the most beautiful flush he had ever seen. He bent to kiss her and when his mouth closed over one nipple she arched against him, crying out with a small muffled groan and clasping his head to her breast.

He glanced up at her and his body pounded with heat and need as he saw her head flung back, her eyes blind with passion. Mastering his own needs, he moved his attention to her other breast, and was rewarded by a long shuddery moan.

Daniel slowly divested her of her clothing, piece by piece, for once not feeling impatient with the quantity and complexity of the underclothes women wore, because as he slid each garment over her skin, she blushed most deliciously and shuddered sensually under the warmth of his hands as they pushed the soft cotton slowly over her skin. He hazily made a note to get her silk underclothes. A few minutes later he changed his mind. It would be better if she wore no underclothes at all…

Finally she was naked, soft and peachy in the flames of the fire he had built. Blushing, she glanced at the bedclothes and then back at him and he realised she would want to cover herself while he disrobed. She was shy and modest, his little Ellie.

She surprised him. "My turn, I think." Eager hands made short work of his neckcloth and shirt buttons. She hesitated when it came to the fastenings of his breeches, then reached for him. He gritted his teeth, fighting for control as she fumbled with the buttons, frowning with concentration, her hands brushing against his arousal, her breasts swaying softly.

She unfastened the breeches and slowly pushed them down his legs. And stared. It was almost as if she had never seen a naked man before, the way she stared, enthralled. And then she reached out and touched him and he could hold back no longer. He tumbled her back on the bed, and, with none of the finesse he prided himself on, entered her in one long powerful thrust. She was hot and moist and ready for him and she arched against him, her body pulling him in, closing in, welcoming him…and as his body claimed her, totally out of his control, she stiffened, her eyes suddenly wide with shock.

"Daniel," she panted. "What is happen—?" She arched all around him and her body began to shudder uncontrollably.

"Let yourself go, love. I am here," he gritted out, himself on the brink of climax.

"Oh, Daniel, Daniel. I love you!" And she shattered around him, sending him over the edge of bliss into oblivion…

He had never known it could be like that. Daniel gazed at his beautiful, rumpled sleeping new bride with bemused wonder. He had thought he would be the one to initiate Ellie into a new world of lovemaking between a man and woman. But if he had shown her a new world, she had shown him one too, a world he'd never even dreamed existed. The world of making love with the woman you adored. Physical pleasures, he'd realised, were shallow ephemeral moments, compared with how it had been with Ellie. The moment when she'd come to climax—her first ever…

Would he, could he, ever forget that look in her eyes as she gazed into his, shouting that she loved him…as she shattered with pleasure, sending him into oblivion with her?

It was like looking at a painting all your life and not knowing there was a living breathing whole new dimension waiting on the other side of the canvas. Like eating all your life and not knowing there was such a thing as salt…

No, there were no poetical images to describe making love with Ellie. All Daniel knew was that he wanted to live to a very ripe old age so he could love her every day of his life.

He leaned down and began to wake her with his mouth, smiling as she squirmed with sleepy pleasure, reaching for him even before she was awake…

At mid-morning, a coach arrived to take them to Rothbury. It bore a crest on the side panel. Ellie glanced at Daniel in surprise. It seemed rather a grand coach for a farmer.

He grinned at her. "It belongs to the Dowager

Viscountess, Lady Rothbury, my love. When I told her I was bringing a bride to Rothbury, she insisted I use her carriage.''

"She must be a very kind-hearted lady.''

"You might say that,'' agreed Daniel wryly. "I put it down to a managing disposition, myself. The woman has made my life a misery since she lost her husband and her eldest son.''

"Oh, the poor lady. She must be lonely, Daniel.''

He nodded. "Yes, she has not enough to do. However, she is expecting her first grandchild any day now and I am hopeful that the child will keep her out of my hair in future.'' He picked up a bundle of Ellie's possessions and winked. "At any rate, having no conveyance of my own as yet, I wasn't about to look her gift-carriage in the mouth.''

"I should think not.'' Ellie frowned thoughtfully as she hurried to collect her things. It was clear that Daniel was a little irritated by his employer's managing ways. She hoped she could smooth the way between them.

Because of their imminent eviction, Ellie was already packed. She left her chickens for Ned to take, as Daniel said he already had plenty. There was nothing else. In a few minutes, their meagre possessions were placed in the boot of the coach and they'd picked up Amy and the sergeant and were heading north.

The trip to Rothbury was long, but not tedious. They passed the time with songs and games for

Amy's entertainment. And with small secret glances and touches, which recalled in Ellie the magic and the splendour of her wedding night and morning and raised in her body the shivery, delightful expectation of nights and mornings yet to come.

Ellie thought of how she had told Daniel weeks before that they had already "made love," without having joined, flesh with flesh. She remembered the look on his face as she'd said it, a little quizzical, a little knowing...indulgent.

How naïve she'd been. She hadn't understood that the act of making love with Daniel would bring another dimension to that love, a deep, powerful intimacy that was not merely physical...though it was intensely physical. She would never forget that first, almost terrifying intimacy, the intensity as she'd exploded into helpless, splintering waves of pleasure under his eyes.

She'd assumed that because the physical act had been unimportant in her marriage to Hart, it would be the same with Daniel. She'd believed it was, by its nature, crude, furtive and only necessary for the procreation of an heir. Because that's how Hart had seen it.

But nothing was the same with Daniel. With Daniel it was...a joyous celebration. A glorious, elemental claiming, in which they united in a way that she had never imagined. It was not a mere fleshly joining—it was...everything. Body, mind, soul. She shivered with remembrance. And pleasure. With Daniel it had been an act of reverence as well as earthy delight. They had made love so many times and the echo of it was with her still. It was as if in one night their bodies had become forever joined, with invisible, unbreakable threads.

The coach swayed along. Awareness shimmered between them, recalling moments of shattering delight. She did not simply love Daniel, she was part of him. And he of her.

With tender eyes she watched him, playing a children's clapping game with Amy, pretending bearish clumsiness with his big, calloused hands. She felt a ripple, deep within her body, as she watched. There was nothing clumsy about those big, beautiful hands. They had taught her body how to sing; it was singing still, within her, deep and silent.

He had transformed her in the night, murmuring endearments, caressing her in places never before caressed, creating sensations she'd never known…nor even imagined. It was as if he knew her body better than she did herself.

Ellie caught his eye, and saw the lurking wolf-smile in it. His gaze sharpened, as if he knew what she'd been thinking, and she felt herself blush as his look turned suddenly intense and hungry. He wanted her. In the course of a single night he'd loved every part of her with hands and mouth and eyes, bringing her alive as she'd never known was possible. And she'd gloried in it so that the wonder still spilled from her…

She couldn't wait for the night to come. Last night she had been the novice, reduced to a blissful jelly by his loving attentions, but it hadn't escaped her that he seemed to enjoy being touched the same way she did. Tonight it would be her turn to explore him. She felt herself smile, a small, secret triumphant feminine smile, and then she caught his eye again, and blushed scarlet as if he'd read her mind.

Passion. She'd never understood it before. An incendiary mix of primitive power...and sublime pleasure. Explosive. Ready to reignite at a look, a touch, a thought...

Though it was only afternoon, dark was falling by the time they turned in at two large stone gateposts, topped by lions. They received their first sight of Rothbury House a few moments later.

It was ablaze with light. The house was huge with dozens of windows. In every window there were candles burning. As they drew closer, Ellie could see they were red candles. Christmas candles.

"Remember how you told me about your wishing candle?" Daniel addressed Amy. "Those are wishing candles for us, to bring us all home safe and sound."

Amy's eyes shone. Ellie lifted his hand and held it against her cheek. It wasn't true—it was probably a tradition of the Big House, but it was a lovely thought, to make a little girl feel welcomed. Daniel put his arm around Ellie and smiled.

The coach pulled up at a flight of steps. "The front door?" whispered Ellie, surprised.

Daniel shrugged. "I'm under orders to present you to the Dowager without delay. She prides herself on knowing everyone on the estate. And it is her carriage, don't forget."

"Oh, dear!" Ellie nervously ran a hand over her hair and tried to smooth her travel-crushed clothing. She hoped the Dowager would not be too demanding an employer.

In the magnificent hallway, an elegant lady awaited them. Silver-haired, she was the epitome of elegance, dressed in the first stare of fashion in a black gown, a black shawl in Norwich silk dangling negligently from her elbows.

"Ellie, I'd like you to meet the Dowager Viscountess, Lady Rothbury," said Daniel.

Ellie curtsied to her new employer.

"Mother, this is my wife, Elinor, the new Viscountess of Rothbury."

Ellie, still curtsying, nearly fell over. Daniel bent down and helped her up.

"But I thought I was to be the new housekeeper!" gasped Ellie. "You mean, you're, you're—"

He bowed. "Viscount Rothbury, at your service, my dear." His blue, blue eyes twinkled wickedly as he kissed her hand in a way that made Ellie blush.

"My son is tiresomely reticent about some things," the lady said sympathetically. "He told *me* he was bringing home a cottage wench, but you are as beau-

tiful and elegant as any of the suitable young ladies
I have been flinging so uselessly at his head this age.''

"Much more beautiful," growled Daniel's deep
voice and he grinned down at Ellie, who looked flustered and adoring at the same time.

The Dowager Viscountess gave a small, satisfied
nod. She moved forward and drew Ellie into a warm,
scented embrace. "Welcome to the family, my dear
girl. I think you will do very nicely indeed for my
scapegrace son.''

"The scapegrace son agrees with you, Mother."

Lady Rothbury's eyes dropped to where Amy was
loitering in the shadows of her mother's skirts, a little
overwhelmed by everything that had happened. "And
who have we here?" she said softly. "Can this be
my beautiful new granddaughter? My son promised
me I would love her instantly."

Ellie's chest was suddenly tight. Such welcome as
this she had never dared to dream of. Her daughter
would be loved in this house.

Amy examined the older lady with wide, candid
eyes. "Are you really Mr. Bruin's mama?"

"Mr. Bruin? Is that what you call my son? Yes, I
am his mama. May I ask why you call him Mr.
Bruin?"

"That's 'cause he looked just like a bear when he
came to me and Mama. He was all prickly."

Lady Rothbury laughed. "A most perspicacious
young lady. A prickly bear is exactly how I would
describe my son at times." She smiled down at Amy.

Amy looked thoughtful. "I haven't got a grand-mother," the little girl said shyly.

The Dowager Viscountess held out her hand and said softly, "You have one now." Amy glanced at her mother for permission, then, beaming, took the older lady's hand.

Lady Rothbury smiled at Ellie through tear-blurred eyes. "Thank you, my dear. You have made my son and me happier than I would have believed possible."

Ellie couldn't say a word. She was blinking away her own tears.

"Now," continued the older lady, "I have some-thing for my beautiful new granddaughter—a wel-come home present which I hope she will enjoy. It isn't new, I'm afraid—it was mine when I was a little girl. I kept it for my daughters, but I was never blessed with any, so it has remained untouched in the attic these many years. When Daniel told me about his Ellie and her Amy, I had it brought down and cleaned up and I must say, it looks almost as good as it did when I was a child."

Ellie looked quizzically at Daniel. He shrugged and murmured, "No idea."

"Come along, Amy." The little girl's hand held fast in hers, Lady Rothbury swept down the hall.

Grinning, Daniel called, "She's a princess, Mother. You have to call her Princess Amy."

His mother turned, regally. "Of course she's a princess. She's my granddaughter."

"Come on, I want to see, too," said Ellie. But his arm restrained her.

"In a moment, love. You don't mind if I call you love, now, do you?"

Ellie shook her head, barely able to talk for the happiness that swelled within her.

"Before we see what my mother has up her sleeve for Princess Amy, you have your first duty as Lady Rothbury to perform."

"Oh, yes, of course," said Ellie, suddenly apprehensive. "What must I do?"

He tugged her half a dozen steps to the left and then stopped. And waited.

"What is it?"

His eyes drifted upwards. Her gaze followed. A branch twisted with mistletoe.

"Ohh," whispered Ellie. "A kissing bough. That duty I can see is going to be very arduous. I might need help." And, standing on tiptoe, she reached up and pulled his mouth down to hers.

After a moment, they separated reluctantly. "You have a choice, my love—we go into the drawing room, or straight up to the bedroom."

Breathlessly, Ellie straightened her gown. "I think it had better be the drawing room. And then…" she looked at his mouth and pressed a quick, hungry kiss on it "…the bedroom."

Arms around each other they strolled towards the drawing room, pausing every few paces for a kiss. At the threshold they stopped. Lady Rothbury sat on a small footstool beside a low table. Amy stood beside her, her little face a study. Ellie gasped.

Amy turned. Her eyes were shimmering with wonder. "Look, Mama," she whispered. "Have you ever, ever, *ever,* seen such a beautiful dolls' house?"

Ellie speechless, shook her head, smiling as the tears spilled down her cheeks.

"Look, Mr. Bruin."

"You can call me Papa, if you like, Princess." Daniel turned Ellie in his arms and began to dry her tears. "I thought you told me you weren't a watering pot," he grumbled softly, making her laugh, even as she wept.

"Can I, Mama? Can I call Mr. Bruin Papa?"

"Yes, darling. Of course you can. He is your papa now."

"Good," said the little girl in satisfaction. "I told you that my Christmas wishing candle was special, Mama. It did bring Papa to us."

"Yes darling, it did."

"Look, everyone," said Lady Rothbury suddenly. "It's snowing."

Outside the long windows, across the bright, dancing flames of the red Christmas candles, it began to snow, softly, gently, blanketing the world with white, making everything clean and new and fresh again.

And so it was Christmas Eve. Filled with peace, love, and the promise of joy to come.

* * * * *

Author Note

My Darling Echo is truly a story straight from my heart. The two central characters, Arabella Simmons and the gallant ex-soldier Alexander Coltrain, seventh Earl of Huntingdon, have lived in my head a long time, just waiting for their chance to come alive. I'm very grateful for the opportunity to tell you about them.

Actually, they were inspired by two of my favourite stories, both written in the early 1900s, a period when writers such as Ethel M. Dell were creating intensely romantic novels that are seldom read today. *Man and Maid* by Elinor Glyn and *Leave It to Love* by Pamela Wynn have been on my keeper shelf for years. Of course, I've always loved to read stories about strong, imperfect heroes, and now I love to write them.

Hunt, as the earl's friends call him, has long believed he would never marry because of his disability. As a result of a heroic military action during his service with Wellington ten years ago, the earl was blinded. Now a member of the House of Lords, Hunt's life is both productive and meaningful. It is also lonely, at least until he employs as his reader the widow of an old schoolmate and finds himself falling in love with a woman's voice.

Arabella has struggled since her husband's death to support her small family in a society in which gentlewomen do not work. The employment Huntingdon offers her is a salvation, and she is enormously grateful. And then, as she comes to know her employer, gratitude and admiration are not the only emotions she begins to feel for him.

It is only with the behind-the-scenes machinations of the earl's faithful valet, however, that two lonely people are tricked into a marriage of convenience, which will in the end, of course, become something very different. And something I hope is as romantically satisfying for you as those old stories on my keeper shelf have always been for me.

I sincerely hope you enjoy *My Darling Echo*, my small tribute to some of the pioneers in the field of romance who have been virtually forgotten by modern readers.

My Darling Echo
by
Gayle Wilson

For Tracy Farrell, with my admiration,
love and deep gratitude

Chapter One

London 1823

He would rather be facing the advance of a line of French cavalry, the Earl of Huntingdon thought, as the strained silence deepened. At least during his service on the Peninsula, he had been able to tell something about what was happening. Now, however—

"Marriage, my lord?" Arabella Simmons said faintly.

Yesterday he would have claimed that he knew every subtle nuance of her remarkable voice, but there was something in that breathless inquiry he had never heard before. Shock, certainly. And after all, he had expected that. Was there disgust there as well?

Damn you, Ingalls, Hunt thought. *Damn you for talking me into this. And damn me for being fool enough to let you.*

"Purely as a matter of convenience, Mrs.

Simmons,'' he said aloud, his voice betraying none of that mental self-castigation. ''If the idea is distasteful to you, however, we need never mention it again. I assure you I meant you no disrespect.''

''And I took none, my lord,'' Arabella said.

There was now a hint of amusement underlying the pleasantly husky timbre of her reply. And hearing it, the sickening sense that he had made an irretrievable blunder began to ease.

''An offer of marriage can seldom be considered insulting,'' she continued. ''And certainly in our case...''

The words trailed. There were, however, so many aspects of their case that were unlike other couples who might be contemplating matrimony that a dozen interpretations could be put on the unfinished phrase.

The most obvious was the difference in their stations, of course. Mrs. Simmons was in his employ, and he was Alexander Coltrain, the seventh Earl of Huntingdon, the last of his immediate family who would bear that old and distinguished title. A match between them would be, therefore, a misalliance by almost every standard the ton might apply.

Since he had determined more than ten years ago that he would never marry, Huntingdon was unconcerned about any opinion society might venture about the proposal he had just made. A proposal that was as unexpected to him, he acknowledged, as it would be to those who knew him.

To the few remaining members of his family,

whom he had informed long ago about his intention not to marry. To his friends, who had chided him often enough about that decision. To his servants, who were more familiar than anyone with the relationship he and Mrs. Bertrand Simmons had enjoyed for more than two years.

A relationship which had never, at least until today, strayed anywhere near the personal. Unless, he amended, one could consider as personal the undeniable pleasure he had felt from the first day Arabella had read for him.

At that time, Hunt had endured his blindness for eight years without giving voice to any sentiment that could possibly be interpreted as a complaint, so he felt he had earned the right to Mrs. Simmons's voice. He had known the first day that, having once heard it, he could never go back to the dry recitations he had suffered before she had arrived on the doorstep of his London town house, the advertisement he had had placed in *The Times* clutched in her hand.

Employing a female reader was highly irregular, even in these modern times. However, Bertrand Simmons had been a schoolmate. And during the course of the interview he had granted Arabella, strictly on the basis of that long-ago friendship with her deceased husband, the earl had learned of her straitened circumstances.

That and her voice had guaranteed his decision to employ her, despite what anyone might think. He considered Mrs. Simmons his one self-indulgence—and had decided that day that surely one was allowed. Now, however, he was suggesting something which would cause far more comment among his set.

"In our case?" he repeated when she didn't go on.

Had his pride prompted that query? he wondered. Or a simple tendency to masochism?

"I doubt your family would be pleased should I accept your offer, my lord," she said.

He was relieved to find that the trace of amusement he had heard before had not disappeared.

"I think we are both of an age to make our own decisions. Your birth is perfectly acceptable, Mrs. Simmons. And whatever objections my family might pose will be of no concern to me, I assure you."

There was little enough family left. His mother had died when he was only ten; his father while he was at Cambridge. His older brother, to whom the title had belonged, had been killed in a riding accident while Hunt was still in Iberia. Rather than sell out, the new earl had decided to stay at least until the army had successfully pushed across the frontier into Spain. That had proved to be a fateful decision and had led, of course, to his decision not to marry.

The occasional guilt he felt about letting the direct line of descent die with himself had a great deal more to do with the unsuitable cousin who would ultimately inherit both the title and the estates than with the opinions of the other members of that small familial band. Of course, neither of those considerations was what had prompted his offer today.

"Past our primes, are we, my lord?" Bella suggested, the hint of laughter he had heard before still running through the words. He wondered if her eyes were smiling as well, and if they were, he wished that he might—if only once—see them.

"My apologies, Mrs. Simmons," he said easily. "My social skills, as you of all people must be aware, are sadly lacking. I should have said *I* am of an age when I no longer need seek my family's approval."

"And what age is that, my lord?"

Hunt found he had to think about it, and when he had, he was surprised by the answer. "I am thirty-eight years old."

There was another small silence, but apparently they had both recovered from the initial shock. This one was almost contemplative.

"I am twenty-six, my lord," she said.

He tried to remember what he had been doing when he was that age. It seemed a hundred years ago, but in actuality...

Deliberately destroying the sudden mental images from those days, because he was unwilling to dwell on the years of camaraderie and adventure he had spent with his regiment, he concentrated instead on trying to read her voice.

"Then certainly too young to consider a marriage of convenience," he suggested, his own tone carefully avuncular. He forced his lips into a smile. *Damn you, Ingalls,* he thought again, fighting embarrass-

ment and an incredible—and incredibly surprising—
sense of disappointment.

"I didn't mean that," she said quickly. "A man of
your age is indeed in the prime of life. There must
be a hundred highly suitable young ladies in London
right now who would welcome your suit, my lord."

"I take it then, you are not one of them."

"You may take it that I am *not* considered to be
in my prime. Nor could I be considered a suitable
candidate to be your wife. Not by anyone's standards.
Not even my own," she added, her tone verging on
laughter.

"I believe it is *my* prerogative to decide who is
suitable for me to take to wife."

"Forgive me, my lord, but my understanding was
that it was your long-held intention never to wed. Or
was I mistaken in that belief?"

Trust Bella to go straight to the heart, Hunt
thought. He couldn't even remember when he had
come to think of her as Bella. He didn't know if anyone else had ever called her that, but at some time in
the course of a dark winter's afternoon, the only
sounds in his study the pleasant crackle and hiss of
the fire and the far more pleasant tenor of her voice,
reading to him from some deadly dull parliamentary
bill, she had become Bella. His Bella.

It was a fantasy, of course. And a harmless one. Or
so he had believed. He had never had any intention
of stepping beyond the carefully prescribed boundaries of their relationship. He had fallen in love with

a woman's voice, and that he had was a secret he would take to his grave. Because, of course, the alternative was unthinkable.

"I long ago determined never to marry. Not in the conventional sense," he said truthfully.

"So what you have proposed between us is...*not* to be a conventional marriage?"

"You may think of it as a business proposition."

Pompous ass, he mocked himself, as soon as the words left his mouth.

"I see," she said.

The tone he had been unable to place at the beginning of the conversation was back, and he still couldn't identify it.

"However—" he began, prepared to cut his losses and sound retreat. It was obvious, no matter what Ingalls had suggested, that she found his proposal to be repugnant.

Why wouldn't she? he asked himself bitterly. And then, because that corrosive bitterness was something he had long ago recognized as skirting too near self-pity, he blocked the thought, arranging his features in the same bland expression with which he pretended to listen to debates in the House of Lords.

"Why would you suddenly offer to marry me, my lord?" she asked.

"I believe I have explained my thinking."

"To have me at your beck and call, available to read to you at any hour of the night and day," she said.

"I don't believe I was so gauche in my phrasing." Again, he allowed the small, controlled smile, inclining his head towards her in an assenting salute.

"You are never gauche," she said. "You are careful. And considerate. Thoughtful. Occasionally impatient," she added after a moment. "More frequently of yourself than of others. But you are *never* gauche," she said again.

"There seems no sense in your braving the elements each day," he said, ignoring her commentary on his character. "I was merely offering you room and board here in my home in addition to your salary. And I am offering those in the only way that would be acceptable to society. I assure you, I have no ulterior motives."

"The salary you give me is more than generous, my lord, providing amply for my room and board."

"You need not look for excuses, Mrs. Simmons. A simple no will suffice," he said, wondering why she was drawing this painful interview out. "Nothing in our situation will change as a result of your refusal."

"I have...dependants," she said.

"Dependants?" he repeated blankly, having no idea what she meant.

"My son and my aunt, who serves as his governess. They are my responsibilities. I could not leave them."

My son. Huntingdon's brain echoed the words as if they had been spoken in some exotic language in which he was only vaguely conversant. Bella had worked in his home, had worked closely beside him day after day for two years, and he had never known she had a child.

"Indeed," he said. "I did not know."

"His name is Christopher. After Bertrand's father. He is four years old."

"You've never mentioned him," he said.

The earl had seen little enough of his own mother during his early years. A succession of nannies and later a rather strict governess had raised him. Obviously, Bella's arrangements were similar. After all, she spent every day except Sunday in this very room, reading to him. When he realized that, Hunt felt another twinge of guilt at the length of the hours he required of her. Ingalls was right: he was a brute.

"There has been no occasion for us to speak of him," Bella said.

Which was true enough. They did not engage in social chitchat. He realized with a sense of surprise he had no idea where she lived. He supposed Ingalls had her address, or perhaps his man of business, but he couldn't remember having ever heard it.

"Surely—" he began, only to be interrupted.

"A child might disrupt your household's routine," Bella warned.

A child. A little boy. There was always the possibility that his presence would be disruptive. The house was huge, however, and as far as he was aware the nursery wing was much as it had been in his childhood—far enough removed from the rest of the living quarters to preclude any such problems.

"Surely one small boy couldn't accomplish so much," he said, smiling at her again.

Another silence. He wished he could see her face. That was the thing he had found hardest to deal with through the years. Not being able to read expressions. Of course, voices could be equally revealing, but not in a situation like this.

"Then…may I have time to think about your very kind offer, my lord?"

Again, she had taken him off guard. He'd thought she had already indicated her intent to refuse, and instead… Despite his avowals, a sense of anticipation, almost a physical reaction, stirred within him at the possibility that she might accept.

"Of course," he said. "Take as much time as you need."

"Thank you," she said.

He listened as she began to gather up the papers they had gone over this afternoon. He knew that the twilight shadows outside would be lengthening as people hurried home in the early-falling winter darkness. He tried to imagine Bella being greeted by her "dependants." He wondered if they would be as glad to hear the sound of her voice as he was each morning.

That was another part of the fantasy he had no right to indulge in, he admonished himself. They had a right to delight in her arrivals. He did not. And even if she accepted his proposal, he would still not have that right. At least not to do so openly.

"Good night, my lord," she said softly.

He could tell she was standing, probably looking down at him as he sat at his desk. He lifted his eyes, wondering what she saw when she looked at his face. He had long ago forbidden himself to think about that because it was something else he could not change.

"Good night, Mrs. Simmons."

It seemed there must be other words they should say to one another. Apparently she felt that as well, for she stood before his desk a long heartbeat before she turned and walked across the room. He didn't move until he heard the door close behind her.

Then the Earl of Huntingdon slowly lifted his hands and with trembling fingers touched the scarred skin around his unseeing eyes.

"Did you know she has a son?" the earl asked his valet that night as Ingalls helped him remove his waistcoat.

"She mentioned once that the boy had been un-well. A fever or a cough. I can't remember, but some childhood ill. That was some time before Christmas, I believe. She was fair anxious about him, I can tell you."

"And it never crossed your mind to inform me of the child's existence?" Hunt asked, his tone coldly demanding.

"Before you proposed to her, do you mean?" John

Ingalls asked. He considered his master's dark, handsome face, and his thin lips twitched at the corners as he suppressed a smile.

"You know exactly what I mean," the earl said. "You suggested that Mrs. Simmons was in danger of suffering a nervous exhaustion from the demands I have made on her time and her patience. You painted a vividly heart-wrenching portrait of a woman worked far beyond her strength by a brute of an employer. A woman who was also forced to travel to and from her place of employment every day in the bitter cold."

"An accurate portrait, my lord," Ingalls said calmly, as he folded the waistcoat. "Nothing about it has changed."

"What has changed, John, is that I have offered marriage to a woman who has, I now discover, a small child."

"You don't like children, my lord?" The subtle movement at the corners of the valet's mouth flickered again.

"You know damn well what I'm talking about," the earl said.

"You're talking about installing a small boy in a household that's large enough for an army of brats to rattle about in without your ever running into one of them. I can't see what all the fuss is about."

"The fuss, as you term it, is about deception."

The earl's voice was carefully controlled, but it was a tone Ingalls had certainly heard on more than one occasion. This was an officer's voice, demanding an explanation from his subordinate. And that had been their roles when they had met.

Through the last ten years, John Ingalls's position in the Earl of Huntingdon's life had evolved into something very different. Despite the outward appearance they maintained, their relationship was a friendship. The mantle of authority that Alexander Coltrain had worn since birth, however, had not diminished. Not even with his blindness. It was in full force tonight.

"You're making a mountain out of a molehill, my lord," Ingalls said soothingly. "This marriage proposal is nothing but a business proposition. The fact that the woman has a boy changes nothing."

"What if—"

When the sentence was abruptly cut off, Ingalls glanced again at his master's face. The finely shaped lips were flattened, as if determined to keep the rest of that question from emerging between them. A muscle jumped in the hard line of the earl's jaw and the blue eyes seemed focused at a spot beyond the valet's shoulder. So intent was the focus that in spite of himself, Ingalls turned, briefly contemplating the empty corner behind him.

"What if?" he repeated cautiously, turning back to consider the classic features of a man he had known and loved for more than a decade. A man he admired more than any other of his acquaintance. A man who in battle knew no fear. Ingalls couldn't imagine, therefore, why the thought of adding a little boy to his bachelor household had so disturbed the ex-soldier.

"Nothing," the earl said.

Then his fingers, long and aristocratic and always sure in their movements, despite his blindness, began to tug impatiently at the intricate arrangement of his neckcloth. Ingalls understood him well enough not to interfere. The earl had said everything he intended to say on the subject, and questioning him would elicit no more information. It might even poison the delicate negotiations the valet had worked so hard to bring about.

However, as John Ingalls tossed and turned that night on his narrow mattress, a rare situation for a man who had never in his life suffered from self-doubt, the earl's words repeated over and over in his head. *What if...* And no matter how much he pondered on what could be worrying his master about the existence of that little boy, he had found no answer before he fell asleep.

"Marriage?" Fanny Hargreaves repeated disbelievingly.

"Marriage," Bella said, savouring the freedom finally to speak aloud the word which had haunted her thoughts all evening. She had said nothing about the earl's offer until Kit had been fed his supper, properly cuddled and then tucked into his bed.

"But why?" her aunt asked, honest bewilderment in her voice.

"I have no idea," Bella said truthfully. "He *said* it was for his convenience, but somehow..." Still puzzling over what might be behind the sudden offer, Bella shook her head.

"Perhaps he has fallen in love with you, my dear," the older woman suggested.

Despite her advancing years, Fanny had never lost her belief in romance. Which must be a comfort, Bella thought. She herself was of a far more practical nature. As enticing as it might be to believe that the Earl of Huntingdon was in love with her, she knew better.

Never once in the two years she had worked for him had she allowed herself to think about him in those terms. It was all well and good for Fanny to entertain romantic notions, of course, but Bella was the one who was responsible for seeing that there was a roof over their heads and food on the table. She had known from the first that she could not afford to put a foot wrong with her self-contained employer.

She could not now. Desperately in need of advice, she had turned to the one person in all the world she could trust to have her best interests at heart, even if that heart were cloyingly sentimental.

"I think I should have known if the earl had suddenly developed a *tendre* for me," Bella said, smiling at her aunt.

"But he has asked you to *marry* him, my dear," Fanny said.

"Strictly as a matter of business."

"Business?" the old woman repeated. "In my day, marriage was not a business. Not for the likes of us."

Bella understood what Fanny meant, of course. For someone in the earl's position, marriages were often decided on the basis of how much wealth, land or distinction they would bring to the families involved. Only those who had none of those things to consider might marry for love.

Bella did not believe that Huntingdon had suddenly fallen in love with his penniless reader. If he had, he might have asked her to become his mistress, but certainly not his wife.

And even if he *had* fallen head over heels for a woman he'd never seen, he was, just as she had told him this afternoon, far too controlled to do something as impetuous as proposing marriage to her. However, try as she might, Bella had been unable to come up with any logical reason for his offer, especially since his determination never to marry was well known to his household.

"He said he wants me to live in the house because it would be more convenient. Apparently, he thinks of things he would like for me to do for him after I've gone home. Perhaps there is something he would like to hear read again for clarification. Or some letter that needs to be written. A speech. And since it's impossible for him to jot down those instructions…"

"Poor man," Fanny said. Her kind heart had always been touched by the earl's plight, since the first night Bella had come home, incredulous, despite

Bertrand's connection, that she had been given the position.

"If we *did* move into his household," Bella began to warn, couching the possibility in terms her mind could deal with and not in those the earl had used this afternoon, "you must never let him hear you voice anything of that nature."

"A proud man, is he?" Fanny suggested.

"A man who does not recognize he has limitations," Bella said. Unconsciously, her voice had softened.

In the beginning she had been nervous about working so closely with a man who was blind, but she had very quickly been made aware that the earl made no allowances for his disability—at least none he could possibly avoid.

"He would not appreciate your concern for his 'plight,'" she added, smiling.

"Are you sure, Bella, my dear, that you have not developed a *tendre* for *him?*"

Shocked, Bella glanced up from the piece of needlework she had been toying with. Fanny's eyes were on her face, and in response, she blushed.

"Of course not," she said, recognizing that her denial was too abrupt.

"Is he…disfigured?" Fanny asked, the question holding the slightest edge of trepidation, perhaps even a fascinated horror.

"No," Bella said quickly, and then, knowing that she had not been completely honest, she added,

"There *is* some scarring, but it is very faded. Not at all noticeable."

"You must be sure to caution Kit not to mention that. Little boys are apt to be curious."

"Of course," Bella said, but she wasn't really thinking about Kit's reaction to the earl. Or that Fanny's words seemed to imply the two of them would eventually meet.

She was picturing instead that beautifully stern visage. Of course, she admitted, it wasn't the earl's features she had come to admire, as fine as they admittedly were. It was, rather, the man himself. His character. And his courage.

A man who had asked her to marry him, she thought with a sense of wonder that had only grown stronger in the hours since he had spoken those shocking words this afternoon. A business proposition, she admonished herself, fighting against the romanticism that was Fanny's great failing. What Huntingdon was proposing was a true marriage of convenience. An arrangement simply intended to make both their lives easier.

"Are you going to accept, my dear?" Fanny asked.

"He'll probably have come to his senses tomorrow and tell me it was all a mistake."

"A gentleman would never do that."

"An employer might," Bella said, smiling.

"And if he doesn't? Oh, my dear, you would be a fool not to accept. It would put an end to all our problems. Never again to have to wonder how we shall pay the coal merchant or the greengrocer. Kit's education would be assured, as would his place in society. Why, of course it would,'' Fanny said, her voice suddenly full of awe. ''After all, you would be a countess, Bella. The Countess of Huntingdon. Just think of it, my love.''

And although she shook her head at Fanny's list of enticements, Bella was thinking of it, of course, as her eyes stared unseeingly into the fire. Finally, her lips curved into a small, secret smile.

Whatever happened tomorrow, she thought, she would always have this night to remember. The Earl of Huntingdon had asked her to be his countess, and she would treasure that offer, no matter what justification he might wish to give for having made it.

Chapter Two

"Come in by the fire," John Ingalls said as he opened the door to the earl's study the next morning. "Did they bundle you up right and tight in the carriage, Mrs. Simmons? It's cold enough out to freeze the Thames."

"Then we'll have another frost fair," Bella said, smiling.

She was accustomed to Ingalls's presence in the study, at least early in the morning. He was frequently the one who ushered her in, the earl already seated behind the huge rosewood desk that dominated the room. Automatically, her eyes sought his familiar figure, a peculiar feeling in the pit of her stomach as she did. Today, the chair behind the desk was empty. Her gaze quickly scanned the room before it returned to meet that of the earl's valet. He smiled at her.

"Lord Huntingdon will be down shortly," he said.

Not once in the two years she had worked for him had the earl broken his own rigid schedule. Despite what she had told herself during the journey to the town house this morning, she felt the strongest disappointment that he had done so today.

Not disappointment that he had thought better of his proposal, of course. She had expected him to do that, just as soon as he realized how ridiculous it was. Indeed, she herself had pointed out the impropriety of the match to him, so there was no need to be embarrassed by his apparent, if belated, recognition of that fact.

In any case, she had come this morning prepared to give him her refusal. Even if he had, during the intervening hours, failed to realize how impossible a marriage between them would be, she had not. But still...

She took a calming breath. She had thought the earl would have the courage to tell her himself instead of asking Mr. Ingalls to act on his behalf. Perhaps he had felt it would be less humiliating for her to do it in this way. After all, Bella knew that nothing went on in the earl's household that his valet wasn't aware of. Not even, it seemed, a patently ridiculous offer of matrimony.

She met John Ingalls's eyes, holding on to her smile and attempting not to let her expression reveal anything of what she was feeling. "I hope his lordship isn't indisposed."

"His lordship suffers from an incompetent staff who cannot seem to tie a cravat properly," a deep voice behind her said. "*Not* from an indisposition."

Bella turned and found the earl standing in the doorway, his shoulders almost filling the opening. He was dressed in a coat of navy superfine and a pair of fawn trousers that fitted without a wrinkle over his flat belly and strong thighs. And despite the twenty-six years through which her heart had beat quite normally within her breast, it fluttered.

There was no denying Huntingdon cut a handsome figure, but she had never before allowed herself to openly admire it. She wondered with a touch of unease if things would ever be the same in their relationship. If they ever *could* be.

"You have my sympathies, my lord," she said, controlling her smile, as her eyes found Ingalls's again.

"And mine," the valet said, his voice almost unctuous.

"Indeed." The earl's eyes seemed to consider his man.

That was something Bella had noticed before. An uncanny knack Huntingdon had of appearing to focus on the speaker. On more than one occasion she had felt as if he were really looking at her. More fanciful than poor Fanny, she thought, remembering, in spite of her intentions, her aunt's excitement last night over the earl's offer.

"Shall we begin?" Huntingdon asked.

"As you wish, my lord," she said.

"Have you had your tea, Mrs. Simmons?" John Ingalls asked.

"Of course," Bella said, surprised by the question. It was not her custom to take tea in the earl's study, not even on a morning as cold as this. She was not a guest, after all.

"Bring Mrs. Simmons tea when you bring my coffee," the earl ordered as he crossed the room, his long stride unhesitating.

He touched the corner of the rosewood desk as he approached it, his fingers finding the edge unerringly. When he slipped into the chair behind it, Bella relaxed a little, feeling as if things might be returning to normal.

The morning light from the windows beside the earl illuminated the strong planes and angles of his face, accenting the high cheekbones and playing over the slight hollows in the lean cheeks and delineating the strength of his jaw. It touched the curling raven hair with blue-black highlights.

When she heard the valet's steps on the hardwood floor of the hall and realized they were finally alone, Bella still didn't move. Instead, she stood watching the man who had yesterday asked her to be his wife, trying to fathom any possible reason for that request.

"And have you reached a decision about my suit, Mrs. Simmons?" Huntingdon asked, as if he had just read her mind. His eyes were focused almost on her face. Heartbreakingly almost.

And that, my girl, will not do, Bella admonished herself. *Not if you wish to keep this position.*

There was no doubt in her mind that the earl would

dismiss her in a heartbeat if he suspected she had felt that quick surge of pity. From the beginning, that was the one thing she had known instinctively this man would never tolerate, not from her. Not from anyone.

"My lord," she began and was amazed to find that her voice trembled over the words.

She was not a woman prone to vapours or a quivering voice. Of course, she had never before been invited to become a countess, she thought. The idea of trying to assume that position was so ridiculous that, despite her nervousness, despite her tangled emotions, her sense of humour came to the rescue.

"Mrs. Simmons," he said politely, mocking her tone.

The earl's voice didn't tremble, of course. She couldn't imagine that it ever had during his entire life.

"Do you really intend that *I* should become the Countess of Huntingdon?" she asked him. The quiver was gone, replaced by her own mockery. Not of him, but of the image of her attempting to play that role.

"It is incumbent upon my wife to assume the position. You have my apologies for any inconveniences the title may cause."

One corner of his mouth had tilted, and that small sensation in the very bottom of her stomach happened again. This time, however, she was able to identify its cause.

After all, she was not an eighteen-year-old virgin, the sort of wife this man should be angling for. She was a widow, who had been married to a normal, healthy man for more than five years. And who had, in that time, enjoyed a normal, healthy relationship with her husband.

"And so, despite the drawbacks we both acknowledge as inherent in my offer, may I have your answer, Mrs. Simmons?" the earl said, his tone deliberately as light as hers had been.

Fanny was right, she realized. No matter how much he might now regret having made that outrageous offer, as a gentleman he wouldn't renege on it. So it was up to her, she supposed, to put them back on some sort of footing that would hopefully enable her to continue to work for him.

Never again to have to wonder how we shall pay the coal merchant or the greengrocer. Kit's education would be assured, as would his place in society.

Fanny's words echoed suddenly in Bella's head, momentarily closing her throat with their promise. All she had to do was say yes, and everything her aunt had predicted would become a reality. And besides that…

Her eyes again traced over the features of the man awaiting her answer. Despite the fact that no one would ever have known, she had fought against studying him like this through almost every day she had worked here.

Perhaps she had understood the temptation he represented. Because it was *so* tempting to dream, to fantasize that one day a man like this, a good and strong man, might step in and make all the hardships of her situation disappear. All she had to do was say yes, and just as Fanny had promised, they really would.

"I am very aware of the honour you do me, my lord," she began, choosing her words carefully.

"Don't let me interrupt," Mr. Ingalls said briskly, coming through the open door with a laden tray.

He carried his burden across to the earl's desk, the aroma of freshly brewed coffee and hot scones permeating the room. He set it down, and then took his master's coffee off the tray and placed it on the desk.

"Your coffee, my lord," he said. "Two inches above your right hand."

The earl's hands, clasped together on the surface of his desk, didn't move. His mouth tightened minutely, but Bella wasn't sure if that were in response to his valet's interruption or to his annoyance with those quite unnecessary instructions.

Ingalls had never before done anything like that in her presence. A little shocked, she looked at the valet's face. His eyes were on her, rather than on his master.

As she watched, they fell, and hers followed to see the earl's fingers move to locate the handle of the cup, a task which they accomplished without the slightest fumbling. Then Ingalls's gaze lifted once more to her face. One dark brow cocked, as if in question.

"Cream and sugar?" he asked after a few seconds.

She understood, however, that that was not the inquiry he had been making with that suggestively arched brow. "Cream," she said.

He fixed her tea, the spoon tinkling annoyingly in the silence. He brought it over to where she was still standing, like a visitor, in the centre of the huge room. As he placed the cup in her hand, he held her eyes. And his mouth moved. The words his lips formed were perfectly clear, if soundless.

"Say yes," the Earl of Huntingdon's trusted valet mouthed. And then he turned back to face his master, as if that extraordinary exchange had not occurred.

"Will that be all, my lord?"

"Thank you, Ingalls. I believe it will be," the earl said.

There was some element in the tone of Huntingdon's response that Bella couldn't identify, but then, considering all the things that had happened yesterday and today that she didn't understand, she supposed that hardly mattered.

She held the cup of tea she had been given, her eyes on her employer's handsome face, as his valet turned towards the door behind her. As he passed, his eyes focused again on hers, and feeling the intensity of his gaze, she looked directly at him. He nodded encouragingly, and then he winked at her before he walked by her and through the door. The silence he left behind lasted a long time, and it was the earl who finally broke it.

"I believe you were about to give me your answer," he said.

So simple a thing, her heart whispered. One word, and everything about her life would change for the better. One word, and this man, who had for two years been her employer, would become something very different.

A marriage of convenience, she reminded herself. A business proposition. An arrangement suggested for his benefit. As it would be for hers, she admitted honestly. And perhaps...

Her eyes again traced his features. He was no longer looking at her. He had turned his face towards the windows on his left, lifting it to the warmth of the sun. The thin morning light outlined his profile, emphasizing its strength. Her eyes fell once more to his hands, which were lying on the top of his desk, so tightly entwined that his knuckles had whitened from the pressure.

Say yes, John Ingalls had urged her. And no one knew the Earl of Huntingdon better than he. No one, she thought.

Suddenly, as if he had realized how revealing his hands might be, the earl's fingers disengaged and he reached for the coffee the valet had brought. For the first time since she had known him, his fingers faltered, searching futilely for the cup and saucer he himself had put down only minutes before. And by the time they had been located, her decision had been made.

"Yes, my lord," Arabella Simmons heard herself say. "If you are sure this...arrangement is really what you wish, then I shall be honoured to be your wife."

* * *

Wife, she thought, looking down on the thick gold band she wore on her left hand. Becoming someone's wife should surely effect more of a change in one's life. Since she had married the Earl of Huntingdon more than four weeks ago, however, there was very little difference in the even tenor of her days.

It was true that rather than being conveyed home every evening in his well-sprung coach, she simply retreated to the rooms she had been assigned upstairs to be greeted by Fanny and Kit. But other than that...

And what did you expect? she chided herself. *He gave you fair warning that to him this was simply a business arrangement. It was your own imagination that tried to believe it would become something else.*

Her imagination, spurred on by Fanny's romanticism, she supposed, and John Ingalls's mysterious behaviour. She had even screwed up enough courage to ask the valet what he had meant by what he'd told her that day, and his answer, made with eyes widened in surprise, had simply echoed the earl's stated intentions. *Easier for everyone all around,* Ingalls had said, leaving her as bewildered by his motives as she had been by her husband's.

Her husband, she thought. There was so much that word should mean, which in this case it did not. Their relationship had not changed, and she had finally been forced by her own sense of disappointment to admit that she had secretly hoped it would.

As fanciful as Fanny, she thought in disgust, putting her hairbrush down on the dressing table.

Kit was standing beside her, his small body pressed against her side. There had been a low, distant rumble of thunder all evening, and she knew that was why her son was delaying the journey to the nursery upstairs. Bella had sent poor Fanny, who was suffering from the headache, to her room with the promise that she herself would see the little boy safely tucked into the narrow bed his stepfather had once occupied.

And that was another fanciful notion she should disabuse herself of, she decided, putting her arm around Kit's small yet sturdy shoulders. The idea that the earl would assume any sort of fatherly role in her son's life. That hadn't been part of the bargain they had made, and she had been very foolish to suppose that someone as self-contained—as rigid—she amended with a spurt of anger, might suddenly become paternal.

Self-contained and rigid for very good reasons, she admitted with a remorse as sudden as her anger. It would be very difficult for a blind man to attempt to interact with a lively four-year-old, however much that might please her. Not part of the bargain, she thought again, trying to be fair.

"I could sleep with you tonight," Kit said. "If you're lonely." The last was added almost hopefully.

"And what makes you think I'm lonely?" she asked, hugging him close and putting her lips against the soft fragrance of his curls that were the same dark copper as her own.

"You seem lonely. Since we moved here. Sad and lonely. Are you sad, Mama?"

"Of course not," she said, turning and putting her hands on his shoulders. She held him away from her so that she could look into his face. "I'm very happy here. Aren't you?"

Solemnly, he nodded, his eyes on hers. He should be happy, she thought. The nursery upstairs was full of toys, and he and Fanny had the whole floor to themselves during the day. There were always fires burning on the hearths, so that the rooms were warm and cheerful. Fanny had assured her that their meals were not only on time, but hot and the food plentiful. Which had certainly not always been the case when they had lived in the small house they rented in Wattington Lane, Bella admitted.

"Are you afraid of the storm?" she asked, knowing this was at the heart of Kit's reluctance to leave her.

He was usually as adventurous as the next boy, full of curiosity, but thunder and lightning, for some reason, terrified him. For the most part he had learned to mask his terror, but night and a storm and a new and rather strange house were proving to be beyond his ability.

"There's nothing to be afraid of," he said, repeating a lesson she and Fanny had reiterated often enough.

"Of course there's not," Bella said, soothing the tumbled curls off his forehead. "There really isn't, you know," she added softly, smiling at him.

She had worked very hard not to turn Kit into a mama's boy, a timid child afraid of his own shadow and clinging to her skirts. She wanted him to grow up to be the same kind of brave man... The kind of brave man he should be, she corrected, wondering as she did why the earl's face had come into her mind.

Perhaps because he had been so honoured for his bravery. An acknowledged war hero, he had also handled the blow fate had dealt him with an undeniable courage. She could certainly do worse than to hold Huntingdon up as a model for Kit to follow.

That had been a part of what she had hoped for when she had agreed to this marriage. It didn't appear, however, that that would come to pass. Any more than any other of the foolish dreams she had cherished.

"I know," Kit said, his voice very low.

"Then...it's past time for bed," she suggested.

She could feel the depth of his sigh, but he made no complaint as they climbed the narrow stairs and he allowed her to tuck him in. It seemed that the storm might have moved on, content to threaten with the occasional low rumbling.

When all the rituals of bedtime had been completed, she found that she hated to leave Kit alone up here in the dark. She knew, however, that this was exactly what she must do if she didn't want him to grow up frightened of everything. If she wanted him to be the kind of brave Englishman who had defeated the Corsican monster on the battlefields of Europe.

Her mind seemed focused on military heroism to-night, she admitted, and of course, she was well aware of the reason for that near-obsession, she thought, as she hurried back to her own chamber. She pulled her dressing gown more closely about her against the chill. Not even the well-maintained fires in the bed-chambers could heat the wide, drafty halls.

Bedchambers. Her mind seized on that word out of the tumbling thoughts. There had been no pretence, not even before the servants, that the arrangement be-tween her and the earl was anything other than what it really was. She honestly couldn't decide if she were pleased by that or not.

But she had become adapt at meeting the some-times speculative eyes of the earl's staff. Which, she admitted, always fell. After all, whatever the narrow bounds of her marriage, she was still the Countess of Huntingdon, and, overtly at least, she was treated with the respect that title demanded.

Of course, they might not treat her so if they could see her now, running shivering in her nightclothes through the near maze of hallways. She was certainly not behaving with the decorum due her position.

You have my apologies for any inconveniences the title may cause. At the remembrance of her husband's comment her lips tilted again. Hunt, at least, would see the humour in this.

And then, at that unthinking choice of words, her smile faded and her steps slowed. He might very well be the only person in this household who would find the spectacle she was making of herself amusing rather than shocking, but he would never "see" her like this.

She was the Earl of Huntingdon's wife, but he would never see whether she carried out her role with dignity or like the hoyden she appeared to be right now. He would never see her at all, and for some reason, that realization was extremely painful.

Wife, the Earl of Huntingdon thought. Surely there must be something more, some change that should have occurred in their relationship when Bella had become his wife. And yet, by design, *his* design, there hadn't been.

Her son was installed in the nursery, watched over by his governess, who was also his great-aunt. And other than that...

And what did you believe would change? he asked himself angrily, pacing back and forth across the thick Turkish carpet of his bedroom. *Did you believe that she would suddenly fall in love with you?* The short laugh that answered his mocking question held no trace of amusement.

Maudlin and self-pitying, he told himself. And those were two things he had determined never to be. He had been satisfied with his life until she had come into it. Even as he thought it, he knew how unfair that accusation was.

It wasn't that he had been satisfied. It was that he had been numb, deliberately cutting himself off from emotions that he had thought he no longer had the right to feel. Or to expect a woman to feel for him.

Of course, he had had a mistress, at least for a while. He had hoped she would satisfy the physical cravings that had not been destroyed when he had lost his sight. He had found, however, that he could not endure her solicitousness and annoying helpfulness. After visiting her less and less frequently through the years, he had finally given her the house he'd furnished for her and the freedom to use it as she saw fit since he had no intention of ever darkening its door again.

Perhaps that had been a mistake, brought on by his pride, no doubt, as most of them were. Surely a mistake, because right now…

He took a deep breath, fighting the aching response of his body. Fighting for the control which had stood him in good stead for the last ten years. And why should he have to fight those very natural urges? he asked himself. He was a married man. A man with a wife.

Wife. The word reverberated again in his brain, echoing there as if he had shouted it into a cave. *His wife.* Who lay sleeping in a chamber only a short distance from here. A room to which he could find his way without a moment's hesitation.

And when he had? That, of course, was the question that kept him pacing the floor of his chamber night after night, unable to sleep. Unable to escape into a far more forgiving darkness.

Maudlin bastard, he thought in disgust.

He walked over to one of the windows, and working by feel, pushed the draperies aside, throwing open the sash. The cold night air rushed in, carrying with it the scent of rain. The electric vigour of the storm.

He had always loved storms. The beauty of the lightning, splitting the dark sky with threads of fire. The crash of thunder that followed. Storms made him feel more alive. And they still did, perhaps even more so now than before. He could feel them. Smell them. Hear them rage and threaten.

He lifted his face into the moisture blown in by the wind, his nostrils distended to catch every subtle nuance of the forces that had been unleashed outside. He wondered if she were also awake, listening to the thunder, wincing with each brilliant flash of lightning which he could no longer see. He wondered if she were frightened, lying alone and trembling in that vast, canopied bed.

And if you knew she were? In response to that unanswerable question, he slammed the window closed and turned back to the room, which was now chilled and uncomfortable, the banked fire unable to conquer the sudden influx of cold air.

Which left him with a choice of alternatives. He could go to bed, which any sensible man would do, or he could find somewhere warmer. More comfortable. Comforting.

The progression of thought was as irritating as the

question about Bella had been. Comforting? He hardly needed comforting. What he needed...

He took a deep breath, knowing very well what he needed. And knowing that was one thing he wasn't going to seek out.

There was brandy downstairs in his study. If it didn't help him sleep, it would warm him. Not as well as some other remedies perhaps, but at least it represented no risk. And there were damn few other elements in the current situation about which that could be said.

Chapter Three

The brandy was smooth, burning a passage all the way down to his stomach. Hunt closed his eyes, trying to will the tension away. Trying to let the liquor relax him.

The crack of thunder made him jump, probably because he hadn't been aware of the lightning that preceded it. He was aware, however, of the gasp that followed on its heels.

He turned, instinctively seeking the source of the sound, his senses more attuned to his surroundings than they had been when he had entered the room. His mind had been on something quite different from the possibility of an intruder then.

He realized as he listened that he was not alone. He could always tell, whether from the subliminal sound of the other person's breathing or from some primitive warning system that had grown stronger in the years since he'd been blinded.

He was not alone. And yet, whoever was in the

room had not spoken when he'd entered. Deliberately hiding?

"Who's there?" he demanded. He waited, hardly daring to breathe, but the silence stretched unbroken. Unbearable. "Answer me, damn it," the Earl of Huntingdon said, his voice rising as his fury grew. "Who are you, and what the hell are you doing in my study?"

"It's only me, sir," a small voice said.

It had come from the direction of his desk, Huntingdon realized. And his mind, although expecting a very different voice, quickly arrived at its proper identification. "Kit?"

He had never spoken the child's name, since they had not yet been formally introduced. It seemed strange to him now that they hadn't been. Of course, for reasons of his own, he had not questioned that strangeness. He wondered briefly if Bella could possibly have understood his reluctance to meet her son.

"Yes, sir," the boy said.

"Where are you?" Hunt asked.

"Under the desk."

"Under it?"

"Yes, sir," Kit reiterated, the note of unease clear in the quavering voice.

"Are you hiding from me?"

The child had probably been told he wasn't to enter this room, which would explain his original refusal to answer.

"No, sir," the boy said.

"Then why the hell—"

The earl cut off the profanity, wondering if he should apologize, perhaps more appropriately to Bella. Just at that moment, however, a clap of thunder rocked the house, eliciting a scrambling noise and another soft gasp from under the desk.

"You're afraid of the storm," Hunt realized, speaking the words aloud as soon as he thought them.

"Please don't tell Mama," Kit begged. "There's really nothing to be afraid of." It was obvious that was something the boy had been told, and just as obvious that at the moment he didn't believe it.

"There really isn't, you know," Hunt said, some of the tension that had driven him here draining away in the face of the child's desperate attempt to be brave.

Whistling in the dark, the earl guessed. Something with which he himself had a long and intimate acquaintance. *You have my sympathies, lad,* Hunt thought, but he didn't say that, of course. He could almost hear Bella's voice assuring the child there was nothing to be afraid of. Sometimes, however, even when one knew the truth of that, the demons refused to listen.

"It's only that it's so very loud," Kit said plaintively.

"It is that," Hunt agreed, moving across the room, nearer the desk under which the child was cowering. "But I confess, there's something about the roar and grumble that I like."

"You *like* storms?" the small voice asked, disbelief writ large in the question, along with the merest hint of awe.

"I'm afraid so," Hunt said humbly. "I find them exciting."

"I expect that's because you can't see them."

"Perhaps," Hunt agreed, fighting a smile at the boy's honesty, "but I think I have always liked them."

"Even when you were little?"

"Even then," the earl acknowledged.

The gasp he heard was warning. It had obviously been elicited by another lightning bolt, which was rapidly followed by the noise of more thunder. Almost before it had faded, the Earl of Huntingdon felt a small, trembling hand slip into his. His fingers automatically closed over those of the child, who grasped them like a lifeline.

"It's all right," Hunt said. "Nothing can happen to you here."

"You won't let anything happen to me?" the child whispered.

It required a simple enough reassurance, but the request produced an unaccustomed thickness in his lordship's throat. After all, it had been a long time since anyone had expected him to offer protection.

"Nothing can happen to you here," he said again, unable to rephrase his answer to accord with the real question the child had asked.

The hand holding his eased its grip somewhat. After a moment, Hunt walked over to his desk, leading the child with him. He touched the edge and then eased down into his chair. The little boy followed him as willingly as a puppy on a string.

As soon as the earl was seated, a small warm body pressed against his leg. He resisted the urge to run his hands over the boy's frame. With Kit's obvious relief at having company in the midst of the terror of the storm, he doubted the child would object to his examination. For some reason, however, Hunt found himself reluctant to make it, despite his curiosity about his new stepson.

"This is your study," Kit said. It was not a question.

"Yes, it is. Your mother and I work here."

"Doing important things for England," Kit said, a hint of pride in his voice.

Hunt's lips moved into a smile, which he hoped the darkness would hide. There was a time when he had been as convinced of that as Kit seemed now.

"I'm trying to," he said.

"And my mama helps you."

"Yes, she does."

"That's why we came to live with you. So she could help you even more."

Hunt couldn't imagine why he found that explanation disappointing. After all, it was the same one he had given Bella when he asked her to marry him. It hadn't been his reason, of course, which had had far more to do with the picture Ingalls had painted of

Bella's supposed suffering than with any concern for his work.

In the weeks she had lived in his house, however, he had gradually been forced into an admission of why he had really gone along with Ingalls's suggestion. And it was not because he had decided he had no more interest in women and might as well marry for the sake of convenience. It was, rather, because he had a great deal of interest in *one* woman. An interest that had only grown since that woman had become his wife.

"And because I thought it would be nice if you all lived here," Hunt said aloud. "Do you like living in my house, Kit?"

"Most of the time."

"When it isn't storming?" the earl guessed.

"I like the nursery. And all the toys. Mama says some of them were yours."

"Your mama's right. Which do you like best?"

"The soldiers," Kit said promptly. "I play with them every day."

"So did I," Hunt said, his voice softened by remembrance, and not only of days spent in that room upstairs.

"And the fire," Kit said. "Mama says Aunt Fanny and I may have a fire at any time we wish. Is that true?"

"At any time," the earl agreed, wondering at what deprivations in the child's past would prompt that question.

He felt the boy's physical shrinking, and it prepared him this time for the following roll of thunder. It did not prepare him for the small, solid body that suddenly came clambering onto his lap. Or for the childish arms which wrapped themselves fiercely around his neck.

Unthinkingly, Hunt pulled the boy closer, sheltering the trembling body against his own. Even when the thunder had faded into an indistinct and distant rumble, neither of them seemed eager to move. After a long time, the small, curly head that rested against the earl's shoulder turned. The child's breath sighed out, warm against Hunt's cheek.

In relief? the earl wondered. And then the breathing settled down into a regular rhythm. Far too regular to indicate anything other than sleep.

Again, that unfamiliar thickness settled in the Earl of Huntingdon's throat. It seemed that whatever the terms he and Bella might come to in regards to this "arrangement," his stepson had his own idea about what the boundaries of their relationship should be. And although Hunt could never have envisioned what his first meeting with this child might be like, he had to admit he was not disappointed in the outcome.

Perhaps he had the darkness to thank for the child's ready acceptance of him, but still… Not disappointed at all, he thought again, moving his hand up to soothe over the softly tumbled curls at the back of the little boy's head.

*   *   *

The crash was loud enough that Bella paused in her reading, her voice cut off abruptly midsentence. Together they listened a moment, the sound of the rain outside, beating against the room's tall Palladian windows, drowning out the low noises of the fire.

Hunt waited for her to go on, but the silence lengthened. There were voices raised in the distance, and then Bella said, "Would you excuse me a moment, my lord?"

He heard her put down the newspaper she had been reading aloud to him. He heard the rustle of her skirts as she crossed the room, and then, when the door was opened, the voices from the hall, much louder now.

The words were still indistinguishable, but he could identify the speakers: Mrs. Crutchen, his housekeeper; Ingalls; and occasionally the deeper, more sonorous tones of Blair, his majordomo. And then finally Bella's voice, her dismay quite clear.

"Oh, no," she said.

Curious, the earl rose and walked across the room, still listening to the hubbub. It was evident Mrs. Crutchen was extremely upset. Ingalls's tones, however, were soothing.

And Bella? he wondered. *What the hell had become of Bella?*

He touched the frame of the study door, and then he walked forward, counting his steps without being conscious of what he was doing. The habit was ingrained now, requiring no thought.

"What's going on?" he asked into the din.

The resulting silence was instantaneous. He had the feeling that every eye had focused on him. It wasn't a particularly comfortable experience.

"Nothing, my lord," Ingalls said. "At least nothing that need concern you."

"It's your great-grandmother's Vincennes vase," Mrs. Crutchen said indignantly. "Smashed to smithereens," she added with a sniff. "I should think *that* would be of concern to your lordship."

"Indeed it is," he said, wishing he hadn't interfered.

Whichever of the servants had been careless enough to break such a valuable piece of porcelain would have to be punished, of course, but that was Blair's domain. Hunt supposed all sorts of things would go into the decision of how to handle that punishment. Blair and Mrs. Crutchen were privy to information about each member of the staff he himself couldn't possibly know. He would be told if the servant were to be dismissed as a result of this, but he would bow to their judgment.

"Mrs. Simmons?" he said, and realized his mistake. Bella was no longer Mrs. Bertrand Simmons. She was his wife.

Perhaps that was why she had come out here, he realized. He hoped she would be wise enough not to intervene in whatever punishment Blair meted out, but if she did, he would have to stand behind her. Even if it meant going against his butler's decision.

"I didn't mean to."

It was the same plaintive voice Hunt had heard last night at the height of the storm and hearing it now, everything fell into place. Including Bella's dismayed exclamation.

"You shouldn't have been downstairs," she said to her son. "If you had only done what you were told, Kit, this would never have happened."

"Have someone clean it up, Blair," the earl ordered, deciding that since his great-grandmother had been dead more than three decades, far too much fuss was being made over the loss of her vase.

The decision might have had something to do with his sudden suspicion as to why Kit was in this hall this morning, a place he had obviously been told to avoid. Last night he had come downstairs to find not only welcome, but solace. The possibility that the boy had been seeking him created a warmth in the centre of Hunt's chest that meant far more than a broken pot, no matter its age or value.

"Yes, my lord," Blair said obediently, but Hunt could hear the displeasure in his tone.

"And nothing further is to be said about the accident," he added, the order edged with the same politely iced tone his father had used with such effect.

"Come on, lad," John Ingalls said cheerfully. "I'll take you back upstairs. We'll have another look at those soldiers you are so fond of. I'll show you how Boney set up his forces at Waterloo, if you want me to."

His voice faded as he directed the boy towards the

massive staircase. The child said something in response, but they were far enough away by then that the words were indecipherable. The earl had the urge to ask them to wait for him, but of course, no invitation to join them had been issued.

"That will be all, I should think," he suggested, raising one brow, as if to question any objection to that pronouncement.

"Very good, my lord," his butler said.

Mrs. Crutchen sniffed again, but he could hear her bustling away, perhaps to round up the maids to take care of the mess.

"Bella?" he said softly.

"I'm here, my lord," she answered.

The note of dismay, or perhaps even of something more profound, was still in her voice. And she was nearer than he had anticipated. Near enough that he could reach out and squeeze her arm reassuringly. Except he couldn't be certain she would welcome his comfort.

"Shall we," he asked, indicating the direction to his study with one outstretched hand.

"Of course," she said, her voice too subdued. Definitely not Bella's voice. Not the way he was accustomed to hearing it.

When he reached the door, he waited beside it until she had gone through, slipping past him and leaving a gentle waft of rosewater in her wake. When she was inside, he stepped into the room and closed the door behind him. His hand on the knob, he stood before it a moment. He needed to apologize for his earlier slip of the tongue and was not quite sure how to go about it.

"I am so sorry," Bella said. "I know that the vase must have had great sentimental value to you and that it was terribly expensive as well. I don't suppose…" She hesitated.

"What don't you suppose?" he asked finally.

"That you would allow me to pay for it. It might take me a long time, but I assure you—" The halting words stopped in response to his shout of laughter.

"Good God, Bella, you're my wife. I don't expect to become your creditor. Besides, you have leave to smash anything in this house. Leave to get rid of the lot and redecorate the whole if you like. This is not a museum. It's your home. As it is Kit's home," he added, remembering the pleasantly solid weight of the child in his arms as he had carried him upstairs last night.

The darkness had been no deterrent to him on that journey. And when he had laid the boy in the very bed he had once occupied, he had stood in the room for a long time, breathing in the scents—and the memories—of his own childhood.

"Even so, he must be punished," Bella said, bringing him back to the issue at hand.

"He's a child. Accidents happen."

"Not accidents of this magnitude. And not if Kit does as he's told," she said. "I can't imagine why he would have disobeyed."

He could hear the anxiety and the disappointment in her voice. The fact that Kit had felt free to come downstairs was as much Hunt's fault as it was any failure of discipline on the boy's part. Perhaps if Bella understood Kit's reasons, she might be more willing to forget and to forgive.

Besides, if Hunt remembered correctly, and he knew that he did, the vase in question had stood on a tall pedestal at the foot of the stairs. He might just as easily have broken it himself.

It wouldn't be the first household object he had disposed of in that fashion. Of course, that sort of accident hadn't happened in years, but had he been the one who demolished the heirloom, no one would have said a word about *his* carelessness. They would all have pretended it had never happened. He wished he had been around when Kit had knocked the vase off its stand. He would have taken credit for the destruction, and the scene in the hallway would have then had a very different tone.

"I think perhaps Kit was coming here," he said.

"Here?" Bella repeated.

"I found him at the height of the storm last night hiding under my desk."

"Under your desk?" Again, she echoed his words. "But…"

"He was afraid. And I promised him I wouldn't tell you that, so please don't betray to him that I have. The desk seemed safe, I suppose. In truth, it's as solid as an oak."

"And were *you* afraid, too?" Bella asked. "Is that why *you* were down here at the height of the storm?"

Trust Bella to ask the one question he didn't want to answer, Hunt thought. He found he was far less willing to explain his reasons for being here last night than he was to explain Kit's.

"I couldn't sleep," he said. "The noise of the storm perhaps. I came down for a glass of brandy, and found Kit. At first…"

He stopped, knowing that what he had thought at first was not something he was willing to share. Not yet, anyway.

"At first…" she prompted.

"Dear Echo," he said, smiling at her, "are you to repeat everything I say?"

"No, my lord. Only the things you *don't* say."

"And that is something else that must change," he said. "We can't go on in this fashion."

"In what fashion?"

"You are not Mrs. Simmons. And I am not your lord."

"And *master*," she said sotto voce, but the amusement was clear, even in the whisper, and he was relieved to hear it.

"I shall call you Bella, and you shall call me…Hunt? My friends do. Or Huntingdon if you prefer. Anything besides my lord."

"And when we're alone?" she asked.

He could have sworn there was something else in the husky timbre of that question. Something carefully hidden under the laughter. Perhaps it was simply the intimacy of the phrase. *And when we're alone.* They were alone now, of course, but her tone seemed to imply a future situation entirely unlike this one.

"My name is Alexander," he said.

"I know."

The silence grew, and then he heard the rustle of the newspaper she had been reading from when they had been interrupted. It seemed she had crossed the room to take it up again from his desk where she had laid it when she heard the commotion. Apparently, she was ready to return to work.

Fighting disappointment, he walked across the room. As he reached out to touch the edge of the desk, which he had done every morning for years, his fingers encountered something quite different from its hard wooden surface.

"I beg your pardon," he said, mortified that he hadn't known she was there.

And she was still there, he realized. Close enough that the subtle scent of rosewater washed over him in a great roiling wave of heat and desire. There. Near enough that he could grasp her shoulders and pull her to him. Bend her pliant body to his and hold her in his arms. Put his mouth over the soft trembling sweetness of hers.

He did none of those things, of course. He took one step back, away from his desk. Away from his wife. And then he waited.

"My mistake, my lord," she said after several long tense seconds. "Please forgive me."

He heard her move to the chair she usually occupied. Clearing his passage to his own, he realized.

All afternoon, as he listened to her beautiful voice, moving smoothly from one topic to the next, it moved also within his heart. And the Earl of Huntingdon knew he was truly lost. He was no longer in love with a woman's voice. He was in love with the woman.

"I have come to apologize, my lord," Kit said, stumbling only slightly over the word.

"I thought perhaps you had come to visit me," Hunt said, smiling at the child.

He had been surprised when Ingalls had ushered the boy into his bedchamber, but perhaps, given the scene downstairs today, his valet had decided that coming here would be less traumatic for Kit.

"I am forbidden to visit you," his stepson said softly. "I have been very disobedient."

"Would you like to visit me, Kit?" Hunt asked, hearing the wistfulness of the reply. "If we can obtain your mother's permission, of course."

"She's very angry."

"Only angry that you disobeyed her, lad," Ingalls said. "She's not angry that you wished to visit the earl. Perhaps if his lordship spoke to her…?"

Huntingdon was surprised that John had taken a hand in the conversation, but since he was probably better informed about what went on in this household than his master, the earl could only defer to his valet's assessment of the situation.

"Would you do that, sir?" Kit asked anxiously. "I should like to visit you above all things."

"And perhaps the earl might return the favour. He knows more about those soldiers you've found in the nursery upstairs than anyone. I believe they were his. Weren't they, my lord?" Ingalls asked innocently.

Knowing quite well when he was being manipulated, Hunt raised a questioning brow at his valet, but he didn't deny the truth of the assertion, of course.

"They once were mine. Now, however, they belong to Kit."

"You could come play with them if you wish," the child said magnanimously.

"Would you like that?" Hunt asked, flattered despite John's rather blatant attempt to solicit this invitation.

"Very much. If my mama doesn't mind you coming to visit me. Aunt Fanny doesn't mind anything I wish to do."

Both men laughed at the honest admission.

"Then I shall ask your mama for permission for us to exchange visits," Hunt said.

"Now say good-night," Ingalls advised, "like a good boy, and I'll tuck you in upstairs."

"You come, too," Kit invited.

Again the small hand slipped into the earl's. Hunt

tightened his fingers around it, savouring the feeling the trusting warmth of that hand resting in his gave him.

"His lordship needs to speak to your mama, remember," John reminded. "And then maybe tomorrow..." he said enticingly.

Huntingdon could only imagine the exchange of looks that passed between the two, but Kit's fingers freed themselves, reluctantly it seemed.

"Good night," the boy said politely. "Come and play with us if you can. If Mama will let you," he added.

Stifling the grin that remark produced, the earl put out his hand, accurately finding the child's head. He ruffled the soft hair, as fine as silk under his fingers. "Sleep tight," he said softly.

"Don't forget to ask," Kit begged.

"I won't."

"Tonight," John suggested.

There was a brief silence.

"Come on, lad," Ingalls urged, perhaps realizing he'd gone far enough. "We don't want to make your mama angry again by missing bedtime."

Hunt listened to them cross the room. When the door opened, Kit rushed out into the hall, but Ingalls turned back to say, "Her ladyship hasn't gone to bed yet, my lord. Just in case you were wondering."

"I wasn't," the earl said succinctly. "And I must thank you for your concern for my entertainment. Are you up to something, Ingalls?"

"Me, my lord? Now what would I be up to?"

"I can only imagine," Huntingdon said.

"Well, it doesn't take much imagination to know that the two of you had better work out some accommodation for the boy. He likes you, my lord. And that's quite a compliment. Don't you go disappointing him. It won't do, you know. He thinks you're brave enough to face any challenge. Even this one."

The door closed before the earl had a chance to ask the questions that sprang to mind. Why would his stepson think him brave, when he knew nothing about him? Unless, of course...

Ingalls had obviously been telling war stories. And he would put a swift end to that. Bella would not appreciate John filling the boy's head with tales of derring-do. Hunt definitely didn't appreciate them if they dealt with any of his own military exploits.

War was not a fit subject for a child, he thought, walking across to the window and opening it as he had last night. There was no storm tonight to electrify the air. Only the crisp bite of the cold. He lifted his face, thinking about the other thing Ingalls had said before he ran off without giving him a chance to respond. *He thinks you're brave enough to face any challenge. Even this one.*

Perhaps because he knew John so well, Hunt understood, despite the rather cryptic reference, the challenge his valet had referred to. It seemed that his feelings for Bella were no more a secret from Ingalls than anything else about his life had been. And he was forced to wonder, since he had obviously betrayed himself to his valet, if Bella could possibly be aware that his motives for this marriage were much different than he had portrayed them to be. And if she did, he also wondered what she felt.

What she felt about him. That was the real question, of course. And finding the answer to it was the challenge John thought he was up to. He only wished he himself were half that confident.

Chapter Four

It had been a very long day, the Countess of Huntingdon decided as she sat before her dressing table that night. And a most distressing one. Of course, that confession was made only to her mirror, so she was betraying to no one the doubts that plagued her.

First had been Kit's "accident," as the earl had referred to what had happened this morning. Despite his kindness in minimizing the loss, she deeply regretted that her son had destroyed an item of such monetary and emotional value.

Kit had always been a well-behaved child, but given the confines of his previous existence, perhaps that had simply been a lack of occasion for mischief. In this house, however, which he must naturally be eager to explore, the opportunities for getting into trouble seemed endless.

Poor Fanny was no longer up to watching over such a lively and inquisitive little boy, Bella admitted.

She herself couldn't watch Kit, not and do the job for which she had been hired. *And wed,* she added, with an unaccustomed tinge of bitterness.

Despite the seriousness of the rest, this was, she admitted, the crux of her despair. She was married to a man who had no interest in her as a woman. The trouble was that she was most definitely a woman. A woman with needs and desires she had discovered during her first marriage and for which she had hoped to find fulfilment in this one as well.

Instead, she had found a husband who seemed to have no appetite for a physical relationship. He didn't even want to touch her. When his hand had accidentally brushed against her body this morning, he had moved away as if he had been scalded. Or contaminated.

The lips of the woman reflected in the mirror tightened. She had known there was a gulf between them when she had agreed to this marriage. A looming gap composed of differences in position, family, wealth, education and experience. Too wide a distance, apparently, for the Earl of Huntingdon to wish to span.

And worst of all, she had no right to complain. He had been quite explicit about the parameters of this marriage. He wanted the convenience of having her live in his home. Marrying her was the only way society would accept that arrangement, since her family and her birth, if not noble, were certainly respectable.

Convenience, she thought, her bitterness growing. That's all she was to him. Despite his calling her

"Dear Echo," a phrase she had examined in her memory again and again throughout the day, trying to believe it might have some significance. Despite his kindness about Kit. Despite—

The knock on her door interrupted the mental tirade. Her immediate thought was that Kit had got into trouble again, but surely he was safely tucked into bed by now. She had had Ingalls's promise about that when she had left them playing with the battalions of metal soldiers before the nursery fire, so she wondered what this could be.

"Come in," she called, half turning on the satin-covered bench of her dressing table so that she was facing the door...which opened to reveal her husband. Her heart stopped and then resumed its familiar rhythm, beating as fast as it had this morning when she had seen the shards of that priceless French porcelain vase scattered all over the gleaming hardwood floor of the hall.

"My lord?" she said. Her voice sounded slightly breathless, but considering that Huntingdon's visit was unprecedented, perhaps he would put its thready quality down to surprise.

"May I come in?" he asked politely.

"Of course," she said.

She rose, hurrying to the door, and realized belatedly that she was wearing nothing but her night rail and dressing gown. Luckily, the latter was of velvet and thick enough to be unrevealing. Even as the thought formed, she remembered that it could not matter to her husband if she were wearing sackcloth and ashes. Or nothing at all.

"Is something wrong?" she asked anxiously, denying that quick surge of regret. *Not allowed,* she reminded herself, her eyes anxiously searching the dark, handsome face.

"Not that I'm aware of," he said, sounding puzzled by her question.

And then neither one of them said anything for what seemed a very long time. She fought the hope that was slowly filling her heart as those silent seconds ticked by. After all, he had come to her room. Surely...

"Forgive my intrusion, but...I have a favour to ask," he said finally, his mouth tilting.

"A favour?"

"A favour, Echo," he said, the slight smile widening. "Only a small one, so I'm very hopeful you'll agree."

"Of course," she said, struggling to control the disappointment that had replaced the tender green shoot of hope. A "small favour" did not seem to imply he was seeking what she had been hoping for when she saw him in her doorway.

"Is something wrong, Bella?"

She fought the urge to say "Wrong, my lord?" *Echo, indeed.*

"Of course, nothing's wrong," she said instead.

"You sounded..." He hesitated, and then he shook his head. "Forgive me. When one is forced to rely on the nuances of voice, one sometimes reads too much into them.''

"Is that what you do?" she asked. "Read our voices?"

"Tone. Inflection. It helps me know what people are thinking, I suppose. So much of communication is unspoken, and when one is deprived of those telling clues of posture, gesture, and expression, one attempts to compensate. Sometimes I overcompensate."

It was the first time in the two years she had known him that he had spoken to her of his blindness. She drew an unsteady breath, knowing that how she responded to this confidence might affect their relationship for a very long time. Perhaps forever.

"I should think it would be difficult not to."

Non-committal enough, she decided. Not fawningly admiring, which he would hate. And, she hoped, not cutting off this unexpected discourse. Which *she* would hate.

"Perhaps," he said. "However, I didn't come to talk about my failings."

"I didn't know you had any," she said, her voice tinged by the bitterness she'd admitted before his arrival.

"I beg your pardon."

"You never seem to fail at anything," she explained, realizing anew how true that was.

Despite the long hours of preparation it took him to become acquainted with every aspect of the topic under debate in the House of Lords, he was frequently the one whose well-reasoned opinion the papers quoted. When she read those articles, sometimes reading them aloud to him, more often perusing them in secret, she felt a sense of pride that she had helped him accomplish his goals. And undeniably a sense of pride in him.

"No obvious failing, anyway," she said. "Not since I've known you."

"I'm flattered, of course, but…perhaps you haven't known me long enough," he said, smiling at her again.

"Two years," she said.

"That hardly seems possible," he said softly.

It seemed he had been a part of her life for far longer than that. And of course, this was another indication that she was the one whose expectations of this marriage were out of line.

"Bella?"

"I'm sorry," she said, gathering her wits. "We seem to have strayed from the purpose of your visit."

"Of course. The purpose of my visit," he repeated, as if he had only now remembered there was one.

With a great deal of self-discipline, she denied herself the pleasure of calling *him* Echo.

"Do you suppose we could sit down?" he asked unexpectedly. "If I remember correctly, there are two chairs before the fire. Or have you rearranged the furniture?"

"This was your mother's room," she realized. The housekeeper had told her that, along with the cherished information that his lordship had expressly chosen his mother's suite for her.

"She would sometimes let me come in and watch her dress for the evening," he said. "Only the finishing touches, of course. The placement of a patch, perhaps. The selection of an ornament to go in her hair. Her jewellery."

"Did she let you choose them?" Bella asked, fascinated by the revelations, far more personal than he had ever made before.

"Occasionally. Occasionally, she even wore whatever I had selected. More often she explained why it wouldn't do."

Although his voice was full of amused nostalgia, Bella was horrified. She couldn't imagine doing that to Kit. If she had given her son freedom to choose something for her toilette, then she would certainly wear whatever he had chosen.

"Perhaps her early lessons account for your excellent taste," she said, trying to find something positive to comment on in the sad little vignette he had shared.

"I'm forced to rely now on Ingalls's taste, I'm afraid. Which I can only *hope* is excellent."

She could feel the blush rise into her throat. For the first time since she had known him, some of his reserve seemed to be melting, and she had had to spoil it by a thoughtless remark.

"You may rest assured that it is," she said stiffly.

"Thank you," he said. "And *now*, Bella, we really need to talk about Kit."

"Kit?" she echoed, taken by surprise.

She waited for him to tease her, and when she realized he didn't intend to, there was a frisson of disappointment to go along with her sense of dread. What could he want to say to her about her son? Obviously, something important enough that it had brought him to her bedchamber for the first time.

"By the fire?" he reminded softly.

A new anxiety stirred in her chest. Should she offer him her arm? If he had not been in this room since his mother's death, then it might be difficult for him to negotiate, perhaps even dangerous.

"Forgive me, Bella, if I'm being obtuse," he said in response to her silence. "Had you rather we talk tomorrow? Downstairs?"

"I would rather you tell me how to go about guiding you to those chairs," she said truthfully.

His laughter sounded almost as relieved as it made her feel. "Is the room a total maze?"

She looked across at the inviting fire and realized it really wasn't. There were almost no obstacles between it and them. "Not really."

"Then this should do," he said, holding out his hand.

She hesitated only a second before she took his fingers, which were warm and hard, especially when compared to the trembling uncertainty of hers.

"Are you sure you trust me to do this?" she asked, slanting a glance at his face, which seemed perfectly composed.

''Implicitly,'' he said, the thread of laughter still lurking in his voice.

She said a quick prayer that nothing disastrous would happen, and then she began to lead him to the wing chair that sat on the right-hand side of the fireplace. When they reached it, she hesitated again, and he simply waited.

Finally, she placed his hand on the back of the chair. She watched as his fingers brushed along the top and down the arm. Then he stepped past her, keeping his hand always in contact with the chair, and sat down.

A sense of accomplishment—and gratitude—overwhelmed her. When she moved to take the other chair, she realized that her knees were trembling. Delayed reaction? Or fear of what he was about to say?

Oh, please, she prayed, *not that Kit and Fanny must leave.* The earl hadn't sounded upset this morning. Perhaps this was to be a simple admonition that she must make Kit keep to the nursery wing. Since she was in complete agreement with that restriction, she would readily accept it. That was what she had intended all along.

''I think that we must make some other accommodation for Kit,'' he said.

And her heart sank. ''Indeed?'' The word was only a breath.

''I confess I enjoyed his visit last night. And Kit seemed to enjoy visiting me. I hope you will not forbid him to come to my study again.''

"*Not* forbid him?" she asked, unsure that she had heard him right. Even by firelight, she could see the quick tilt of his lips, but he didn't point out that she had done it again. "You want him to come?" she asked carefully.

"He seemed to enjoy his visit as much as I enjoyed having him. I thought at the time—"

He stopped, and she waited until it was obvious he didn't intend to complete the sentence.

"Yes?" she prompted.

"He doesn't mind these," he said, raising his right hand to touch those long, dark fingers to the scarred skin.

Her own eyes filled with quick tears, but she blinked them away, determined he would not hear them in her voice. "Why should he mind them? They are very faint, I assure you."

His lips tightened quickly before he said, "I thought it was simply that he hadn't seen them clearly in the darkness, but this morning and even tonight—"

Again the sentence was cut off, and she knew then that this was something he had not intended to tell her.

"Kit came to your study tonight?" she asked. She couldn't believe that her son would disobey her again, not after this morning's fiasco.

"No," Huntingdon said quickly. "Forgive me, Bella. Ingalls brought him to my room to apologize for breaking the vase. In the course of that visit, Kit invited me to come to the nursery and play with the soldiers.''

''And you want to,'' she said.

It wasn't hard to see that he did. He was fighting a grin, looking almost as young as Kit. And something very peculiar happened within her chest.

''They *are* my soldiers,'' he said, smiling openly now.

And with that smile, the fear that she hadn't even realized she had been living with these weeks disappeared.

''You like him,'' she said.

''Of course. More importantly, I believe Kit likes me. At least he doesn't seem to be afraid of me.'' His hand lifted, making what was almost a gesture towards his eyes. ''Nor does he seem to be unduly uncomfortable about…this. So, with your permission, of course, we should like very much to continue to exchange visits.'' The earl stood, his left hand maintaining contact with the chair. ''Do we *have* your permission, Bella?''

''And my blessing,'' she said softly, denying again the sting of tears.

''Thank you,'' Huntingdon said, his voice as low as hers.

''Thank *you*, my lord.''

''Hunt,'' he corrected. ''Or Alex, if you prefer.''

When we are alone, she had said this morning. They were alone now. Alone in her bedchamber.

''Hunt,'' she agreed.

"That wasn't so bad, was it?"

"Not nearly so difficult as I had imagined."

"Good," he said. "Then I shall bid you good night."

"Do you need me to—"

"Not now. I know the way," he said, but he didn't move.

"Was there something else?" she asked finally, watching the play of the firelight over the strong features of the man she had married.

"Any regrets, Bella?"

She knew what he meant, and she searched her heart for a truthful answer. She had no regrets about marrying him, of course, but many about the nature of their relationship. Despite tonight's disclosures, however, those were something she still couldn't share with him. Not yet.

"No," she whispered, forcing the words through the tightness in her throat. "No regrets."

"Good," he said again. He turned, and stepped away from the chair, moving without hesitation towards the door.

As he put his hand on the knob, her question stopped him. "And you. Do *you* have regrets?"

She couldn't see his face, and she realized this was what he had meant about missing those subtle clues of gesture and expression. She wanted to see what was in his eyes when he answered her. And it was a very long time before he did.

"Only that I waited so long," he said softly. Then

he opened the door and disappeared into the darkness of the hall.

Had he made a fool of himself? Hunt wondered as he sat at his desk the next morning, waiting for Bella to come down. When she greeted him, he thought he would be able to tell if he had from her voice, which was so richly textured that it expressed far more than her words. And there had been something in it last night—

"Planning to get an early start on the work, are we, my lord?" Ingalls said as he came into the room.

John Ingalls had obviously expected his employer to wait until his normal hour to come downstairs, although he was certainly aware of how early Hunt had sent for him to help him dress. What he probably hadn't been aware of was how little his master had slept last night.

"Why not?" Hunt said.

Ingalls set the tray on the desk, but there was no clink of china to indicate that he was removing the earl's cup and saucer.

"Something troubling you, my lord?"

Hunt briefly debated asking for John's opinion. After all, very little that went on in this household escaped Ingalls's notice. This seemed too private, somehow, despite all they had shared through the years. And he couldn't be sure, in spite of its importance, that John would tell him the truth.

"Only the lack of my coffee," he said.

"Of course. And I took the liberty of bringing in the most recent invitations. Now that the Season is upon us, they are beginning to pour in. I thought you and her ladyship might wish to confer together on which to accept."

Ingalls certainly knew that he declined almost all of the invitations he received. Most were sent as a matter of course by those with whom he associated in Parliament or strictly on the basis of his title. The few he did accept were for very private entertainments at the homes of close friends.

"You know—" he began, when John's voice continued, just as if he hadn't spoken.

"Her ladyship must be excited. It's been a long time, I should imagine, since she's been out and about in society. And that's a shame, as young and as lovely as she is. If you'll forgive me for saying so, my lord, she'll be even lovelier when she's a bit more fashionably dressed. I've been expecting her modiste to call any day now."

"Have you, John?" the earl said softly.

There was no doubt of Ingalls's intent. And no doubt he was correct about everything he'd said. Unforgivably correct. It had been too long since Bella had been in society. And too long, apparently, since she'd had a new dress.

"Indeed I have, my lord."

"Are you implying that Lady Huntingdon is dowdy?"

"I'm saying it's a crime that a woman who looks

like that isn't the most fashionably dressed in the capital. And if you could see her, my lord, you'd be agreeing with me."

If you could see her.... It was the perfect opportunity, of course, to do something he had wanted to do for a very long time. Long before he had considered asking Bella to marry him. Despite their friendship, however, he had never asked Ingalls to describe his wife to him. He didn't now.

"I have received Lady Huntingdon's permission for the boy to call on me," he said instead. "I would appreciate it if you could bring Kit here this afternoon. If he wishes to come."

"Oh, he'll want to come. Don't you be worrying about that. He has a thousand questions to ask you, my lord. He's very excited about the possibility."

"Questions about what?"

"About you, primarily. About your experiences on the Peninsula. And don't be angry at the lad about that. It's my fault, I'm afraid. I told him a little about what we did there."

"A rather blood-thirsty topic of conversation for so young a child. I'm not sure his mother would approve."

"Maybe not," John allowed. "But he's got a good mind and a lively intelligence that won't be put off with short shrift. He'll pester you until he's satisfied about a subject."

"I'm afraid I haven't been around many children," Hunt said.

He was beginning to wonder if attempting to further his relationship with his stepson was a good idea. And at the same time beginning to recognize the fine hand of his valet in far too many of the changes that were suddenly taking place in his life.

"It's time you were," John said. "Time you had some of your own, if you ask me."

"I don't believe I did, thank you, Ingalls," Hunt said, allowing the coldness in his voice to convey his displeasure with the direction of this conversation.

"That's half your trouble, my lord," Ingalls said, setting his coffee down with a clink. "You never do ask me."

"Good morning," Bella said from across the room.

Hunt wondered if she had heard any of that, especially John's suggestion that he needed children of his own. Despite his belief that he could read her voice, he couldn't tell a thing from the two words she had spoken. She sounded exactly as she had every other morning she had come to work.

"Your ladyship," John said. "And will you be having tea this morning?"

"Thank you, but no, Ingalls. I've had my tea."

"We may manage to stretch the household budget to allow you another cup," Hunt said. Thankfully, his voice seemed to betray none of the nervousness he felt.

"Thank you, Hunt. It's very good to know we aren't in dun territory," she said.

He could almost sense John's listening stillness. It

must be obvious that there had been a subtle change in their relationship. He wasn't certain what aspect of his visit to her boudoir last night had effected that change, but he was encouraged by it.

"Of course, the Season hasn't properly begun," he said, remembering Ingalls's admonition. "Your dressmaker's bills may change all that."

"My...dressmaker's bills?"

"That will be all, I think," he said in an aside to John, amused by the knowledge that his valet would be very reluctant to leave now that the subject he'd brought to his master's attention had been broached. There was no doubt in Hunt's mind that John would give his right arm to hear the rest of this.

"And her ladyship's tea?" John asked.

"Perhaps later," Hunt instructed, struggling not to smile.

"Very good, my lord," Ingalls said, his voice stiff with indignation.

John played with the dishes on the tray a moment, prolonging his departure as long as possible, but as the silence stretched, it must be obvious that Huntingdon didn't intend to go on until he and Bella were alone.

Two can play at manipulation, my friend, Hunt thought in satisfaction. A petty victory perhaps, but after what Ingalls had been doing, he deserved this defeat.

When the door closed finally behind the valet, he

said, "You haven't been fitted as yet for the gowns you'll need for the Season?"

"I didn't realize we should accept enough invitations to require new gowns," she said.

We. Hoist on his own petard, Hunt admitted wryly, but he realized with surprise that this was a sacrifice he was willing to make. Because John was right, of course. It had certainly been too long since Bella had been to a party.

He, of all people, understood how hard her life had been since Bertrand's death, especially in the years before she had come to work for him. Both Bella and her husband had been orphaned, and neither had family in a position to offer financial assistance when Bertrand died. Or to offer Bella a home. She had told him quite openly during the initial interview how she had hoarded the small sum her husband left her, spending it only on necessities, until it had been used up and she had been forced to seek employment.

Necessities. And knowing Bella that would mean nothing for herself. He wondered how long it had been since she had had a new gown. He realized in self-disgust that Bella had been his wife for over a month, and he had never even thought about enlarging her wardrobe. Despite the change in her circumstances, he knew she would never have undertaken to do that herself.

Nor could she have, he realized. Dawkins, his man of business, would quite naturally have assumed that he would no longer pay the Countess of Huntingdon a salary. Which meant...

"You have no money," he said aloud.

She laughed. "If you were expecting to receive marriage settlements, then you will be disappointed. I thought you understood that *before* we wed."

"Forgive me, Bella. I meant that I have made you no allowance since we've been married."

"Pin money, do you mean?"

"Of course. You are my wife."

"The Countess of Huntingdon," she said, her voice still amused.

"And you must dress the part," he advised, deciding he could manipulate as well as John.

"So I won't embarrass you at all these entertainments we shall be attending." Her voice was mocking.

"Of course. What I have got away with as a bachelor will not be tolerated in a man who is newly married."

"Do you seriously intend..." she began before her voice faltered.

"To take you dancing?" he suggested softly, realizing even as he said it that it was exactly what he wanted to do. He wanted to take Bella in his arms, even if only briefly, and lead her slowly around the floor.

He had once been accounted a very good dancer, a skill that was as necessary for a member of Wellington's staff as being a good shot or a good rider. There was no reason why he couldn't manage one waltz. Was that so much to ask?

Into her shocked silence he asked, ''Do you have a favourite modiste, Bella?''

''If I had,'' she said brusquely, ''she is probably dead or out of business by now. Or she would refuse my custom after such a long, dry spell of inactivity.''

''Then it's settled,'' he said.

''What's settled?'' she asked in bewilderment.

''You shall have a new wardrobe, one suitable for the Countess of Huntingdon. And it shall come from the most fashionable dressmaker in London. With your permission, of course.''

It seemed a very long time before she answered, and in her voice was a tone he had never heard before. Of course, in this case, it was only the words that mattered.

''Of course,'' she said softly. ''Whatever you wish. I shall be very honoured to go out into society on your arm.''

Royally hoist on his own petard, Hunt thought in amusement, and found he had no regrets.

Chapter Five

"That fabric is perfect with your colouring, my dear. And the style could not be more becoming. You are truly a picture, Bella. A picture!" Fanny said proudly. "Don't you agree, my lord?"

The silence that fell after that unthinking remark was suddenly full of tension, almost as tense as Hunt himself felt, as he stood at the foot of the staircase waiting for his wife to descend. Not over what poor Fanny had said, of course, but because he really wanted to see. To see Bella. And for the first time in almost ten years, the anger he had vowed never to reveal threatened his control.

"Please forgive me, Lord Huntingdon," Fanny said, her voice trembling. It was obvious the old woman was deeply embarrassed.

"There's nothing to forgive, Mrs. Hargreaves. I'm sure Lady Huntingdon is indeed 'a picture,'" Hunt said, holding the years-old facade in place.

Inwardly, he wondered how he would manage to

get through this night. Despite what Ingalls had said, despite what he'd felt when he'd suggested taking Bella into society, this was a mistake. He had known that long before it was time to don his evening clothes. No matter how much he wanted Bella to enjoy herself, no matter how much he had fantasized about holding her in his arms as they slowly circled the floor, he knew neither of those things was likely to come to pass.

Instead, other uncomfortable remarks would be made during the course of the evening. There would be whispers as Bella led him into the ballroom. Although he was certainly accustomed to the curiosity his appearance aroused, she would not be, and he wondered what she would feel. And he knew he would never find the courage to propose the waltz he had dreamed about in the fortnight since he had foolishly accepted an invitation to tonight's ball.

Hunt realized suddenly that Bella was standing beside him, the subtle scent of roses surrounding him. It was indicative of his state of mind that she could be this close and he hadn't even been aware of it. He knew his distraction didn't bode well for the remainder of this evening.

It would take every ounce of his concentration tonight to keep from making a fool of himself. A fool or an object of pity. Except, if some embarrassing disaster did occur, the pity of the ton would be reserved for Bella, of course.

"Here," she said. She took his hand, carrying his

fingers to touch the silk of the gown she was wearing. "It truly is a remarkable fabric. The colour of moonbeams and as fine as a cobweb. I can't imagine how they fashioned the cloth, but they tell me it was made in Cathay."

At the lack of tension in her voice, Hunt began to relax. Or perhaps that was because she had not released his hand and seemed in no hurry to do so. He brought her gloved fingers to his lips, pressing his mouth against the soft kid.

"You'll be the most beautiful woman at the ball," he said softly. By design, his tone was so low over the next words that only she might hear. "And I wish more than you can imagine that I could see you."

Her fingers trembled in his, and he released them, immediately regretting his confession. She would undoubtedly hear enough references to his blindness tonight, most of them unintentional and as harmless as the one Fanny had just made. He could only hope none would be truly malicious. He wanted nothing to spoil her evening.

"It's far better that you can't," she said, her voice equally low, the words laced with self-mockery. "I should so hate to disabuse you of the notion that I could be the belle of this or any other ball."

More of his tension dissipated at the wry amusement in her tone, and he presented his wrist. She placed her fingers, no longer trembling, on his arm, and he led her to the wide doors of the town house. This was the easy part, Hunt acknowledged, as the footman helped them into the waiting carriage. Everything would be much harder once he was away from the safe familiarity of home.

It was always so damn hard. Meeting new people. Trying to keep track of the changing speakers in a conversation, despite the music and the flow of noise around him. Negotiating his way through a totally unfamiliar place, which would be crowded with people. Having to depend on the guidance of others, something he hated.

For Bella's sake he could survive one night, he told himself sternly, calling on the courage that had sustained him through the years with Wellington. And more importantly, on that quite different kind of courage which had carried him through the long, dark years since his last battle. This was simply another, and the greatest enemy he would face tonight would be, as always, his own stubborn pride.

The evening had been nothing like what she had anticipated, Bella thought, as she was whirled competently around the floor by another of Huntingdon's friends. This one had served with him in Iberia, as had several of the gentlemen who had asked her to dance. Of course, ex-soldiers weren't the only ones paying quite flattering attention to the new Countess of Huntingdon. Bella had danced with some of the most prominent men in the current government as well.

As the evening wore on, their names and faces had

begun to run together. All she knew for certain was that she had not been without a partner for any set.

Had she been vain, she might well have attributed her popularity to her own person. Or perhaps to the gown she was wearing. Hunt's promise about choosing the most fashionable modiste in London had certainly been fulfilled. This was the most beautiful dress in the room, and her mirror had confirmed that its elegance was vastly becoming to her.

Not being vain, however, Bella had quickly begun to suspect there was a conspiracy afoot among her husband's friends. And even to suspect that Hunt himself had taken a hand in it.

Her gaze went straight to her husband, despite the throng. He was standing across the ballroom, his dark head bent slightly because of his height, the better to hear what the prime minister, who was on his other side, was saying to him. As she went mindlessly through the motions of the waltz, Bella continued to watch the small group gathered around her husband.

It seemed she had been aware of exactly where Hunt was throughout the evening, although she had spent most of its long hours away from him, in the arms of some handsome man or another. *Never in his arms,* she thought with regret. And of course, she had no right to have expected that she would.

She only wished that he might display a little more reluctance in sending her onto the floor on the arm of each gentleman who applied to him for permission to dance with her. He hadn't, seeming instead to be pleased at the attention she had garnered.

Knowing him now as well as she did, however, she knew Hunt would be finding this evening a dead bore. The ball was, by its nature, devoted to dancing, an activity in which he obviously did not participate. To her certain knowledge his social calendar during the last two years had never included this kind of entertainment. Not until tonight.

As soon as she had realized she was to be partnered in every dance, almost certainly by prior design, she had known Hunt was here only because he believed this would give her pleasure. And it had, of course. The greatest pleasure had been the knowledge that her husband had carefully planned this evening with her enjoyment in mind. Now if only—

"Am I boring you, Lady Huntingdon?" her partner asked. "That's the second comment I've made to which you've failed to respond. At this rate, even I, acknowledged wit that I am, shall run out of commonplaces with which to entertain you before the music ends."

Startled, she pulled her gaze away from her contemplation of her husband and looked into a pair of very fine brown eyes, sparkling with amusement.

"One is supposed to converse with one's partner, you know," the man holding her in his arms said in a confiding whisper. "I don't know who began the custom, but by now it's rather widely accepted."

"I am *so* sorry," Bella said, feeling the blood rush

into her cheeks. "Forgive me, please, Lord…" For the life of her, she could not remember his name. And her blush deepened when he laughed.

"Ardley. Actually, it's quite refreshing to see a lady in love with her husband. Very rare in our set, even for newlyweds, I'm afraid. Hunt's a lucky man," he added. "Swept him off his feet, did you?"

His eyes were still smiling at her, so she didn't take offence. "I think that's supposed to be phrased the other way round," she countered, and then lowered her own voice. "I don't know who began the custom…"

He laughed, just as she'd intended.

"But you *are* in love with him," he said. "It's quite useless to deny it, as unfashionable as that may be. You're in love with your own husband, as much, perhaps, as he is with you."

"In love with *me?*" she repeated, remembering with a jolt in the region of her heart how Hunt teased her about that unfortunate habit. *Dear Echo.*

"Of course," Ardley said. "We all wondered when we heard the news of your marriage, since Hunt had sworn he'd never burden a woman with…what he has become. And then, when we saw you, we understood why he would—"

Their eyes met and held, the laughter disappearing suddenly from his. "But Huntingdon has never seen me," she said softly.

And he never will. That was somehow harder to bear now than it had ever been before, perhaps because of the words her husband had whispered as he kissed her hand at the foot of the stairs.

"Did he tell you how he lost his sight?" Ardley asked.

"No," she said, wondering if this was a story she wanted to hear. Wondering if her husband would want her to hear it. She knew that Hunt would never tell her, however, and she would never have dared to ask him. And so, although she felt that she should, she didn't stop Lord Ardley when he began.

"He was a staff officer. One of the Beau's pets. Everyone knew it, but no one resented the favouritism. Hunt had earned our respect in more ways than I could possibly recount to you. Earned it again and again. The more difficult the mission, the more certain one could be that it would fall on Hunt's shoulders to carry it out."

He took a breath, deep enough that his shoulders lifted, moving against her hand as it rested lightly on top of the left one. "There was a rather reckless young lieutenant, newly out from London, who believed that war was all glory and honour and tilting at windmills. He was the kind of nincompoop that battle-hardened veterans like Hunt were sure to avoid as bad, mad and *very* dangerous to know."

She laughed. "And was he?"

"Oh, far more than you can imagine. It took him less than a month to get into trouble. No one was surprised by that speed, of course, and most of them would have said, 'Devil take him.' The only trouble was he had got the men under his command into trouble, too. And a lot of them stood to die because of his foolishness.''

He paused again, his eyes finding Huntingdon in the throng as surely as Bella's had earlier. The earl was laughing at something someone had said to him, his head thrown back a little in what appeared to be genuine enjoyment. Bella hoped it was.

When Lord Ardley's brown eyes came back to hers, however, they were sober. ''Huntingdon was sent to the rescue, of course. And he even found a way to get most of the troop out of the ridiculous mess our stalwart young hero had got them into. Most of them,'' he said. His lips tightened, and his eyes briefly sought Hunt again.

''And the lieutenant?'' Bella asked.

''Took a French ball in his arm and fell off his horse. Grandly heroic, ain't it?'' he said mockingly.

''And he died?''

''Oh, no, Hunt rescued him, too. Fought off a French dragoon who was about to use him for saber practice. Put the lad up on his own mount and sent horse and rider off in the direction of our lines with a good hard slap on the rump. The horse's, not the lieutenant's. The boy got back behind his own lines to discover that the ball he'd taken had gone through the flesh of his arm without touching bone. A miracle, the sawbones said.'' Again, he paused, his face set and his mouth grim.

''And Hunt,'' Bella whispered, knowing the answer from the question that had begun this story. She had been right from the first, she realized in regret. She did *not* want to hear this.

"A French shell exploded almost at his feet. And since he had given his horse away…" Again, the handsome mouth flattened before Ardley went on. "No one who saw what happened expected Hunt to live through that explosion, but when the patrol was sent out that evening to bring back the bodies, they found him still alive. The shell had set the grass where he had fallen on fire. Hunt had managed to crawl away, but the heat—"

"Don't," she commanded.

The horror of the story made her steps falter until they were standing unmoving in the midst of the swirl of dancers.

"Forgive me," Ardley said softly. "I should never have told you all that, but I wanted you to know the calibre of the man you married."

"I knew already," Bella said, fighting the power of the terrible images his words had produced.

"You're quite pale, Lady Huntingdon. If I take you back to Hunt in this condition, he'll have my hide. And rightly so. Some fresh air?" he suggested.

Bella realized they were beside French doors that led into the garden. Perhaps she *would* feel better for a breath of the cooler night air. It had grown very close in the room. And much too warm. Besides, Ardley was right. Hunt would know from her voice that something was wrong. He knew her far too well.

Lord Ardley was already leading her towards the doors, and as soon as she stepped through them, she knew she had done the right thing. Hunt wouldn't miss her, and she would only stay outside a moment or two. Only long enough to put the story from her mind and regain her composure.

"May I bring you some refreshment?" Ardley asked.

"Oh, yes, please," Bella said. "You are so very kind."

"No, Lady Huntingdon. What I have done is unforgivable. And I have no excuse, except that it seems I am still the same reckless, unthinking fool I was that day in Spain."

He bowed to her, his eyes meeting hers briefly before he turned and disappeared into the crowded ballroom.

The same reckless, unthinking fool I was that day in Spain. He was the lieutenant whose life Hunt had saved, Bella realized. Ardley was the man whose foolhardy exploit had cost her husband a price greater than any man should have to pay to the gods of war. And if Hunt had had his choice that day, she suspected that he would rather have died.

She took another deep, fortifying breath, trying to put the story and its implications from her mind. It had all happened more than ten years ago, and surely Hunt no longer felt that way. He had certainly by now come to terms with the consequences of his heroism.

She had truly understood only tonight how well he

coped with his blindness, whether he was dealing gracefully with the unspoken discomfort of others, quickly putting them at ease, or enduring the confusing bombardment of sound that came at him from every direction, or putting up with her own inept and hesitant guidance through those close-packed bodies.

None of those were skills any man would have wished to acquire. Certainly not the man Ardley had just described. Not that gallant and respected soldier.

''Bella?'' he said from behind her.

She turned in time to see Ardley slip away, leaving Hunt alone in the wide frame of the French doors. He tilted his head slightly, listening for her answer, despite the noise from the ballroom behind him.

''I'm here,'' she said.

She did not move towards him, her emotions too raw and exposed. Too vulnerable. A careless word or the hint of pity in her voice would be fatal to her cause. She knew that, although her instinct was to rush to him as she would have to Kit, taking him in her arms and kissing the hurt away.

This, however, was a ten-year-old hurt that no one, not even she, could ever make well. Nor was it her place to try. She was his wife, not his mother. Perhaps it was time she undertook to fulfil her proper role.

''Ardley said you were ill,'' Hunt said.

He sounded both concerned and puzzled. And why shouldn't he be? she thought in quick amusement. She had not been ill a day since he had hired her. Why would he believe that on a night he had planned as carefully as he might have planned a military campaign she, of all people, would succumb to a fit of vapours? She could hardly believe it herself.

"Not ill," she said. "Only stifled by the heat and the noise. And quite tired of having my toes trod upon."

"Shall I call him out?"

"Who?" she asked, feeling a flutter of anxiety that Lord Ardley might have confessed that he had told her.

"The cad who trod on your toes, of course."

She laughed, the tension of the last few minutes melting away in the face of his calm serenity. In the security she always felt in his presence. Hunt did make her feel secure, she realized, because she knew that he would always take care of her, just as he had tonight.

"I shall forgive him if you'll take me home," she said softly.

"Tired, Bella?"

"Only of this," she said truthfully. "Only of the ball and the noise and the heat."

"I thought you would enjoy it. You were quite the belle, despite your doubts."

Her lips lifted, knowing full well why that had come about. "The dress, perhaps," she suggested.

"The woman wearing it," Hunt corrected. "Two score people went out of their way to tell me what a lucky man I am. Most of them shortly after they had danced with you."

"Well, *I* didn't tread on *their* toes," she said.

She was rewarded by his laughter. This time, the impact of that ghastly story fading, she was able to laugh with him.

"I'm sure they should not have minded if you had," he said.

"Would *you?*"

Her voice was teasing, the suggestion lightly made, though it had been carefully worded. Despite her tone, she watched his face change, the laughter disappearing to leave the spare planes and angles arranged in the same austere lines they assumed whenever he was concentrating on something very difficult to comprehend.

As she waited for his answer, the silence grew and then expanded. Through it the sounds of music floated to her, spilling from the dance floor out into the cool darkness. And when he spoke again, it was not in response to her question.

"As soon as we've made our farewells and apologies, I can take you home. I'm sure you'll feel better when you're away from this mob."

She had accomplished nothing, other than to embarrass them both. And to put a damper on an evening that had been planned strictly for her pleasure. It was a mistake she would not make twice.

"I'm sure you're right," she said.

She raised her chin, holding her head high, and walked across the terrace to take his arm. Then she turned, prepared to lead him into the ballroom, but he didn't move.

"Did you enjoy yourself, Bella?" he asked.

"Thank you, yes," she said, the words sounding more formal than she had intended.

"Then...perhaps another night?" he said softly, the inflection almost a question.

He took a step forward, forcing her to move with him or send him into the throng without guidance. And he never spoke to her again on the way home.

Chapter Six

"*I'm sure they should not have minded if you had.*"
"*Would you?*"

There was no other logical interpretation that might be put on that question, the Earl of Huntingdon decided, as he paced back to the window of his bedchamber, mentally reviewing the conversation, something he had done a hundred times since they had returned from the ball.

Bella had wanted to dance with him. And, fool that he was, he had ignored her suggestion. As he had feared at the beginning of the evening, his pride had defeated all his expectations.

Not all, he amended. Bella had said she had enjoyed herself. Since that had been his primary purpose in accepting the invitation, he could not regret that they had gone, despite the strain the evening had proven to be.

It was over now, thank God, and alone in his room

he could finally relax. He had allowed Ingalls to help him off with his coat, and then he had sent the valet away.

He didn't want to answer the questions he knew John would be eager to pose. After all, his valet's anticipation of tonight's success had perhaps been as great as his own. And from the beginning they had both been destined for disappointment, he acknowledged, still pacing restlessly.

Bella had, however, been introduced to a number of his friends, who could now be called upon to provide an escort for any of the Season's events she might wish to attend. From that aspect the evening had been a success. An unmitigated success, he thought bitterly, remembering the many comments about his wife's beauty. Which had only reinforced—

The soft tap on his door was unexpected. Ingalls, he thought, come to question why he was still up. More and more frequently of late John had been poking his nose into things that were really no concern of his. The earl felt an unaccustomed spark of anger, which, had he been honest, he would have admitted had nothing to do with his valet's actions, but rather with his own. Or the lack of his own.

He walked over to the door and threw it open, ready to chastise Ingalls for hovering over him like some damned mother hen. As he drew breath to begin that angry lecture, the subtle scent of roses surrounded him. He fought the urge to close his eyes and savour the fragrance, as he had during the carriage ride home.

"Bella?" he questioned instead. "Is something wrong?"

"Most wives would take offence if their husbands greeted their appearance at the bedroom door with that question."

But Bella was *not* most wives. Nor was he, of course, most husbands. He was a blind man, who had felt more blind tonight than he had at almost any other time in the last ten years. A blind man in a marriage of convenience. A blind man in love with a woman he had never seen.

A woman who was, according to his friends, incredibly beautiful. A woman to whom he had offered a home and financial stability. There had been nothing else, stated or implied, in that arrangement. And no matter how he felt, he didn't see how he could legitimately expect to change the terms of their agreement now.

"May I come in?" Bella asked.

"Of course," he said, more from a lifelong habit of politeness than because he was eager to add to the chaos of emotion that had tormented him since their return.

"Thank you." Her voice seemed almost amused.

She came into the room, and when he heard the door close behind her, his heart rate accelerated. Unaccountably accelerated. After all, he was alone with her every day. Not in these circumstances, he admitted, which somehow seemed even more intimate than the night he had gone to her bedchamber to speak to her on Kit's behalf.

Kit. Perhaps Bella had come here for that same purpose. To talk about her son. He took another deep breath, controlling his wayward imagination, which had stupidly been suggesting that Bella might have sought him out for a very different reason.

"I wanted to thank you for tonight," she said. "The evening was almost perfect."

There was something in her voice—some subtle undertone—that he was aware of, but couldn't identify.

"*Almost* perfect?" he asked, smiling at her. "Did you wish to lodge a complaint, Bella?"

"Your friends are delightful. And I very much enjoyed being treated like a diamond of the first water. That's flattering, of course, for any woman, especially for one of my...advancing years," she said, the amusement back in her voice. "However, I must confess..."

And then she didn't. He waited through the long silence, still uncertain where this conversation was headed.

"What I wanted most of all was to dance with *you,*" she said finally, and his heart rate, which had almost returned to normal, began to race again.

"Forgive me, Bella. I no longer dance. I thought you understood."

"Why?" she asked.

There were, of course, a number of quite legitimate reasons he could give her. He chose the truth instead.

"Because I'm very much afraid I should make a fool of myself if I tried," he said, and then to soften the harshness of the words, he smiled at her again.

It was not a plea for pity, and he believed that by now he could trust her to understand that. This was simply the ultimate truth of his situation. Making a fool of himself, especially before her, although he did not confess to that, was the one thing he feared above all others.

And it was why, of course, he had never told her what was in his heart. He still didn't, although the silence stretched beyond comfort as he waited for her response.

"Isn't it strange that we've been afraid of the same thing and didn't know it," she said.

He shook his head. "The same thing?"

"Yes, my darling Echo. We've both been too afraid of making fools of ourselves to admit how we feel."

My darling Echo. He had revealed too much of what he felt for her that day. And yet, hearing what was in her voice, he could not regret that he had.

We've both been too afraid of making fools of our-

selves to admit how we feel. How we feel. Which could only mean...

And then, the old doubts flooded his heart, forcing out that sudden glorious certainty. This was the same battle which had kept him from taking her in his arms tonight and swirling her around and around to the music drifting through the terrace doors.

Fear was his enemy. Fear and his own stubborn pride, which had told him for years that he could never reveal to anyone how vulnerable he felt.

He knew, however, that he must somehow find the courage for this. The same courage he had called on when the surgeons told him he would be permanently blind. The courage that had been required then simply to face each day. To decide to make something meaningful of his life. To accept every challenge this eternal darkness had presented. A darkness which he still hated, even after all these years.

We've both been too afraid of making fools of ourselves to admit how we feel.

"And if I tell you how I feel, Bella? Will I be making a fool of myself?" he asked.

"Love makes fools of us all. I'm surprised you didn't know."

"Then...I love you, Bella," he said, forcing the words through the constriction of his throat.

"And I love you, my darling," she whispered.

She moved into his arms as if they were not only dear to her, but familiar. He lowered his head, finding her mouth unerringly, as though he had kissed her a thousand times.

Her lips trembled under his. He caressed them with his own, trying to control the flood of desire and longing that swept through him so fiercely he was terrified he might frighten her. He need not have worried. Her mouth opened, her tongue seeking his to engage in a dance more primitive than any a London ballroom would ever witness. That slow, tender waltz of mutual passion.

The kiss seemed unending. Their mouths met, melded, and then released, only to seek the same sweet pattern again. And then again. To cling. To break apart. To reunite.

Learning. Learning one another. After a very long time, he put his hands on her upper arms and set her away from him, positioning her body almost at arm's length from his. As he did, her lips still clung, as if they could not bear to be separated from his.

"Bella," he said, almost in wonder. "My darling…"

He wasn't sure she would understand, but this was something he needed to do. Something he had wanted to do far longer than she could know.

"What is it?" she asked. When he didn't answer, she put her hand on his cheek, her thumb pulling slowly and sensuously across the fullness of his bottom lip. "What's wrong?"

Because there were no words to tell her what was

in his heart, he said nothing. Instead he raised his hands, putting his fingertips lightly on either side of her face. His thumbs brushed over her forehead and then more boldly down the narrow bridge of her nose. And when they had finished there, his fingers examined her brows, following the arch of bone they outlined. As they trailed across her eyelids, her eyes closed, the long lashes lying like fans below them, allowing his examination.

The movement of his fingers didn't stop until he had traced over all the delicate structures of her face: brow, nose, cheekbone and jaw. They had moulded each feature, following not only the outline of her eyes and brow, but tracing the bow of her top lip and the sensual fullness of the bottom. He even followed the shape of her ears and touched the softly curling tendrils that floated against her cheek.

When his hands finally rested unmoving around the slender column of her throat, their journey of exploration complete, with the smallest of pressures, he urged her to him again. He bent his head, putting his lips against the soft skin below her ear, his tongue trailing provocatively along the underside of her jaw.

The progress of his mouth was as unhurried as that of his hands had been. He stopped to examine the pulsing hollow at the base of her throat. To follow the fragile line of her collarbone, returning to glide over the beginning swell of her breasts. Her sudden intake of breath as his tongue delved into the shadowed darkness between made him pause. He lifted his head, listening to the subtle change in her breathing.

"Don't stop," she whispered.

"Are you sure, Bella? Because once I touch you, my darling, there can be no turning back. If you can't endure the fumbling caress of a blind man..."

She stopped the words by the simple and effective expedient of stretching on tiptoe to put her mouth over his. Briefly then, hers was the guidance, but only until she had convinced him that whatever doubts he had, she did not share them.

As his hands dealt efficiently with the intricacies of feminine apparel, a task at which he had excelled in his younger and admittedly wilder days, the Earl of Huntingdon found there are some skills one never forgets. And he was inordinately delighted only a short time later to realize that darkness had never, in the history of the world, been any impediment to making love.

"Yes," She breathed, the word softly sibilant, almost a whisper.

"And here," he said.

His breath was moist against her skin. His tongue circled her nipple, laving it lazily, applying no pressure. Teasing. And tantalizing.

Everything he had done during the long dark hours of the night had tantalized her, arousing feelings she had not known she was capable of experiencing. She had never dreamed there were so many ways to give pleasure. Or to receive it. It seemed she had learned new ones with each touch of his lips and every movement of his tongue.

"And here," he said, his mouth leaving her breasts to glide downward over the sweat-dampened skin of her stomach. She didn't have the strength to speak again. Or the will to deny him. Not anything.

And he wasn't really seeking her permission. Any barrier she might have thought to erect between them for modesty's sake had long ago been destroyed. Every portal had been thrown open. Lovingly invaded. The citadel of her body joyfully surrendered.

This was only the shivering aftermath. The heated shimmer of nerve endings tested beyond their endurance, so that they, too, quickly surrendered again before the knowing touch of his lips and his tongue and his hands.

Those long, dark skilful fingers had caressed her body as if it were infinitely precious. As if every part were beautiful, something to be cherished. And they had moved with a sure mastery which proclaimed she belonged to him. After tonight, of course, there was no longer any doubt that she did.

Love makes fools of us all, she had told him. Until now, lying in his arms, boneless and spent, she had not realized how true that was. Her fingers tangled idly in the dark silk of his hair, allowing the strands to curl around them. Savouring the texture against her palm as she drew her hand through its thickness.

She had willingly entered his world of sound and touch and taste. There was no light in the room, nor had there been any throughout the night. In the darkness, they had discovered one another tactilely, and for her that had meant a freedom from inhibition she had never before experienced.

He had delighted in her body, but she had been given an equal liberty to explore his. To daringly run her fingers over its hardened contours. To draw her bare insole along the muscled ridge of his calf. To caress the broad, hair-roughened chest. To lay her cheek against it, exhausted by his lovemaking and content to listen to the rhythm of his racing heart slow and finally steady.

She had believed they were both sated, beyond need or desire, long past satisfaction. She *had* believed that until suddenly his tongue flicked against the very core of her sexuality. Heat spiralled upwards, running along those same over-stimulated nerve pathways, liquid fire leaping through veins and arteries and rushing like a reviving drug through still-trembling muscles.

She gasped, fingers reflexively tightening in his hair. There was no response. His tongue didn't cease to caress, and slowly, despite her shock, she began to relax into the waves of sensation that poured like torrents from a seemingly endless spring throughout her body. No one had ever touched her like this, and in her wildest fantasies, she would never have been able to imagine that he would.

She felt as if she should protest, in spite of the fact that he was her husband. Despite all they had already shared. This was too intimate, the feelings it created too powerful, almost frightening in their intensity.

Before that thought was fully formed, however, she knew she didn't want him to stop. Despite her satiation, that slow, spiralling journey had already begun. Fulfilment awaited, hovering just beyond her reach, and her body strained wildly against the movement of his mouth.

This was something she had wanted almost as much as she had wanted the acknowledgment of his love. This had been a part of that longing. To know that he wanted her physically. And now, after tonight, after this, there could be no doubt that he did.

Racked with need and desire, her body writhed, trying to hurry him. As through every moment of the long dark hours they had spent together, however, he would not be rushed. The control was his, and ultimately she surrendered her will to his as completely as she had given him her body.

Again and again, he brought her to the very edge and then retreated, deliberately allowing the sensations to ease, to withdraw their dominion until she could again think. And she didn't want to. Tonight was not about thinking, and she had welcomed the permission his lovemaking had given her to allow her mind to simply drift, all the intellectual decisions already made.

She had again reached the cusp, and she knew this time there would be no turning back. Apparently, he knew it too. His body shifted, moving over hers in the darkness. Suddenly his mouth again sought hers, which was open and waiting, as her body waited breathlessly for his entrance. And it was as powerful as the first time he had taken her.

With his thrust, she cried out, her nails scoring his back as she rode the crest of sensation that caught them both. His body arched and then convulsed, and she could feel the hot, jetting release. In response she wrapped her legs around his waist, pulling him closer, trying to become one with him forever. Holding him to her as the darkness spiralled around them.

His darkness. And he had taught her tonight there was nothing in it to fear.

Slowly his body stilled, and then he pushed himself up a little, propping on his elbows, just as if he were looking down on her. And she could see him, she realized, his face pale against the blackness that was beginning to fade with the faint light of dawn. She put her hand against his cheek, the gesture almost consoling.

He turned his head and pressed his lips into her palm. And when he turned back again, once more seeming to look down into her eyes, he said, "I wish I could see you when that happens."

She tried to read the tone. There was regret, she thought, but no sadness. A simple statement of fact.

"I know," she whispered.

She thought about telling him that only now, with the breaking day, could she see him. And then, looking at his face, she decided there was no reason to tell him that for her the darkness they had shared all night had broken. As it would each morning for the rest of their lives. Instead, she raised her head and put her lips very gently against his.

There was no passion in their touch. The driving need that had guided their actions had been exorcised—at least for now. It was time for other things. The simple but important tasks of living, as well as they could, new each day. Beginning with this.

"What was that for?" Hunt asked, smiling at her when she lay back on the pillow, her eyes still feasting on the sight of his face, emerging from the shadows.

"Just in case you've forgotten."

"Forgotten?" he asked, tilting his head a little, the familiar gesture more endearing than it had ever been before.

"My darling Echo," she said softly, touching the tips of her fingers against his lips. "Just in case you've forgotten how very much I love you. Even when you are *not* making love to me."

"And when I am?" he asked, his tone wickedly suggestive. The smile had become a grin, and it destroyed the slight melancholy she had felt with the arrival of dawn.

"Then you shouldn't have to be told," she said. "It should be obvious."

"Even to me," he said softly. The smile slowly faded. "And will you eventually tire of telling a blind man all the things that should be obvious?"

She thought about what he had asked, wondering if she might. "Did you tire of explaining all those parliamentary bills to me?" she asked.

And was relieved to see the grin return. "Occasionally," he admitted, "but not often. Those are things I feel very passionate about."

"Exactly," she said, and pulled him down to her again.

When Bella awoke, she could tell by the sun it was very late. She turned her head and found the pillow beside her empty. As was the room, she discovered. She was alone in her husband's bedchamber, and he was probably downstairs, forced to make do with Ingalls's less than fluid reading of the day's headlines.

It was not until she had found her dressing gown, thoughtfully laid out for her on the foot of the bed that she remembered it was Sunday. Her day off, she realized with a smile. And in all honesty, after last night she needed one.

There was a discreet knock, so well-timed she wondered in amusement if the servants had been spying, ears against the door. In response to the permission she called, however, Ingalls entered with a tray bearing a pot of tea. His face was perfectly controlled, his eyes averted from her state of undress.

Bella was just as glad that she didn't have to meet them. She knew she'd blush, which was probably not the response a *proper* countess should make to being found *en dishabille* in her husband's bedchamber.

"Will that be all, my lady?" Ingalls said after he'd put the tray down on the table before the windows.

"Thank you, Ingalls. Is the earl already at breakfast?"

"I believe Lord Huntingdon is in the nursery, my lady."

"The nursery?" she repeated, and then realized that was where she wished to be as well. With the two people she loved more than anything else in the world. Especially today.

"Shall I ask him to join you?"

"Thank you, no, Ingalls. I think I shall join them instead."

"Very good, my lady," the valet said, bowing in preparation for leaving.

"And John?" He turned back, his eyes meeting hers for the first time. They were alight in a way she had never seen them before. "Thank you," she said softly. "Thank you for everything."

"Sometimes Quality don't know what's good for them, my lady. Those of us in service occasionally have to give them a push in the right direction, if you take my meaning. After that, things are generally better for everyone concerned. As I'm sure your ladyship will agree," he added. And then he winked at her.

The blood she had denied before rushed into her cheeks. Seeing it, Ingalls grinned, and then, without another word, he crossed the room and went out, leaving her alone.

Bella could hear Kit's piping voice, full of excitement, even before she opened the nursery door. She hadn't taken time to return to her own room to dress. Luckily, she hadn't encountered any of the servants in the halls or as she'd climbed the stairs to the third floor. Facing Ingalls's knowing grin had been quite enough embarrassment for one morning, she thought.

She opened the door in time to hear Kit offer magnanimously, "Now *you* may be the Iron Duke, if you wish. I'll help you set up your army exactly the way that he did at Vitoria."

"Thank you," the Earl of Huntingdon, who had had a hand in the strategic planning of that battle, said humbly.

By that time, however, Kit had seen his mother standing hesitantly in the doorway. "Mama!" he shouted, jumping up and running across the battlefield, which was really only the worn rug before the nursery fire. More than one of the gallant tin soldiers inadvertently broke ranks as the little boy flew across the room to throw himself into his mother's arms.

Bella bent just in time to stop his headlong rush by scooping him up. She hugged him tightly, as if they had been separated for days rather than hours. She swung him around once or twice before she set him on his feet again.

"Did you have a good time last night?" Kit asked.

Despite herself, Bella's eyes lifted to find her husband, still lying on his side on the rug. His dark head was propped on one hand while the other toyed with the soldiers scattered before him. Even from where she stood, she could see the amused quirk of his lips in response to Kit's question. And again she blushed.

"A very good time, thank you, Kit. The earrings you chose to go with my gown were the perfect touch. I was quite the belle, I assure you."

"Good," Kit pronounced in satisfaction, and then moved on to a subject of far more importance. "Did you come to play soldiers with us?"

"Only to watch, perhaps," she said, her eyes still on her husband.

"I suspect girls aren't very good at playing war," Kit said.

"Perhaps they have other interests," the Earl of Huntingdon suggested. "And other...talents."

The long fingers of his left hand were still arranging miniature men into formation before the cheerful blaze. As Bella watched, knowing quite well what he meant, the memories of what had happened between them last night produced a different kind of heat.

"Thank you," she said softly.

"Thank *you*," he answered, his lips tilting again.

"Hunt says I'm to have a brother," Kit announced, drawing her eyes back to him.

"A brother," she repeated.

"Darling Echo," Hunt said, still arranging his troops.

"Or perhaps a sister. He doesn't know yet for sure."

"The earl seems to be making quite a few... assumptions this morning. I only hope you won't be disappointed if you have to wait a while, Kit."

"Only the requisite nine months," her husband said confidently. "I've explained all that."

"Indeed?" Bella said faintly, putting her hand on the back of Kit's head and directing him towards the fire. The little boy sprawled happily across the battleground from his stepfather, his eyes excitedly taking in the formations of both armies. "You seem to be *very* sure of yourself this morning, my lord."

"Oh, I am. I have it on the best authority. Ingalls assures me it's time I should have children."

He lifted his hand to her, an obvious invitation to join them on the rug. Smiling, she complied. And when she was seated on the floor beside him, he didn't release her fingers until he had brought them to his mouth and kissed each one individually, much to Kit's fascination.

"And I *never* argue with Ingalls," Hunt said, smiling at her. "If there is one thing I've learned, it's that he truly does always know best."

Bella thought of that cold winter day when she had come to his study to refuse the Earl of Huntingdon's offer and had watched John Ingalls's mouth those fateful words. *Say yes,* he had told her, and for some inexplicable reason, she had. And now...

She breathed a silent prayer of thanks for her husband's valet. She had no idea, of course, what other role he might have played in this, but it was obvious by Hunt's remark there had been one. Perhaps he had influenced the earl's decision to propose as much as he had hers to accept. If so, she owed him a debt she would never be able to repay.

"If you tell him I said that, however," Hunt continued, still holding her fingers in his, "there will be no living with him, I'm afraid. Shall we pretend we were unaware of his manipulations?"

"Pretend we thought this marvellous arrangement up all on our own?" she asked mockingly, setting a fallen soldier upright and in his proper rank. "But my dear, no one would believe a member of the nobility would have the rare good sense to fall in love with his own wife."

"I must confess I am finding that rather convenient,'' Hunt said, smiling at her over the small curly head of their son. Their first son.

''Of course you are,'' Bella said contentedly. ''That's exactly why a match such as ours is *called* a marriage of convenience. I'm surprised you didn't know.''

Then the Countess of Huntingdon leaned forward to kiss her husband, dealing Wellington's army such a defeat as it had never before known.

And properly distracted, the commander of all the British forces in the field that day didn't even seem to notice.

* * * * *

Author Note

Regency England, with its wit, elegance and style, has always fascinated me—and what could be more elegant, stylish and romantic than a Regency wedding? When I was invited to write this story I remembered the romantic poem by Sir Walter Scott where the bride elopes on her wedding day, and this inspired me to write my own story about a runaway Regency bride. When Thea Shaw leaves her bridegroom at the altar and runs into the arms of the handsome rake, Jack Merlin, the sparks start to fly!

I loved writing this story so much that I wanted to write about another Regency bride! Look out for THE CHAPERON BRIDE in March 2003 which is linked to THE EARL'S PRIZE, available in November 2002. Both published in Mills & Boon Historical Romance™. I hope you enjoy reading this story as much as I have enjoyed writing it!

The Rake's Bride
by
Nicola Cornick

For Andrew

Chapter One

The April sunlight was as blinding as a flash of gunpowder and the rattle of the bed curtains sounded like distant artillery fire. For a moment Jack, Marquis of Merlin, wondered if he had gone to hell and ended back in the Peninsular War. He rolled onto his back and flung an arm up to shield his eyes.

"Hodges?"

"Yes, my lord?"

The Marquis opened his eyes and looked at his valet. His gaze was dark blue and very unfriendly and his voice held a dangerous undertone. "Hodges, what is the time?"

The valet remained impassive. "A little after nine, my lord."

"That would be nine in the morning?"

"Indeed, my lord."

The Marquis stretched, with a ripple of honed muscles. "As I recall, I asked you to wake me at twelve of the clock and not before. No doubt you can account for the discrepancy?''

"Yes, my lord." Hodges opened the wardrobe and took out a coat of blue superfine. Truth to tell, he had been relieved to find that the Marquis was at home—and alone—for neither circumstance was a foregone conclusion. There had been plenty of occasions on which the Marquis had spent twenty-four hours in one sitting at White's, wandering home only to change his clothes before another spell at the faro tables. There had been many other mornings when Hodges had come to wake his lordship only to discover one of his *chères amies* sprawled naked in bed beside him. It was a sight that would have shocked a valet of less hardened constitution and a circumstance that would have been decidedly awkward that particular morning.

"Well, Hodges? I am awaiting your explanation."

"If I could encourage your lordship to rise?" Hodges said expressionlessly. "The Duke and Duchess of Merlin are awaiting you in the green salon—"

Jack gave an oath and sat up, clapping his hand to his head as a wave of brandy-induced pain threatened to lay him low again. "Damnation! My parents, you say? Here? What in God's name could induce them to call at such a confoundedly unsocial hour? Surely they are not about to parade some other unfortunate candidate for my affections in front of me?"

"His Grace, your father, did not share such information with me, my lord,'' Hodges said, allowing himself a tight smile. ''However, the Duchess mentioned something about your cousin, Mr. Pershore, finding himself in a difficult position—''

Jack paused, running a hand through his dishevelled black hair and making it even more disordered. ''What, again?''

''Yes, my lord. The matter involves a designing female and a hasty marriage, as I understand it. The country was mentioned, my lord.''

Jack swore. It was hardly the first time that his feckless cousin Bertie Pershore had fallen into a scrape. ''Damn it, that's too much! Why could Pershore not contract his ill-conceived marriage in Town? If I have to go chasing off to Oxfordshire again just to act as nursemaid to my cousin—''

''Quite so, my lord.'' Hodges finished brushing down the blue coat. ''His Grace the Duke did mention one thing, my lord.''

''Yes?''

''He said that if you had not joined them within the half hour he would come up here himself.''

Jack swung his legs over the side of the bed and reached for his shirt. He glanced across at the clock. ''How long ago was that, Hodges?''

The valet gave another small smile. ''A little over five and twenty minutes, my lord. I tried to wake you before but you did not stir. I was about to resort to an ewer of water—most efficacious, my lord.''

''Thank God you did not,'' Jack said feelingly. He

looked from the valet's face to the coat in his hand and gave a sigh.

"Devil take it! I suppose I must…"

"Yes, my lord," the valet said.

"Thea," Miss Clementine Shaw said, fixing her elder sister with an earnest look, "are you marrying Mr. Pershore for his money? He is very rich—is he not?—and it seems to me most unlikely that you could be marrying for love!"

Theodosia Shaw let her needlework fall to her lap. She was trimming the bodice of her bridal gown, adding the scraps of Brussels lace that she had garnered from her mother's old dresses that were still stored in lavender in the chest upstairs. The lace was fine but a little yellow with age now and the village gossips in church tomorrow would quickly divine that the entire dress was secondhand. Thea gave a little shrug; there was no point in pretending, for everyone in the village of Oakmantle knew their parlous financial state.

"Clemmie, you really must learn not to ask questions like that," she said severely. Her sister had never understood the art of polite conversation and at nineteen possessed an outspokenness that would deter even the most persistent of suitors. "The Honourable Mr. Pershore is everything that one would wish in a husband. He is…" Here she paused, desperately trying to think of some positive attributes. "He is gentlemanly and kind and good-natured…'' she floundered. ''And kind…''

''You said that already,'' Clementine observed critically. Her perceptive blue eyes, identical to those of her older sister, scanned Thea's face. ''I cannot dispute that he is kind, for has he not offered to marry you and take all of us on, as well?'' She ticked them all off on her fingers. ''Ned will go to Oxford and Harry to Eton, and I may have my come-out and Clara her harp lessons and Daisy—''

''Pray stop at once!'' Thea said, more sharply than she had intended. To hear her sister itemize the material benefits of the match made her feel intolerably guilty, for she *was* marrying Bertie Pershore for his money and could scarcely deny it. She wished that it was not so; somehow she felt that Bertie deserved better than that she take advantage of him. Yet she was in desperate straits and he was chivalrous enough to come to her rescue. For a moment she thought back to the day when he had made his unexpected declaration and a smile, half rueful, half sad, crossed her features.

''You know I'm dashed fond of you, Thea, old girl,'' Bertie had said that day in the drawing room. His kindly brown gaze, so reminiscent of Theodosia's favourite spaniel, had rested on her with sympathetic concern. ''Can't bear to see you struggle on in this mouldering old place any longer! I'll need a suitable wife one day and you're well up to snuff—we would deal well together! So what do you say?''

Thea had not replied at once. She had got to her feet and strolled over to the drawing room window. It was early spring. The trees were still bare but beneath them the ground was starred with snowdrops and yellow aconites. It was a pretty scene but it failed to distract the eye completely from the general air of shabby neglect that hung over Oakmantle Hall.

Thea had turned back to her suitor, unsure whether to laugh or to cry. There were those who held that the Honourable Mr. Pershore, a Pink of the Ton, cared for little beyond the set of his neckcloth or the polish of his Hessians. Yet Thea had known him since they had been children together and knew him to be good-hearted and kind. She had just had the proof of it in his generous, if unromantic, proposal.

She had given him a rueful smile. "Oh, Bertie, you are most chivalrous, but I know perfectly well that you can have as little desire to marry as I! If it weren't for the rest of my family I would not even countenance it! Besides, that odious guardian of yours will surely kick up a fuss if you marry a penniless prospect such as myself, a woman older than you are, with so many dependants—"

Bertie had tried to shake his head and almost impaled himself on his shirt points. He'd frowned as mutinously as someone of his mournful expression was able.

"Don't see what business it is of Merlin's! I'm of age and may marry whom I choose."

Thea had sighed with all the wisdom of her two

and twenty years. "Bertie, only conceive of the trouble it would cause! The Duke of Merlin would never tolerate so imprudent a match, not even for a distant cousin! Can you imagine what he would do?"

"Probably send Jack down," Bertie had said, his face breaking into a sudden grin. "Jack is forever pulling me out of scrapes! Did I tell you about the time he found me at Madam Annet's when I was on *exeat* from Eton—"

"Yes!" Thea had said sharply, wincing more at the reference to their potential marriage as a "scrape" than the indelicate story of Bertie's foray into one of London's most notorious bawdy houses. From the age of five, Bertie had tired her ears with his hero-worshipping references to Jack Merlin, his cousin and idol, and as a result Thea had taken the Marquis in extreme dislike. She had never met him in person but had formed an impression of an arrogant nobleman who had been granted all of life's privileges and took them lightly, until they bored him. Bertie's assurances that Jack was a great gun and a devil with the ladies did him no favours in Thea's eyes. She knew that Jack Merlin was a rake—even in the village of Oakmantle they had heard something of his reputation.

Bertie had looked abashed. "Sorry, Thea. Dashed improper of me to mention it."

Thea had sighed. It was impossible to feel anything other than a faint exasperation for one whom she had always considered as a rather tiresome younger brother, which made the proposed marriage even more ridiculous. She already had five siblings and scarcely needed a husband who would constitute a sixth child. Yet did she have any choice? Her father had left her with a mountain of debts, a crumbling manor house and her brothers and sisters to care for. And there was scarcely a queue of eager suitors hammering on the door of Oakmantle Hall...

Thea came back to the present and cut her thread with a sharp snap. There was no point in dwelling on that now. She had made her choice and tomorrow the knot would be tied.

"Clemmie, you must understand that one cannot always marry for love." She tried to explain.

"Why not?" her sister said immediately. "Mama was most insistent that we should not compromise our principles."

Thea sighed again. Their mother had been a bluestocking in her day, one of Mrs. Montagu's circle, and had held strong views on women's education and independence. She had brought all her children up to view romantic love as the ideal, which was all very well, Thea thought crossly, but when she had no money and a family to support, high-minded principles were a luxury she could ill afford.

The true extent of their poverty had only become apparent when their father had died some six months previously. Mr. Shaw had been a scholar and a gentleman, but he had had no concept of the importance of more worldly matters such as money. They had lived in the old house at Oakmantle for more years than Thea could remember but on her father's death she had discovered that it was not their own, and now the landlord was threatening to increase the rents or repossess the house. They had no source of income. Thea could never earn enough as a governess or schoolteacher to keep a family of six and though her brother Ned talked wildly of finding work as a clerk in the city of London, he was only seventeen and had no one to sponsor him. They had subsisted on the generosity of friends and distant relatives up to this point but now funds were running short and a more permanent answer had to be found. Bertie Pershore was that solution.

Thea shook the wedding dress out and held it at arm's length for critical inspection. Her pride had rebelled at the thought of Bertie paying for her trousseau, so as a result she would have to go to him in these faded threads.

"There, that will have to do."

Thea sighed again, repressing the urge to bundle the dress up and thrust it to the back of a cupboard, or even into the fire. "I never was much of a hand at needlework but I have done my best. It requires a hot iron."

Clementine closed her book and bent to blow out the single stand of candles. "It requires more than that! Never mind, Thea, you may have no skill with the needle but you will be able to discuss philosophy and poetry and ancient history with Mr. Pershore over the teacups…''

Thea winced but did not reprove her sister. Clementine was a sharp observer but seldom intended malice and it was not her fault that her words conjured up so ridiculous an image. For no matter how amiable Mr. Pershore was, he was no scholar. The thought of making trivial conversation with Bertie day in, day out, for the next forty years was purgatory, but Thea knew she was being ungrateful. There was a price to financial security, and if this was all she had to pay then she had escaped lightly.

The wedding service had barely begun when Thea realized that she simply could not go through with it. The omens had been bad that morning but she had tried to ignore them. A light drizzle had been falling as she made the short journey from Oakmantle Hall to the church, dampening her veil and making the embroidered roses in her circlet droop miserably. At her side, Ned glowered in silence, still smarting over the fact that she was sacrificing herself because he, the head of the family, could not support them. The church felt cold and smelled of dust, and Thea shivered convulsively in her thin silk dress. Clementine, Harry, Clara and Daisy were lined up in the front pew looking scrubbed and subdued. They were a good-looking family—all possessed the cornflower-blue eyes and fair hair of the Shaw family and all were huddling in old clothes that had been sponged down for the occasion by Mrs. Skeffington, the cook-housekeeper. Thea thought that Harry looked like an undertaker's boy in his best black coat and Clara and Daisy were clutching each other's hands and looking as though they were about to cry.

Bertie Pershore was standing before the altar, looking terrified. Thea wondered if he was having second thoughts but was too honourable to say anything. Her heart sank lower than her soaking satin slippers and right down to the gravestones beneath her feet.

"Dearly beloved…" the rector intoned, fixing Thea with a severe look. He had baptized her and all her siblings and had buried her father six months before. The same villagers who had come to pay their respects to the late Mr. Shaw now bobbed and whispered in the pews behind Thea's family, noting the secondhand wedding dress and the groom's terrified demeanour. None of Bertie's family was present and Thea did not know whether she was glad or sorry.

The rector had moved on to the reasons for which marriage had been ordained and was speaking of the procreation of children. Thea, who had managed to avoid all thoughts of her wedding night, was suddenly confronted by a picture of herself and Bertie lying side by side in the ancient tester bed at Oakmantle. Under the circumstances the knowledge of Bertie's experiences at Madam Annet's hands might have been reassuring, since Thea had no experience of her own to draw on. Instead the thought was decidedly off-putting, providing as it did too much information for comfort. Bertie was kind, but Thea did not find him in the least attractive, and whilst she was not naïve enough to imagine that one had to enjoy submitting to one's husband's desires, she had once hoped that she would marry a man who stirred her feelings....

"Secondly, it was ordained for a remedy against sin, and to avoid fornication..." the rector said, glaring ferociously at the congregation, who shifted uncomfortably in the pews. Bertie stared at his highly polished boots and cleared his throat nervously.

Oh, dear... Thea thought.

"I am sorry," she heard herself say politely, "but I am afraid that there has been a dreadful mistake and I have to go now."

There was a moment of absolute silence that felt to Thea as though it went on for hours. The vicar opened and closed his mouth like a landed fish, Bertie went white then red and the congregation started to flutter and whisper as they realized that something was wrong. Then Thea found herself hurrying back down the aisle, holding her skirts up in one hand, the slap of her slippers sounding unnaturally loud on the stone floor. She looked neither left nor right, ignoring the avid faces of the villagers as they craned to see what was going on. Behind her she could hear a swell of voices like the roar of the sea, but she had already reached the door and was fumbling with the latch. Her hands were shaking so much that they slipped on the cold metal. She felt faint and light-headed but she knew that she had to escape.

The door swung open suddenly with a gust of cool spring air. Thea rushed forward, almost tripping over the threshold in her haste, blinded by her veil and the tears that were now threatening her. She stumbled a few paces down the path towards the gate, realized that she would fall if she did not steady herself, and put out a hand. She recoiled in shock as it was caught and held. Strong arms went around her, holding her close.

''What the devil—'' a masculine voice ejaculated, then the veil was pushed roughly back from her face and she found herself staring up at the man who held her.

His face was heart-stoppingly close to hers. As though in a dream Thea noted the dark blue eyes with their ridiculously thick black lashes, the harsh angles and planes of his tanned face, the square chin and uncompromising line of the mouth. She could smell lemon cologne mixed with cold air and leather and it made her feel faint but in an entirely different way from before. Her knees buckled and his arms tightened about her.

A lock of black hair had fallen across his forehead and it looked soft and silky. Thea had a sudden urge to smooth it back, to let her hand linger against his cheek where the stubble already darkened his skin. Her fingers were already halfway to their destination when she shivered convulsively and snapped out of the dream that held her, stepping back and freeing herself.

The man made an instinctive gesture towards her. "Wait!"

Thea ignored him. With no thought to the rain or the slippery stones of the churchyard or the damp, clinging lace of her wedding dress, she ran from him as though her life depended on it.

Jack had seen her as soon as he came through the lych-gate and started up the path towards the church. She was hurrying towards him but he could tell that she had not seen him—there was an air of intense concentration about her that suggested she was completely wrapped up in her feelings. Then she had stumbled on the wet path and he had caught her hand, instinctively pulling her into his arms, as she seemed about to fall.

She had eyes of cornflower-blue, stricken and bright with tears now, but direct and uncompromising still. They widened as she looked up into his face and focused on him for the first time. He felt a jolt of something go through him, something like pain, deeper than desire.

Her fair hair was so soft it looked like spun gold as it escaped the confines of the wedding veil, and he had the near irresistible urge to loosen it and bury his face in the silken mass. Her mouth was tempting and voluptuous, as unconsciously sensuous as the rest of the yielding body that was pressed so intimately

against his. She smelled of lavender and spring mead-
ows and sunshine, and he found that all he wanted
was to hold her closer still. Jack Merlin had never
experienced so strong a reaction to a woman in his
whole life. It was no surprise to find that he wanted
her but it was a surprise to find himself so shaken.

"Wait!" The word burst from him instinctively as
she freed herself violently from his arms. She took no
notice. He saw that her hands were trembling as she
scooped up the yellowing lace skirts of the old wedding gown, then she was running from him down the
path and disappearing through the lych-gate. The
whole encounter had taken less than a minute.

Jack let his breath out in a long sigh and felt the
tension drain slowly from his body. Behind him in
the church he could hear an excited babble of voices
rising to a crescendo. He cast one look in the direction
the girl had gone. Unless he missed his guess, he had
just met his cousin's runaway bride. But whether she
was running away before or after the knot had been
tied was as yet uncertain. Jack found himself hoping
fervently for the former, then sighed again. When he
had set off from London the last thing he had expected was to find himself envying his cousin. The
whole matter of Bertie's wedding was becoming a lot
more complicated than he had envisaged.

Chapter Two

"At least I was able to hold my peace!" Jack said wryly. "I'd have felt a damned fool intervening in the service at the point where the parson asks if anyone has just cause to stop the proceedings."

"Never got that far," Bertie Pershore said gloomily, passing his cousin a glass of brandy. He joined Jack by the fire. "Devil take it, Jack, if Thea didn't want to go through with it she could have told me before that! Making a cake of myself in front of the entire village... Jilting me at the altar—"

They were in the private parlour of the Lamb and Rabbit hostelry, where Jack had abandoned his carriage and his valet an hour previously. Hodges had spent the intervening time bespeaking rooms and making sure that everything was comfortable. Sampling the brandy, Jack observed that he did indeed employ a prince amongst valets.

After the debacle at the wedding, Jack had simply strolled up the aisle, ushered his shocked cousin out a side door, pressed a large financial contribution into the startled rector's hand and suggested that the jilted groom be left in peace to recover. No one had dared to gainsay him.

Jack shrugged, settling himself deeper in the armchair. "Maybe Miss Shaw suddenly realized she could do better for herself, old chap! A title *and* a fortune, perhaps…"

"Thea isn't like that!" Bertie said hotly. He saw Jack's sardonic glance and added, "Oh, I know you think I'm besotted with an adventuress, but you couldn't be further from the truth. Thea and I have been friends for years and I was only trying to help her out—"

"Keep your chivalric instincts under control in future!" his cousin advised dryly. "Not that I can blame you, Bertie. Miss Thea Shaw is devilish attractive and I can quite see why you fell for her charms, but to make her an offer—"

He broke off at his cousin's blank stare. "Attractive? Thea? I'll concede she's not a bad-looking girl, and she's game as a pebble, of course, but she's no diamond of the first water! Sure we're talking about the same girl, Jack?"

Jack raised his eyebrows. He had never felt that Bertie's taste in women was either well developed or particularly subtle and here he had the proof. His cousin had evidently been in the ridiculous position of being blind to the considerable charms of the woman he was about to marry. Jack shrugged philo-

sophically. He was not going to point out the error of
his ways to Bertie for this way he could kill two birds
with one stone. He could ensure that the marriage
would not be revived and he could map out a very
different future for Miss Theodosia Shaw. He already
had in mind exactly what it entailed.

In the hour since he had met Thea outside the
church, Jack had successfully managed to master the
surprising and wholly unexpected feelings that she
had aroused in him. Clearly Thea Shaw was a fortune
hunter, no matter what Bertie said to defend her. That
being the case, she might be receptive to an offer from
him, which, whilst different from Bertie's chivalrous
proposal, might still be as financially rewarding. Jack
smiled, a little cynically. He was certain that he could
satisfy both his own desires and those of Miss Shaw
one way or another.

"I assume you have no intention of renewing your
suit to Miss Shaw?" he inquired casually and was
relieved when Bertie flushed angrily.

"Damned if I will! I have my pride, you know,
Jack! All I ever wanted to do was help Thea out—a
favour because of our long friendship, you know, and
I think she could at least have been honest with me."
He stared gloomily into the fire. "Think I'll eschew
all women! Better off without them! No idea what
makes them tick."

Jack grinned at that. "You and the rest of the male
population, old chap! Well—" he stood up and

stretched ''—I am going to pay a call on Miss Shaw. Wouldn't want her stirring up any trouble in future.''

Bertie shook his head. He looked up. ''Barking up the wrong tree there, Jack! Thea won't take kindly to your interference. Why not let it lie, old fellow? Wedding's off—you can be sure that I won't be making any rash offers again. Fingers burned and all that!''

''All the same, I will be happier when I have made a few matters clear to Miss Shaw,'' Jack murmured. ''It will not take long.''

''Suppose you mean to pay her off,'' Bertie said, adding with gloomy relish, ''Big mistake! Asking for trouble, old fellow! You'll see!''

''I have various offers to put to Miss Shaw,'' Jack said lazily, reaching for his coat. ''We shall see which one suits her best.''

''I cannot believe that I have behaved so badly!'' Thea was curled up in an armchair in the blue drawing room. She had changed out of the soaking wedding dress into a plain gown of grey-spotted muslin and her hair was loose, drying in corkscrew curls about her face.

''Poor Bertie! He will never forgive me. I cannot forgive myself. Jilting him at the altar! How could I do such a thing?''

''Well, it was very bad of you,'' Clementine confirmed with a judicious purse of the lips, ''but far better than to marry Mr. Pershore today and change your mind tomorrow. It will only be a nine days' wonder until the next scandal comes along!'' She pressed a glass of Madeira into her sister's hand. ''Here, drink this. I always think it the best way to ward off a chill.''

''I cannot see what you can know of such strong cures at your age!'' Thea said severely, forgetting her dejection for a moment. Sometimes she felt she was a poor substitute for a mother to Clementine. It was impossible to control her sister's waywardness. She took a sip of the drink and sat back in her chair.

''What happened in the church after I left, Clemmie?''

''Not a great deal,'' her sister said, kneeling to add a couple of applewood logs to the fire. ''The rector appealed to the congregation to keep calm.'' She snorted. ''As well try to dam the river Oak! They were chattering and gossiping when you were barely through the door.'' She caught Thea's eye and said hurriedly, ''It will all die down before you can say 'jilt'!''

Thea glared at her. ''Thank you! And in the meantime we are in as poor and parlous a situation as before. I cannot think what came over me.''

''You did the correct thing.'' Clementine stood up and dusted her palms together to remove the wood chippings. ''No matter how rich Mr. Pershore, it makes him not one whit more attractive as a husband.''

Thea turned her face away. She felt restless and on edge but she knew it had nothing to do with what had happened in the church and all to do with what had happened afterwards. She had not even seen the stranger in the churchyard until she had stumbled into his arms and once she was there she had wanted him to hold her forever. It was extraordinary, it was deeply unsettling, but it was true.

"Did a gentleman come into the church just after I left?" she asked casually. "I thought I saw someone on the path."

Clementine brightened. "Oh, yes! I forgot to tell you! Apparently it was Mr. Pershore's cousin, but I had no chance to meet him as he whisked Bertie away in an instant. He was most prodigiously handsome, though. That I do remember."

Thea sat upright, her heart pounding uncomfortably. "Bertie's cousin, did you say? Oh, no, I do believe that must have been the Marquis of Merlin come to stop the marriage, just as Bertie predicted..." Against her will she felt a blush rising. So it was Jack Merlin in whose arms she had taken refuge! Thea put her glass down with a snap, damning the confoundedly bad luck of the whole situation.

Clementine was sitting back on her heels and eyeing her suspiciously.

"That was the Marquis of Merlin? Is he not the one with the terrible reputation? The rake? The one who ran off with Lady Spence, then decided he preferred her younger sister who had just wed Lord Raistrick?"

"Yes!" Thea said quickly, wondering where on

earth her younger sister had picked up such scurrilous gossip. There was no denying that Jack Merlin was rakish and dangerous—she had assimilated that in less than ten seconds in his arms. Compellingly attractive was another matter, and one she did not wish to admit to her sister.

"And divinely handsome, as well!" Clementine sighed. "Oh, I do so wish I had had the chance to make his acquaintance."

Thea was just reflecting that Clementine had absorbed a great deal of romance along with her mother's more stringent philosophies on life, when her eye was caught by a figure strolling around the corner of the house. There was no mistaking him, for all that she had met him so briefly. This was definitely the Marquis of Merlin come to call. Thea recoiled, stifling an urge to run away and hide upstairs. The doorbell pealed.

"I do believe that you may rectify your omission now," she said faintly, "for that is the Marquis at the door. Though what he can be wanting with us—" She broke off and smoothed her dress down with nervous fingers. Oh, to be wearing her old grey muslin at such a time! This would be the second occasion on which the Marquis would see her in her frumpish clothes, just when she needed the confidence that a really modish dress would give her. But then, she possessed no such thing, so bewailing the fact was immaterial...

"Excuse me, ma'am," Mrs. Skeffington, the housekeeper, arrived at the drawing room door looking flustered and disapproving. Thea squashed the ridiculous suspicion that the Marquis had been flirting with her. "The Marquis of Merlin is asking if you are at home, ma'am—"

"Oh, show him in!" Clementine said, almost hopping with excitement.

Thea sent her a quelling look. "Thank you, Skeffie. I will see Lord Merlin in here. Clementine—" she turned to her sister "—it would perhaps be better if you were to leave us to talk in private."

"Oh, no!" Clementine said, adopting the severe tone her elder sister always used with her, "that would not be at all proper!"

"Lord Merlin, ma'am!" Mrs. Skeffington murmured, frowning sternly. She dropped a curtsy and moved away with a stately tread that managed to imply even greater disapproval.

The Marquis of Merlin came into the room.

Thea took a deep, steadying breath. Her heart was racing and not simply with nervousness. She had the time to study the Marquis properly now as he came forward to greet her, and she was disconcerted to discover that she had the inclination to carry on looking at him indefinitely. It was not simply that he was, as Clementine had said, prodigiously handsome, although this was not in dispute. There was something else, something more compelling than mere good looks. Here was a man who was everything that Bertie Pershore was not. In an instant Thea recognized that she had accepted Bertie because he was straightforward and safe and unthreatening. And even on so short, albeit eventful, an acquaintance, she could tell that Jack Merlin was the exact opposite—complicated, dangerous, a challenge she was unsure she wanted to accept. Such thoughts did nothing to quell the uneasy excitement that was coursing through her body.

Clementine was staring and Thea could hardly blame her. The Marquis was tall, with a strong physique and a nonchalant grace that compelled the eye. His thick, dark hair was dishevelled in the kind of style that poor Bertie could not have achieved even with the ministrations of the best valet. He bowed with ineffable elegance.

"Miss Shaw?"

His voice was low and warm, sending a curious shiver down Thea's spine. She nodded starchily. "Lord Merlin."

She saw a smile touch that firm mouth. "How do you do, ma'am? It is…most agreeable to meet you again."

Thea ignored the intimate implication of his words and gestured to Clementine. "Lord Merlin, may I introduce my sister, Miss Clementine Shaw."

Jack inclined his head. "Your servant, Miss Clementine."

Thea watched with exasperation as Clementine dropped a demure curtsy and smiled enchantingly at the Marquis. She had never behaved as such a pattern card of female perfection with any of their other male acquaintance. Such contrariness was enough to tempt Thea to shake her sister—until she realized that the Marquis was skilfully disposing of Clementine's company and suddenly she was tempted to cling to her as a safeguard.

"I hope you will excuse me if I beg a private word with your sister, Miss Clementine," Jack was saying, holding the drawing room door open. "It was indeed a pleasure to meet you."

Thea sent Clementine a look that was part beseeching, part commanding, but her sister seemed blind to her appeal. She tripped out without demur and Jack closed the door gently behind her.

Thea blinked. She cleared her throat hastily, searching for a diversion.

"Would you care for some refreshment, Lord Merlin?"

Jack's gaze fell on her half-finished glass. "Thank you. I will join you in a glass of Madeira, ma'am."

Thea poured the wine herself, trying to prevent her fingers from shaking. There was something unnerving about Jack Merlin, the direct, dark blue gaze that had barely wavered from her since he had entered the room, the instinctive authority that cloaked him. This was not a man Thea wanted to tangle with. And yet a part of her, a treacherous part, wanted it very much indeed…

She handed him the glass of wine, making sure that their fingers did not touch. The memory of their encounter outside the church was still in her mind and her equilibrium, already fragile, could not withstand another onslaught. She resumed her seat with what she hoped was an assumption of ease, gesturing Jack to take the chair opposite. He did so, his eyes never leaving her face.

"I hope that you are somewhat recovered from your ordeal, Miss Shaw?" Jack raised an eyebrow. "When we met outside the church I thought that you were a little...distressed? I would have assisted you had you given me the opportunity."

There was a warmth in his tone, an intimacy, that brought the colour into Thea's cheeks. His words conjured up the memory of his arms about her, the comforting strength that had somehow been simultaneously protective and inexplicably exciting. Thea smoothed her skirts with a little nervous gesture. She did not—could not—meet his eyes.

"Thank you, my lord. I am much recovered now."

"Good." Jack's tone changed subtly, the gentleness gone. "Miss Shaw, forgive my abruptness, but I wished to speak to you of the wedding. Why did you abandon Bertie at the altar? Having persuaded him to marry you, I cannot understand why you should throw away all your advantages! Unless, of course—" there was a sardonic note in his voice now "—you are contemplating a better offer?"

Thea looked up sharply. He had wasted little time on polite niceties. The gloves were off now, the contempt very clear.

"I fear that you are labouring under several misconceptions, sir,'' she said with cool haughtiness. ''In the first place I had no need to exert undue influence in order to persuade Mr. Pershore to propose! He did so because he is a true friend and most chivalrous—''

She broke off as Jack shifted slightly. ''And then you scorned his chivalry by jilting him at the altar?'' he queried gently. ''That was badly done, Miss Shaw.''

Thea bit her lip, all too aware that he was deliberately putting her in the wrong, but equally aware that her position was indefensible. It *had* been inexcusable to treat Bertie so, but she had no intention of accepting Jack's reproofs. She looked at him defiantly.

''Would you have preferred me to marry your cousin, Lord Merlin? Forgive me, but I thought your presence in Oakmantle indicated an intention to put a stop to the nuptials rather than to dance at the wedding! Am I then mistaken and you are here to persuade me to accept Bertie, after all?''

Jack laughed. ''Certainly not, Miss Shaw! My cousin has told me a little of your situation and I cannot but see it as a most undesirable match! No money, no connections, nothing to recommend you but…'' He paused, and his blue gaze slid over her with a mocking appraisal that made his meaning crystal-clear.

Thea was incensed. She stood up. ''You are impertinent, sir! Since you evidently set great store by wealth and connection, I am happy to tell you that my family is at least as old and distinguished as your own—more so! And we are far more honourable in our conduct!'' She saw him smile and went on sharply. ''So have no fear, I do not intend to importune Bertie to give me a second chance! Your cousin is safe from my attentions!''

''I am happy to hear it,'' Jack murmured. He had also risen to his feet and was standing disturbingly close to her. For a wild moment Thea could almost imagine that she could feel the warmth of his body, smell the faint scent of lemon cologne she had detected when he had held her before. Her senses went into a spin and she felt herself tremble. It was deeply unnerving. She stepped back hastily and almost overturned the table with her wineglass upon it. Jack caught her elbow to steady her and Thea shook him off, appalled at the tremor that slid through her at his touch.

''I cannot believe that we have anything more to say to each other, Lord Merlin,'' she said coldly, moving to pull the bell for the housekeeper. ''I must bid you good day.''

Jack put out a hand to stop her. ''On the contrary,'' he said, gently mocking, ''there are a number of points I still wish to make. Please be seated, Miss Shaw.''

Their eyes met in a long moment of tension, then Thea deliberately moved away to the stand by the window. She was damned if she was going to do his bidding!

"I am sure that whatever you wish to say to me may be adequately expressed with me standing here, Lord Merlin," she said. "Pray continue!"

Jack shrugged carelessly. "As you wish, Miss Shaw. My only concern was for your comfort."

"Pray make your point!" Thea snapped, allowing the tension to overset her naturally good manners.

Jack was not in the least discomposed. "Very well. In recognition of your obliging nature, Miss Shaw, I would like to make you an offer. If you undertake not to see Bertie ever again I shall be happy to contribute something to recompense you for your loss." He looked around the shabby drawing room. "It will help to tide you over until you find another suitor, perhaps…"

Thea drew herself up. She had never previously considered that she had a bad temper, but then she had never been provoked by the Marquis of Merlin before.

"Do I understand you to be offering me a bribe, Lord Merlin?" she inquired icily. "You quite misunderstand me if you think I should be amenable to such a suggestion. I have *every* intention of seeing Bertie again, if only to apologize to him! We have been friends these twenty years past."

"My dear, you are the one who is deluding herself," Jack said, sounding to Thea's infuriated ears both bored and amused. "It may salve your conscience to pretend that the arrangement between yourself and Bertie was based on chivalry, or friendship, or however you wish to dress it up, but the truth is that it was a business transaction no different in essence from the offer I am making you now.''

There was another sharp silence. ''I do not accept bribes!'' Thea said through stiff lips. ''You have my word and that should be sufficient.''

Jack shrugged gracefully. ''The word of a woman of principle?'' There was cold cynicism in his eyes. ''I wish I could believe it, Miss Shaw.''

He was unfurling a roll of banknotes from his pocket and casually placing them on the mantelpiece, stacking a column of golden guineas on top to keep them in place. Thea stared, transfixed. So much money... More than she could earn in a lifetime as a schoolteacher, enough to keep a family of six in comfort for years and years....

''You see, Miss Shaw—'' Jack's voice was very soft ''—principles are for fools! Take it. It is yours...''

With a violent sweep of the hand, Thea scattered the guineas to the four corners of the room. They spun across the floor, clattering against the skirting board and rolling under the furniture. One of them bounced off a particularly ugly sculpture that had belonged to Thea's father and chipped its nose.

Jack picked up the banknotes, folded them and put them back in his pocket.

He grinned. ''I take it that that is a refusal?''

Thea was shaking but she managed to keep her voice steady. ''You are most perspicacious, sir!''

Jack was laughing at her. "A woman of principle indeed! If you wish to save my father the expense of paying you off I shall not argue with you!" He took a step closer to her. "Do not think to come begging for money in future and threatening scandal, however!"

It took all of Thea's will to respond with cool disdain when she wanted to slap him. She glared at him with the angry intensity of a cornered cat. "I have no intention of acting so! That may be *your* preferred mode of behaviour, my lord—"

Jack's eyes lit suddenly with wicked amusement. Thea took an unconscious step back, warned by the predatory brightness she saw there.

"Since you ask, *this* is my preferred mode of behaviour, Miss Shaw."

His arms went around her, hard and fast, and his mouth had captured hers before she even had time to think. Thea's immediate feelings of outrage died a swift death, banished by the warm pressure of his lips on hers. Her lips parted, instinctively obeying the unspoken command; she felt his tongue touch hers and a seductive weakness swept through her, leaving her breathless with shocked desire.

There was no reprieve. Even as Thea's mind reeled under the onslaught of her feelings he deepened the kiss, his mouth skilful, demanding, making no concessions. Thea swayed a little, half astonished to find herself pressing closer to him, half wanton in her need to be closer still.

She moved slightly and her foot struck something against the softness of her kid slipper. A golden guinea. Thea's mind cleared abruptly and she pushed hard against Jack's chest, pulling away from him, utterly appalled. He released her at once.

Thea stepped back. Her voice was shaky. "That was—"

"Exceptional." Thea saw a heat in Jack's eyes that mirrored the desire still shimmering through her own body. His voice was rough. She repressed a shiver. What was it about this man that turned her bones to water? She was no foolish scullery maid to have her head turned by a handsome marquis!

"My dear Miss Shaw," Jack was saying gently, taking her hand in his and reawakening all the latent feelings that Thea was trying so hard to suppress, "might I suggest an alternative future based on the… surprising…harmony we seem to have achieved? In return for your favour I should be glad to help with your financial difficulties…"

It took a second for Thea to understand, but then the shock hit her with what felt like physical force and she found it difficult to breathe. She turned away and moved a few ornaments at random on the mantelpiece.

"I collect that you mean to set me up as your mistress, Lord Merlin?" She was amazed at her own mild tone. "Or do I mistake and you intend only a short but sweet liaison? Not that it matters." She spun round to face him with such sudden violence that one of the ornaments, a pretty little shepherdess, clattered to the floor. "The answer to either suggestion is no— thank you! First you try to bribe me and then you offer me *carte blanche!* Your arrogance, insensitivity and conceit are truly breathtaking! Now leave this house before I throw you out myself!"

Jack raised his eyebrows, seemingly unmoved. "Your indignation is magnificent, my dear, but is it justified? Did you not respond to me just now?" His gaze, suddenly insolent, swept over her and lingered on the curve of her breast. "How many times have you used your undeniable charms to aid you in a difficult situation? When it is the only card to play?"

Thea did not answer. She brushed past him and opened the drawing room door. Then she marched out into the hall, past the startled housekeeper, and flung open the main door of Oakmantle Hall. It crashed back on its hinges, the echo reverberating through the entire house.

Jack had followed her into the hall and was now receiving his coat from Mrs. Skeffington, whose mouth had turned down so far with disapproval that it looked as though the ends would meet. Thea was grudgingly forced to admit that Jack appeared to be taking his eviction with a good grace. He even bowed to her, a twinkle of very definite admiration in those dark blue eyes.

"Your point is taken, Miss Shaw!"

Thea still did not reply. She watched in stony silence as he went down the broad stone steps, then she slammed the door so hard that the crash raised the wood pigeons from the oak trees all along the drive.

Jack strode across the gravel sweep towards the drive, his mind still focused on Miss Theodosia Shaw. *Arrogance, insensitivity and conceit...* He winced. It was a long time since anyone—except perhaps his father—had dared accuse him of any such thing. Perhaps that was half the trouble.

Jack knew that he had mishandled the situation and he also knew that in part he had done it deliberately. He had wanted to test Miss Shaw, to see if she was the woman of principle that she claimed. And yet Jack realized that as soon as they had spoken, he had known instinctively that Thea would accept neither his money nor his amorous attentions. There was an innocence about her, a straightforward honesty that made such transactions seem grubby and demeaning. Which they were, of course. It served him right to have his offers thrown back in his face.

Jack smiled a little. He had ignored his intuition and put her to the test, but Thea had triumphantly proved his instincts to be right and this pleased him more than a little. He frowned whilst he grappled with the implications of this. It would have been so much easier to have either paid her off and forgotten about her, or to have set her up as his mistress until his surprising desire for her had waned. Instead he found that he wanted her to be innocent of deceit. In fact he wanted her to be innocent, full stop. Jack whistled soundlessly to himself. Purity had never particularly appealed to him before—he had enjoyed the attentions of plenty of experienced women and had never wanted it to be any other way. This, however, was different. For a moment Jack allowed himself the luxury of imagining what it would be like to introduce Thea to physical pleasure. She had responded to his kiss with an untutored passion that was wholly arousing. Multiply that effect ten times and it gave some indication of the conflagration that would surely follow...

Arrogant, conceited... Jack acknowledged that he was being both of those things in wanting Theodosia Shaw all to himself. Further, he was certain that given the time and the opportunity he could persuade her to his point of view, convert her to his way of thinking. He did not have the time, however, and there were any number of pressing reasons why he should return to Town at once, not least because he detested country life. Miss Theodosia Shaw would simply have to remain the one lady who had escaped him...

Jack shrugged his shoulders uncomfortably, frustrated in more ways than one. He was not sure why he was hesitating when Miss Shaw had made her aversion to him crystal-clear. If he had not found himself in actual physical discomfort, he would have laughed at the irony. Jack Merlin, the ruthless rake, was aching for a woman he could not have.

To distract himself, Jack looked around at Oakmantle Hall and the neglected gardens that surrounded it. He was surprised to find that they were rather charming. The house was a low building of golden stone, with higgledy-piggledy chimneys and a pale slate roof. It was surrounded by a moat of green water, almost full after the earlier rain, and beyond that the lawn stretched to the deer park, where clumps of daffodils were showing beneath the trees. The air was mild and soft. It was a tranquil scene.

Jack paused on the edge of the moat. He could see paddocks over to the right, where a fat pony grazed undisturbed. It would make the most excellent place to keep stables. Jack told himself, jokingly of course, that if he ever lived in the country he would breed horses and set up racing stables to rival the finest.

He could hear the distant sound of children's voices and wondered whether Thea's younger siblings were close at hand. He thought that he would like to meet them, then paused, frowning. Those were two uncharacteristic thoughts that he had had in the space of a minute. Perhaps there was something in the Oakmantle air that was turning his mind. He had better get back to the inn, and from there to London. Quickly.

There was a shout much closer at hand, and he turned abruptly, but it was too late. He was struck hard on the shoulder, a blow that knocked him to the ground. He felt something sharp hit him on the head and he went out like a blown candle.

Chapter Three

"Thea, come quickly! I've shot him! I've shot the Marquis of Merlin!"

Thea was in the drawing room, tidying her ornaments, picking up the guineas and trying to put Jack Merlin from her mind. So far her mode of doing so had involved going over every part of their conversation and feeling utterly outraged, then moving on to the kiss, and feeling deeply disturbed. The fact that she had spent ten minutes thinking of nothing but Jack Merlin was something that exasperated her even more, but she did not seem at liberty to prevent it.

"Thea!"

Clementine's voice broke through Thea's preoccupation and she hurried towards the door, colliding with her sister in the hall. Clemmie was pale, her hair in disarray, her eyes wild. She grabbed Thea's sleeve and almost dragged her to the front door.

"Thea, I've shot him—"

"I heard you the first time," Thea said soothingly,

noting the bow propped in a corner of the hall. She gave Clementine a quick hug, feeling the tension in her sister's body and noticing that she was close to tears.

"Calm down, Clemmie, I'm sure it cannot be so bad! Now, show me where he is!"

It was a mild afternoon outside and the threat of rain was back in the air. As they came round onto the carriage sweep, a horrid sight met Thea's eyes. Jack Merlin was lying on the gravel by the moat, his head resting on one of the large white stones that marked the edge of the drive. The shaft of an arrow was sticking out of his shoulder, his face was parchment-white and he was quite unconscious.

Thea took a deep breath and knelt down beside him, feeling for his pulse. The gravel felt sharp through the material of her dress. She knew it must be uncomfortable for Jack to lie on, but she also knew that she should not move him until she could ascertain his injuries.

"Clemmie, send Ned for Dr. Ryland," she said over her shoulder, "then go to the kitchens and ask Mrs. Skeffington to heat some water and find some bandages."

Clementine peered at Jack's recumbent form. "Is he dead, Thea?"

"Certainly not!" Thea gave her sister an encouraging smile. "You are not such a good shot, you know! The arrow is not in very deep but I think he hit his head when he fell."

''He wandered straight across my sights.''

Thea squeezed her hand. ''Never mind that now. The best way for you to help him is to fetch the doctor. Hurry!''

She watched her sister run off a little shakily towards the shrubbery where Ned and Harry could still be heard playing at cricket. The archery target was visible on the drive fifty yards away. Thea sighed. Ever since Clementine had skewered the delivery boy's hat with an arrow a few months back, she had been afraid that a worse accident would happen and now she had been proved right. That it had happened to the arrogant Marquis of Merlin was only a small consolation, for Thea found that when she looked at Jack's lifeless body it was concern that she felt rather than triumph.

She turned her attention back to him. His face was still pale, chill and clammy to the touch, but she was a little reassured that his pulse was strong and his breathing regular. She moved his head onto her lap, taking care not to jolt his shoulder. He did not stir. Thea felt a surprisingly strong impulse to brush the hair back from his forehead, and after a second she did so. It was as soft and silky as she had imagined earlier and she lingered over the feel of it before recalling herself and snatching her hand away guiltily. Then she just sat and studied the sweep of his lashes against the hard line of his cheek. It gave her a strange feeling inside, breathless, warm and protective all at the same time. She shifted uncomfortably, then hastily stilled her movements as Jack groaned a little. She held her breath, but he did not open his eyes.

It was starting to rain, the drops pattering down on the drive and dampening Thea's grey muslin dress and wetting her hair all over again. A drop fell on Jack's face and Thea wiped it away gently. She saw him wrinkle up his nose as the cool water roused him. Then he opened his eyes and looked at her. For a moment his gaze was cloudy with pain and puzzlement, then Thea saw him focus on her face, and he tried to sit up.

"What the hell—" Jack broke off with a groan as the movement jarred his shoulder and made him wince. He closed his eyes again momentarily, then opened them and frowned.

"What in God's name is going on? Miss Shaw—"

Thea laid a restraining hand on his sound shoulder. "Please lie still, Lord Merlin. You have had an accident but I have sent my brother for the doctor and we shall have you inside the house in no time."

Jack raised his right hand to his shoulder, twisting awkwardly as he tried to discover the source of his discomfort. "What is this—an arrow?" There was stark incredulity in his voice, overlying the pain. "Good God, ma'am, have you shot me to protect your virtue? I assure you there was no such need."

"Don't be so absurd." Thea said crisply. "You wandered across the target where my sister was practising her archery. It was the veriest accident! Then you hit your head when you fell."

"A veritable chapter of accidents, in fact!" Jack gave a sigh and rubbed his hand across his forehead. "Damnation, I feel as weak as a kitten and my head aches to boot." He shifted again. "This arrow in my shoulder—"

"Dr. Ryland will remove it as soon as he gets here, I am sure!" Thea looked around a little desperately, wondering where the good doctor had got to. It seemed like hours since Clementine had run to fetch help but perhaps it was only a matter of minutes. The rain was falling harder now and she knew she had no way of getting Jack to shelter. There was sweat on his face now but he had started to shiver. Thea felt the worry clutch at her.

"If I could reach it properly I would pull it out myself!" Jack was muttering, sitting up with an effort and straining to reach the shaft of the arrow. He struggled, a groan escaping his lips. "Devil take it."

"Please keep still," Thea besought him. "You will only make yourself worse! If you are strong enough we could attempt to walk to the house."

Jack looked at her, squinting with the effort of concentration. "I would gladly try but I cannot walk anywhere with an arrow stuck in my shoulder, Miss Shaw. It is damnably dangerous and could easily injure you, too, if I were to fall." He shook his head in an attempt to clear the pain. "Perhaps if you were to take it out for me—"

"Oh, I do not think so!" Thea recoiled. "Besides, surely it is too much of a risk."

Jack's eyes, bright with fever now, mocked her. "What, rejecting an opportunity to cause me pain, Miss Shaw? Do you faint at the sight of blood? I assure you, there will not be much and you would be doing me the utmost favour."

There was a silence. Thea looked at him, her face pale. He gave a slight nod, holding her gaze steadily with his. She gritted her teeth, trying to ignore the sickness inside her at the thought of hurting him. She knew she had to do it, but it was so very difficult to screw her courage up. She took a deep breath and set her hand to the arrow shaft, giving it a sharp tug. She heard the breath hiss between Jack's teeth as it came out in her hand, but he made no further sound. The blood spread from the tear across the coat of green superfine, not in a huge rush, as Thea had feared, but in a steady stream.

"One of Weston's best creations ruined," Jack observed dispassionately. "He will never forgive me! Miss Shaw, might I trouble you to lend your petticoat to stem the flow? It is likely the only opportunity I shall get to encourage you to voluntarily remove a garment…"

Thea smothered a smile. For some obscure reason his teasing made her feel much better, as though it was a sign that he was not at death's door.

"I am pleased to see you so much recovered that you can make fun of me, my lord!" she said. "I will gladly donate a strip of my petticoat, although I cannot afford to give you the whole as it is the only one I possess!''

''I will buy another one for you, if you will accept so personal a gift.'' Jack gave her a faint glimmer of a smile as he watched her pull up her skirts a little and hastily tear a strip from the material.

''Make it into a pad,'' he instructed, ''then tie it in place with the loose ends...''

''You are very resourceful, my lord,'' Thea said, following his directions and trying to keep the surprise out of her voice. Such commonsense practicality did not seem to fit her image of the society rake at all.

Jack shrugged, then winced. ''I learned to make shift as I could when I was in the Peninsula. Your petticoat is a very superior sort of bandage, Miss Shaw, compared with some of the dressings I was forced to apply then.''

''You were in the Peninsula?'' Thea asked, this time failing to hide her surprise. ''I did not realize... That is, Bertie did not mention...''

Once again Jack's smile contained a flicker of mockery. He turned his head to watch her hands as she hesitantly wrapped the bandage about his shoulder. A lock of his hair brushed her wrist and Thea nearly jumped away, then schooled herself to carry on. She did not want him to see her vulnerability.

''A little tighter, if you please, Miss Shaw...'' Fortunately Jack did not appear to have noticed her discomfort although his gaze was disturbingly observant for a sick man. It returned to her face and stayed there, thoughtful, disconcerting.

"Perhaps there is much you have to learn about me, Miss Shaw. Does Bertie speak of me often?"

"Incessantly!" Thea said briskly, tying the bandage with a little tug just to put him in his place. "He is quite boring on the subject. Now can you manage to struggle to the house by leaning on my arm, my lord? I regret that we do not have any servants who can carry you indoors…"

"No need, Miss Shaw," the Marquis murmured, "though I appreciate your offer. I believe that must be the good doctor now, and bringing Hodges, my valet, with him."

Thea looked up. Ned was hurrying across the drive, leading Dr. Ryland and a portly man who was carrying a travelling bag and wearing a long-suffering expression. Thea had the impression that the valet was accustomed to finding his master in such unusual circumstances and was wearily weighing up exactly what was required this time.

Thea accepted Ned's hand and struggled a little stiffly to her feet, then hung back as Dr. Ryland and Hodges between them managed to help the Marquis across the gravel sweep and back into Oakmantle Hall. It felt decidedly strange to see Jack Merlin escorted back into the house she had thrown him out of only twenty minutes before and Thea could not be sure if she was glad or sorry that he had not been so easy to dismiss. One thing she was certain of, how-

ever, was that she had to get rid of him again, and
fast. She had no wish for Jack to realize just how
much the whole experience had shaken her and how
protective of him she had felt. Pulling out the arrow
had taken all her courage and she had admired Jack
for the stoical way in which he had accepted her fumbling ministrations. Clearly he was no mere society
rake. There was indeed a lot that she did not know
about him. She was not certain if it was safe to know
any more.

Once inside the house, Thea was confronted by a
new dilemma. Dr. Ryland was insistent that the
Marquis should be put to bed and Thea saw no alternative than to donate her own room for the time being. She saw them safely upstairs then went to check
that Clementine was feeling somewhat improved. Her
sister was in the kitchen regaling Mrs. Skeffington
with the tale of how she had shot the Marquis, but
she broke off, looking guilty when Thea entered.

"A cup of tea, ma'am?" Mrs. Skeffington suggested quickly, pushing the pot towards her, and Thea
sat down gratefully whilst the housekeeper poured her
a cup. She let Clementine's chatter flow over her,
aware that most of it was prompted by relief, and
unwilling to give her sister the scolding she so clearly
deserved.

Thea leaned her chin on her hands, feeling tired
and out of sorts. The whole incident had left her feeling curiously vulnerable and prey to all manner of
conflicting emotions. She did not want Jack Merlin in

the house, but it was not because she disliked him. She knew she *ought* to dislike him intensely after what had happened between them and it was all the more disconcerting to discover that the reverse was true. Jack was too disturbingly attractive, his presence too unsettling for her peace of mind. So he had to go. She would insist that, as soon as Dr. Ryland had seen him, the Marquis be taken straight back to the Lamb and Rabbit, or to London, or to hell for all she cared. For the one thing that she did know was that even in his weakened state, if she gave Jack an inch, he would take a mile.

"Not much harm done!" Dr. Ryland said reassuringly half an hour later as he joined Thea in the library. "The Marquis has a lump on his head but his vision is unaffected and the arrow wound is slight. It may be that he has taken a fever but—" the doctor shrugged philosophically "—with your excellent care, Miss Shaw, I am certain he will be up and about within a se'nnight!"

Thea stared. She had not thought of this, had not really thought beyond the necessity to get Jack out of the rain and seen by the doctor. But for him to have to remain in bed, and for it to be her bed...

"But he cannot stay here!" she said, appalled. "My dear Dr. Ryland, that is quite improper! You know that there is no one here but my family and Mrs. Skeffington. Surely you could arrange to move him to the Lamb and Rabbit."

Dr. Ryland drained his glass of wine and put it down on the drawing room table. He was shaking his head. "Lord Merlin cannot be moved at present, my dear. Leaving aside his injury, which would be aggravated by movement, there is the blow to the head. Besides, it is raining and that may encourage the fever. There are many ways that Lord Merlin's condition could deteriorate!"

Thea pressed her hands together. "Then what is to be done?"

"We can only watch his progress over the next few days and see how soon he is recovered," the doctor said. "Besides, would you condemn Lord Merlin to Mrs. Prosper's somewhat…hit-and-miss nursing, my dear Miss Shaw? The poor fellow would certainly perish within the week!"

Thea gave a rueful smile. Mrs. Prosper's brand of brusqueness was admirable in the landlady of the local inn, but she had little time for invalids and her cooking was desperately bad. Even so, Thea felt most awkward. She did not wish to appear inhospitable but she could not explain to Dr. Ryland that what she dreaded about having Jack Merlin in the house was nothing to do with the expense or the propriety of the arrangement and everything to do with Jack himself and the way he made her feel.

"Besides," Dr. Ryland said cheerfully, picking up his bag and heading towards the door, "you have the valet, Hodges, to help with the nursing. He seems a most accomplished fellow—has been in the Marquis's

service some ten years, I understand.'' His shoulders
shook slightly. ''By George, the things he must have
seen—''

Thea waved the doctor off, having extracted a
promise from him that he would call the next day,
and went slowly up the stairs and along the landing
to visit her unwanted guest. Her hand was raised to
knock on the bedroom door when she heard voices
from within and instinctively froze, listening.

''So what do you think of the place then, Hodges?''
That was Jack, sounding none the worse for his adventure. ''Somewhat picturesque, eh? I feel my opinion of the country undergoing a change, you know!''

''It is most charming, my lord,'' the valet returned.

''As is Miss Shaw,'' Jack added lazily. ''She is
quite an original, you know, Hodges, with her quaint
notions and her fancy dress!''

Thea looked down. It was just conceivable that the
ancient wedding gown could have been mistaken for
fancy dress but her old grey muslin certainly could
not. She bristled.

''She seems a most pleasant and accomplished
lady,'' Hodges replied woodenly.

Thea heard Jack yawn. ''Damned pretty, too,
though I understand from Bertie that the situation is
not precisely as my father imagined.''

''Just so, my lord.'' There was distinct disapproval
in the valet's tone now. ''One can scarce imagine a
lady such as Miss Shaw trapping a gentleman into
marriage.''

Thea drew a sharp breath, the colour flaming to her face. So that was what the Duke of Merlin had thought when he had heard of her wedding to Bertie! She blushed all the harder to think that he had not been far out in his assessment.

There was a noise close at hand and Thea came to her senses and knocked loudly and hastily on the bedroom door. The voices within stopped immediately and Hodges opened the door to her. She thought that she detected a shade of embarrassment in his manner.

"Good afternoon, madam." He slipped past her. "Excuse me. I shall leave you to speak with his lordship alone."

This was not precisely what Thea had intended, but it was too late to stop Hodges, who was already halfway down the stairs. Thea went into the room and made sure to leave the door open.

Jack was sitting up against the pillows, looking faintly comical in one of her father's old nightshirts. Evidently his travelling bag had contained nothing so practical as night attire, and Thea wondered faintly if he actually wore anything when he was asleep, then hastily tried to think of something else. Unfortunately the ancient linen of the late Mr. Shaw's shirt concealed little and only served to emphasize Jack's muscled physique and superb form. Thea hastily averted her eyes, telling herself primly that she should be more concerned about whether or not Jack was running a fever rather than giving herself a temperature simply through looking at him. He gave her a faint

smile that only served to make her feel warmer still
and she just managed to prevent herself from turning
tail and rushing from the room.

"I am sorry to be an additional burden on your
household, Miss Shaw," he said politely. "I shall try
to be as little trouble as possible."

Thea doubted it. "I am sorry that my sister shot
you, my lord," she replied equally formally. "It is all
most unfortunate."

Jack smiled. "Well, I suppose it was a little un-
orthodox of her, but then yours is hardly an ordinary
family!" His smile faded and Thea thought that he
actually looked slightly discomfited. "I meant what I
said, Miss Shaw. I do not intend to be a…a financial
burden to you." He met her eyes, and looked away.
"Forgive me for broaching such a confoundedly delicate subject."

"I see no need for apologies, my lord," Thea said
sharply. "It is but a few hours since you offered me
plenty of money and your guineas are more than
enough to bespeak the best medical care and hospitality for the next few days!"

Jack winced. "*Touché,* Miss Shaw! I can only beg
your pardon once again for assuming in so unsubtle
a manner that I knew your price."

Thea's eyes narrowed. She did not like the implication of that. "I thought that I had made it clear that
I could not be bought, my lord."

There was a cynical light in Jack's eyes. He pulled
a face. "Come now, Miss Shaw. Your price may be

above rubies but any commodity can be bought—
even innocence! It is a question of finding the right
currency.''

Thea's eyes turned a stormy blue. ''And am I to understand that you think you will find my…currency, my
lord?''

Jack laughed. ''It should not be so difficult! Bertie
has told me something of your circumstances and how
much you would do for your family. There is your
brother…Ned, is it? The one who wishes to be a soldier… A commission for him in a good regiment would
be a fine thing, and such matters take influence as well
as money. With my connections I could arrange such a
thing as easily as breathing!'' His blue eyes mocked
her. ''You see, Miss Shaw, it is not very hard to find a
weakness to exploit…''

Thea found that she was shaking. She pressed her
hands together, then put them behind her back to ensure that she did not hit an injured man.

''That is just bribery by another name, Lord
Merlin! It does not impress me. Nor do I believe that
you will find breathing so easy when I smother you
with a pillow!''

Jack's wicked grin deepened. He leaned forward.
''Very well then, Miss Shaw. How about an old-
fashioned wager? No bribery or blackmail involved.
Just my…expertise…against your virtue. What do
you say?''

Thea gave him a scornful look. ''That will be easy,
my lord. You are scarce irresistible!''

Jack inclined his head. "I am willing to believe that you will prove that," he said easily. "How piquant, to pit goodness against—"

"Wickedness!" Thea finished for him. "I cannot believe you so devoid of any sense of morality, my lord! It is most disturbing!"

Jack laughed. "Perhaps you can redeem me, my sweet Theodosia."

"You need not start immediately!" Thea said sharply. "I should warn you that I am on my guard, my lord."

"That's good…" Somehow Jack had taken her hand and his warm touch was already undermining her defences. She snatched her hand away and straightened the already straight bedclothes in an attempt to cover her confusion. She hoped that Jack would feel too weary to continue the conversation, but unfortunately he did not appear in the least bit affected by his injury.

"This is quite an unusual establishment, is it not?" he continued. "Do you have no older relatives living with you, Miss Shaw?"

Thea pursed her lips. "No, my lord. I am quite old enough to run an establishment on my own."

Jack raised his brows. "In the light of our conversation, I was thinking more of the propriety of such a situation—"

"Oh, I am well known in the neighbourhood as a respectable spinster!" Thea said with spirit.

Jack gave a derisive laugh. "I do not doubt it, my

dear Miss Shaw, but wearing a lace cap scarcely convinces me that you are in your dotage. Surely you are forever fending off the advances of unsuitable men.''

''Not at all, my lord,'' Thea said, plumping his pillows with unnecessary force. ''At the least, not before you arrived here. Such things seldom happen in the country and as I said, my reputation is of the most respectable. Besides, I have Mrs. Skeffington to lend me countenance.''

''Oh, the hatchet-faced female who acts as your housekeeper? She doesn't approve of me, you know.''

''One can scarcely blame her,'' Thea said hotly. ''And anyway, Skeffie is the dearest creature imaginable. She has taken care of us all since our father died.''

''Yes—'' the laughter left Jack's eyes briefly ''—I heard that Mr. Shaw died only six months ago. I am very sorry.''

There was unmistakable sincerity in his tone. Thea swallowed hard, wishing that she had not raised the subject in the first place. Jack was confusing her, one moment so infuriatingly arrogant and the next so perceptive. She suspected darkly that it was all part of his planned seduction. He would lull her into thinking that he was not so bad after all, undermine her already-shaky defences, destroy her resolution and seduce her ruthlessly. Thea shivered at the prospect, and not entirely from horror. She started to tidy the bedside table with a certain fierce energy.

"Thank you, my lord."

"A shotgun accident, I understand," Jack pursued gently. "I am sorry if my own accident raised any difficult memories."

Thea looked at him swiftly, then away. The last thing she wanted to explain to him was that pulling the arrow out of his shoulder had been so difficult because she still remembered trying to staunch the flow of blood from her father's injuries. That would make her just too vulnerable. She changed the subject rather abruptly. "Are you quite comfortable here, my lord?"

Jack accepted the change in the conversation gracefully, although Thea had the unnerving feeling that he also understood the reason for it. That blue gaze was very searching and she knew she had to defend herself better against it. Then she saw a wicked glint come into Jack's eyes, which was more unsettling still.

"Yes, I thank you, I am most comfortable. This is a very pleasant room. Yours, I imagine? If you wish to share it with me…"

Thea compressed her lips. Dealing with his flirtation was as difficult as coping with his insight.

"I shall just remove some of my possessions, my lord," she said pointedly, "and leave you to sleep."

She was very conscious of Jack's gaze resting on her as she moved about the room, collecting her bottles from the top of the dressing table and her clothes from out of the cupboard. She hesitated before going to the armada chest to take out her underwear but she had little choice. With her hands full of chemises and stockings she skirted the bed and edged towards the door.

"You need not be shy of my seeing your underwear, Miss Shaw," Jack said softly. "I am sure I have seen items far more shocking."

"I am sure you have!" Thea snapped, trying to hide them behind her skirts and only succeeding in scattering her stockings across the bedside rug.

"Your practical clothing is far more respectable than the apparel I am accustomed to seeing," Jack continued. "Though I can imagine what you would look like in something more...provocative...."

"Pray do not exercise your imagination so!" Thea glared at him. "You are outrageous, my lord."

"And you are so charming to tease! I feel such a slow convalescence coming on, by which time I am convinced that I will have persuaded you to share more than just the secrets of your underwear...."

"You are more likely to find yourself sharing the moat with the swans than my bed!"

Thea vented her feelings by going out and slamming the bedroom door behind her. It was becoming a habit and a very damaging one, since the whole house was so old and neglected that it might fall down around her ears. She could still hear Jack laughing as she made her way down the corridor. The sound was disturbing and her heart sank to think of him occupying her bedroom for another week. Something told

her that he was going to be a very difficult patient
indeed, and then there was the matter of the wager.
Thea paused, leaning against the panelled wall of the
corridor for a moment and closing her eyes. It mattered not one whit whether or not she had accepted
Jack Merlin's challenge, for he would try to seduce
her, anyway. Just for the fun of it, just for the thrill
of the chase, just because he was a rake. Thea's shoulders slumped. She was not at all sure that she could
resist.

Chapter Four

"You will not be able to keep Lord Merlin in bed for much longer, you know, Thea."

Thea jumped, her book sliding off her knee. Had Clementine but known it, her words summoned up all kinds of visions in her sister's overactive mind. Tending to Jack over the past three days had been absolute purgatory, not because he had been a troublesome patient but because of the sheer overwhelming effect of his presence. It had been exactly as she had feared—only worse.

Jack had developed a fever initially, but after it had subsided he had grown bored of his own company and had wanted to talk. It had been difficult, for Thea found that he asked all manner of perceptive questions and challenged her assumptions on a variety of topics in a manner that no one had done since her father had died. In a strange way it was very similar to the sparring matches she had had with Mr. Shaw, but in another way it had been far more stimulating—

and exciting. She would become engrossed in their discussion, then would look up and find Jack watching her steadily. In an instant she would lose the thread of her thoughts and feel herself blushing whilst that lazy, dark blue gaze swept over her so searchingly that she was sure he could read her thoughts.

Their discussions had also been a revelation of Jack himself, for Thea knew that many of her greatest assumptions had been made about him and his lifestyle, and not one of them had survived. Well, she had dismissed all but one. She was still utterly convinced that he was a dangerous rake and that given the right circumstances, he would prove it. The wager was always at the back of her mind, an unspoken thought, troubling her, and the fact that Jack made no overt move to seduce her simply added to her concern. She could not afford to trust him.

Then there were the difficulties engendered by Jack's physical presence. Thea had been happy—relieved, even—to leave the practical nursing to Hodges, who had tended his master with exemplary skill and was fast becoming one of the household to boot.

Then, two nights previously, Thea had heard a sound on the landing and, thinking it was Daisy sleepwalking, had got up to investigate. She had found Jack, his fever returned, about to tumble down the staircase. There had been no time to call Hodges— she had had to catch Jack and support him back to bed, whereupon he had fallen in a heap on the covers and had pulled her down with him. It had taken her some time to extricate herself from his embrace, particularly since her efforts were so halfhearted because the weight of his body on hers was so peculiarly exciting. The whole experience had been deeply disturbing, and if Thea had not known that Jack was ill, she would have been convinced that he had done it on purpose. As it was, he had seemed unconscious throughout and after she had gently bathed his face, she went back to bed and lay awake for hours, tormented by the memory of his touch, the scent of his skin and the warmth of his body.

After that she had not been to visit his room for two days. She dared not.

Thea bent to retrieve her book and looked over the top of her glasses at her sister. "Whatever can you mean, Clemmie? I am not deliberately confining the Marquis of Merlin to his bed—"

"Pshaw!" Clementine snorted. Thea did not even trouble to admonish her. "You know you persuaded Hodges to keep the Marquis in his chamber today when Dr. Ryland said that he was quite well enough to get up! I do believe that you would lock him in if you could. You are afraid of what will happen once he is loose about the house."

"That is a most unfortunate turn of phrase to apply to a man of Lord Merlin's reputation," Thea said, trying not to giggle. "Besides, you make him sound like a wild animal, Clemmie, dangerous to the rest of us."

"Dangerous only to you, I believe," her sister said calmly. "You know he has you in his sights."

"I know no such thing!" Thea said hastily, wondering how Clementine could possibly have guessed. "I am only concerned that Lord Merlin should not overtax his strength, and once he is recovered he will be gone from here anyway. It is quite straightforward."

Clementine muttered something that sounded considerably ruder than "fustian," but Thea chose to ignore it and read on in a dignified silence. After a few moments she gave a sigh and cast her book down again.

"Oh, this is ridiculous! No matter how many moneymaking schemes I read about I can see a flaw in every one! At this rate Harry will have to become a climbing boy and Clara and Daisy can sell flowers in the street, whilst you and I will be teaching spoiled brats their letters and Ned will be apprenticed to some backstreet lawyer!"

Clementine put down her own book on the pedestal next to another of the sculptures that the late Mr. Shaw had delighted in. Thea was intrigued to see that the book was Mrs. Kitty Cuthbertson's *Santo Sebastiano* rather than her sister's favourite, Mary Wollstonecraft's *A Vindication of the Rights of Woman*. She wondered why her sister had suddenly taken to reading romance and hoped that it was not because Clementine was developing a *tendre* for the Marquis. That would become too intolerably complicated. Thea could cope with her own foolish feelings but not Clementine's, as well.

"Well, it might not be so terrible to work for a living," Clementine said slowly. "Only Harry is too big to be a sweep's boy now for he would get stuck up the chimney, and Clara suffers from sneezing fits when she is near flowers—"

"There is no need to be so literal," Thea snapped. "I am sure I shall come up with something, even if it is only to sell lavender pillows or royal jelly! Oh, if only we possessed something valuable to sell." She took a deep breath, anxious not to add further credence to her sister's view that she was on edge about Jack's presence in the house. Her eye fell on the book again.

"What do you think of Mrs. Cuthbertson's writing, Clemmie? It is much lighter than your usual read, is it not?"

"It is all very well." Clementine wrinkled up her nose. "Hodges recommended it to me, you know. He is a great reader of contemporary romances, but I find there are a little too many sentimental parts for my liking." She laughed. "The hero is forever swooning at the lady's feet, you know, and how impractical is that? I fear romance is vastly overrated, Thea! Perhaps you would have done better to marry Mr. Pershore, after all!"

Jack woke suddenly, wondering where he was. For a moment he lay still, taking in the pale candlelight and the worn bed hangings, the daylight fading beyond the windows. Then he remembered. He was at Oakmantle Hall—had been there for almost seven days now—and though the fever had not yet carried him off, the starvation diet certainly would. And soon.

On the first evening after his accident, Thea had sent Hodges up with a bowl of gruel, which Jack had immediately sent back with a demand for a bottle of port and a side of beef. Ten minutes later the gruel had reappeared in Thea's own hands and she had made it abundantly clear that unless he ate it he would receive nothing else at all. Jack had submitted with an ill grace but the starvation diet had continued with a thin soup the following day and bread and cheese the day after, until Jack had wondered if it was simply that Thea's household budget could not afford anything better, the golden guineas notwithstanding. When Hodges had explained that this was Mrs. Skeffington's view of a healthy diet for a convalescent, Jack had been unimpressed, and whether it was the effect of his illness or the unaccustomed frugality of his meals, he had been unable to drag himself from the bed and had been disgusted at his weakness.

He had also been bitterly disappointed that Thea had not been in to see him for the past two days. She had accompanied the doctor upstairs on his visits—Jack had heard her voice outside the door—but she had not been into the room since the third night, the night when she had rescued him from falling down the stairs. Despite his fever, Jack could remember the details of that encounter in vivid detail, the softness of her body beneath his on the bed, the sweet scent of lavender in her clothes and hair, and the way she had extricated herself with what seemed regretful slowness from his embrace… He smiled a little. He had been too ill to take advantage, which was a shame in a way, but he would have needed to be near death not to have appreciated the experience.

Except that Thea had not been to see him since. Perhaps she was only acting out of propriety, or perhaps she was embarrassed at what had happened between them, but whatever the cause, it was deeply frustrating. He wanted to see her, to talk to her. It was a troubling realization for a rake, but he was forced to admit that he missed their discussions, which had broached topics from the London Season to the writings of Shakespeare. He had never crossed swords with a bluestocking before and he had found it a stimulating experience, almost as stimulating as holding her in his arms. But perhaps she would bring his food that night…

On the thought of food, he rolled over and sat up. And blinked.

There was a vision sitting on the end of his bed, a tiny angel. For a second Jack wondered whether he had died in his sleep and whether this was as a direct result of requesting that Hodges smuggle him in an illicit bottle of brandy. When he considered the angel more carefully, however, he realized that she was clutching a ragged toy sheep in one hand and looked about five years old. She also looked a lot like Thea, a miniature version, with tiny fair corkscrew curls and huge blue eyes. Perhaps Thea had looked like this as a child, or perhaps this was what a child of Thea's would look like. Jack felt something twist inside him at the thought. A child with fair curls and a cherubic smile… He grimaced. His illness was turning him quite ludicrously maudlin.

"Hello!" the angel said.

"Hello," Jack replied.

"Thea says that you're trouble," the angel announced, fixing him with a stern blue stare. "She says that we're not to see you."

Jack felt hurt at this apparent treachery. Did Miss Shaw really consider him a monster with whom her younger siblings were not safe? His own sisters had always praised him as a most indulgent uncle even though he had had no thoughts of setting up his own nursery—until now.

He smiled at the angel. "I think that you must be Daisy."

A nod was his only reply. Daisy was still weighing him up.

"So if your sister told you not to come here, Daisy, what are you doing?"

There was a pause. "Seeing for myself," Daisy said solemnly.

Jack grinned. It seemed that Clementine was not the only one who had absorbed Mrs. Shaw's philosophy of independence! If Thea thought that she had problems with her sisters already it seemed that her troubles were only beginning. He raised his eyebrows.

"And what do you think?"

Daisy was in no hurry to commit herself. Her cornflower-blue eyes appraised him thoroughly and Jack found himself holding his breath.

"You look very nice," Daisy said. Her rosebud mouth curved into a smile and she crawled towards him across the bedcover. When she reached his side she simply held her arms out.

"Cuddle," she said.

After a moment of frozen incomprehension, Jack shifted obligingly so that she was curved into the circle of his good arm, her golden curls brushing his shoulder, the toy sheep clutched against his chest. Now that he could see it more closely, he realized that it was moth-eaten and more than a little chewed. No doubt toys in the Shaw household had to last from one child to the next and were never thrown away. He watched as Daisy yawned suddenly and her eyelids flickered closed.

"Story," she said.

Jack's mind was suddenly, frighteningly blank. Although he was indeed a generous uncle, his indulgence had never stretched to telling his nephews and nieces bedtime stories. After all, it was hardly his place. There were nursemaids aplenty to do such a thing. He looked down at Daisy and after a moment she opened her eyes again and frowned at him.

"Story!" she said again, slightly more querulous this time.

Jack felt panic rise in him. He glanced towards the door, but there was no sound from the landing, no rescue at hand.

"Er…does Thea tell you stories?" he asked, playing for time.

Daisy nodded. Her hair tickled his nose. "Stories 'bout the fairies in the garden."

Fairies. Jack took a deep breath, trusting to magic himself. "They live in the garden but you can't see them, can you?"

"S'right." Daisy snuggled down again. "Cos it's magic."

Jack relaxed slightly. He seemed to be on the right track. He dredged his memory for anything that he could recall about the Oakmantle gardens. It was a shame that he had not seen them properly. There were the trees, of course, and there was also the moat…

"Has Thea told you about the water sprites who live in the moat?" he asked.

Daisy shook her head a little. "No…" She sounded sleepy but willing to give him a chance. "Tell…"

Jack started cautiously on a tale about the water sprites who shared the moat with the swans and ducks. He invented a castle for them under the water and a feud with the goblins in the oak trees that had led to much magic and mayhem. He was about to launch into the story of the fairy princess who had been kidnapped and rescued by the sprites, when he felt Daisy shift and relax further into his arms, her breathing soft, deeply asleep.

Jack stopped speaking and looked down at her. Her cheeks were flushed pink, her rosebud lips parted. His arm felt warm and damp and he was tolerably sure that she was dribbling slightly as she slept.

Jack sat still, afraid to move in case he woke her. He wondered why his sisters never told their children bedtime stories when surely it was one of the best bits of having a child. That led him to wondering why the fashionable farmed their children out at every available opportunity and if they knew what they were missing. The warm weight of the child in his arms seemed to load him down with love. He almost decided that he wanted one of his own, but his mind shied away from the implications of that particular thought.

Daisy and Clara and Harry and Ned and Clementine. His heart ached suddenly for Thea, trying to do the best she could as a substitute mother for her siblings. If he could help her… Jack shook his head, as if to dispel the thought forcibly. That was the trouble with the country—he had always sworn that it addled the brain and here was the proof.

There was a step on the landing and the door was pushed wider. Thea herself stood in the doorway, a white apron over her dress, her face flushed, the hair escaping from her cap, as it always seemed wont to do.

''Oh!'' She saw the sleeping child in Jack's arms

and lowered her voice to a whisper, "I am so sorry! I have been looking everywhere for her! It's just that she sleepwalks sometimes—"

"She just wanted a bedtime story," Jack said softly.

Thea's eyes met his. Hers were very dark and unreadable. "Did you tell her one?"

"I did indeed. Fairies and sprites and kidnapped princesses…"

He saw her smile. "I should have liked to hear that."

Jack grinned at her. "I would gladly tell you a bedtime story anytime you wish, Miss Shaw!"

He saw the blush that came into her cheek, but she did not answer. She leant down to take Daisy from him. Her sleeve brushed his cheek. He could smell her scent, lavender and roses, faint and elusive. Jack shifted, pretending that he was simply moving his arms now that the weight of the child was removed. Perhaps it was just hunger that was making him light-headed, or perhaps it was something more.

"You have not been to see me," he observed lightly, watching as Thea scooped Daisy expertly into the crook of her arm. "I could have died in here for all that you knew…"

"No doubt Hodges would have told me if that had happened," Thea said calmly. She smiled at him suddenly and Jack felt his pulse rate increase. This fever was proving damnably stubborn to shift, or perhaps that was something else, too.

"However," she continued, "I am happy to see that you are far from death's door."

"Are you?" Jack quirked one dark brow. "Then why have you been avoiding me, Miss Shaw?"

"I must go," she said hurriedly. "Daisy will wake—"

"But you have not answered my question!" Jack protested. "Surely you are not afraid to be alone with me, Miss Shaw!"

There was a pause. "Not afraid, precisely, my lord," Thea said slowly, "but I have not forgotten your reputation. Now if you will excuse me—"

"A moment." Jack touched the back of her hand and she paused by the side of the bed. His tone was unwontedly serious. "Why did you tell the children that they were not to see me? Am I then *so* disreputable that you think I am not fit company for them?"

"Oh!" He heard Thea catch her breath. "It was not that, Lord Merlin. I simply wished you to have undisturbed rest and I thought that if the children pestered you…"

"You have permitted Bertie to visit me," Jack pointed out.

"That was different. Besides, I wished to make my peace with Bertie myself."

Jack raised an eyebrow. "So that is why he has had the best of your attention and I have had nothing myself."

Daisy stirred then, murmuring in her sleep. "I must

go,'' Thea said again. Jack let his hand fall to his side and watched as she walked slowly to the door.

''Miss Shaw?''

She paused in the doorway. ''Yes, Lord Merlin?''

Jack grinned. ''Is there gruel for dinner tonight?''

He saw the answering smile gleam in Thea's eyes before she wiped it clean away. ''No. Mrs. Skeffington has prepared a nourishing mutton stew for you. Oh, and Lord Merlin...''

''Miss Shaw?''

''I have confiscated the bottle of brandy that you asked your valet to bring up. It is not healthy. But if you are very good I shall allow you one glass of homemade elderberry wine.'' And she closed the door very softly behind her.

Jack lay back on the pillows, a smile curling his mouth. Theodosia Shaw. She might have the upper hand at the moment whilst he was laid low in so inconvenient a manner, but tomorrow he was determined to leave his bed and then she would not find it so easy to avoid him. Then he would progress his acquaintance with Miss Shaw. He was looking forward to it immensely.

''It is plain as a pikestaff that you are still avoiding Lord Merlin!'' Clementine said bluntly, helping Thea to gather up the bunches of daffodils that they had just cut for the house. ''You denied it before, but you know that it is true and you *know* it is because you like him!''

Thea paused, her flower basket over one arm. It was a beautiful morning and she had decided at once to go out into the fresh air for she found that being cooped up in the house only seemed to encourage the feelings of restlessness that she had suffered of late. And Clementine, with her usual sharp observation, had immediately identified the reason why her sister was feeling so on edge—the Marquis of Merlin.

In truth Thea could find very little to dispute in Clementine's words, for she *had* been avoiding Jack, particularly since he had become active again and was wont to pop up in all sorts of unexpected places. She knew he was deliberately seeking her out, and it was all very strange and disconcerting, all the more so since she could not ignore the speculative intensity of that dark blue gaze when it rested on her so warmly, nor the enjoyment she derived from his company. She felt as though she were being hunted—gently, patiently but relentlessly, and the feeling engendered a mixture of fascination and excitement. She knew she was being drawn into a trap, and it was one that she had to avoid, though she had little desire to do so.

"I think Lord Merlin likes you very much, too," Clementine added slyly, and Thea knew she was blushing and felt vexed.

"Lord Merlin is most amiable to everyone," she said, trying to sound indifferent. They started to walk back towards the house, their skirts swishing through the long grass. "He has been giving Harry some coaching on his cricket."

"And talking to Clara about music."

"And telling Daisy bedtime stories." Despite herself, Thea felt a smile starting.

"And chatting to Skeffie about recipes!" Clementine finished with a giggle. "She has quite altered her opinion of him, you know, and praises him to the heavens!"

Thea laughed, as well. "That, at least, is self-interest on Lord Merlin's part! I believe he finds our diet sadly circumscribed and is longing for a side of sirloin and several bottles of port!"

They had reached the edge of the park and paused to look across the moat to the house. The golden stones of Oakmantle Hall glowed warm in the sunlight. The ducks were quacking on the water and the swans stretched their wings in the sun.

"Lord Merlin has also been speaking to Ned…" Thea spoke hesitantly. "About joining the army, you know."

"Capital!" Clementine gave a little skip. "Ned has always wanted to be a soldier and if Lord Merlin can help."

"Ned should be going to university!" Thea said shortly. "And don't say 'capital,' Clemmie—it should not form part of a lady's vocabulary!"

"Stuff!" her sister said, clearly unimpressed. "You know that Ned has no time for book learning and has set his heart on following the drum! If Papa had not died so untimely—"

"I will not allow Lord Merlin to buy a commission

for Ned!'' Thea's words came out in a rush. ''I could not bear to be so beholden to him.'' It was impossible to explain to Clementine the conversation she had had with Jack that first day, when he had spoken of there being a price for everything and used Ned's example to make his point. It only served to prove that he could not be sincere now.

Clementine was looking at her curiously. ''Why not? He is influential and you would not think twice if there were another sponsor for Ned!''

Thea's hand tightened on the basket. ''Lord Merlin is different. He...I... He might expect...''

''Something in return for his generosity?''

''Clemmie!''

Clementine took off her bonnet and swung it by the ribbons in a casual manner that Thea considered deplorable. Not for the first time she felt hopelessly incapable of controlling her sister.

''Has Lord Merlin made such a suggestion to you, Thea?''

''Yes!'' Thea said, goaded. ''Several times!''

Clementine's eyes widened. ''Glory! Oh, lucky you!''

''Clementine Shaw!''

Clementine did a little skip. ''Well, I must leave you to fight the matter out with Lord Merlin himself, for I see him coming this way! I am sorry that I cannot stay to protect you!'' She took the basket of daffodils from her sister and sped off towards the house before Thea could say a word.

Thea turned her head. Jack was indeed walking towards her, one of the spaniels panting at his heels. In Thea's father's day there had been a whole pack of dogs at Oakmantle but there were only three left now and this was the oldest and most arthritic of them all. Thea was certain that Jack had slowed his pace to allow the ancient creature to keep up and she smiled. Really he was very kind and, confusingly, that made him far more dangerous to her.

She thought that Jack was still looking a little pale, but he was immaculately elegant in gleaming black top boots, pristine white linen and a green hunting jacket that was the epitome of good taste. He was bare-headed and the morning sunshine made his dark hair gleam with tawny and gold. Feeling a certain shortness of breath that she knew was nothing to do with her exertions out walking, Thea decided that she had to be firm with him before he undermined her defences completely.

"Good morning, my lord," she murmured as he reached her side, "did you come equipped for a long stay in the country, or do you always come accompanied by a baggage train?"

Jack smiled and Thea's heart did a little leap. He took her hand and her pulse rate increased still further. She tried to tug her hand away; he retained it, tucking it through his arm as he fell into step beside her.

"To tell the truth, it is only Hodges's ingenuity that has kept me so well turned out," he said ruefully. "

shall soon be reduced to asking Bertie for a loan of his linen. And one of his coats.''

''I doubt that it would fit you—'' Thea began thoughtlessly, then flushed scarlet as she realized she was expressing a view on a matter a lady should not even have considered let alone articulated. It was all very well for her to notice Jack's impressive phy-sique—how could she avoid it?—but to give away the fact that she had been studying him... She saw him smile, felt the warmth of that midnight-blue gaze trap and hold hers, and cursed herself.

''I am flattered that you should have been observ-ing me so closely, Miss Shaw,'' he drawled, proving to Thea that any opportunity she gave him would be exploited to the full. ''Should you wish to continue your inspection, I am at your service.''

Thea was determined to not be easy game for his teasing. ''Indeed, my lord? But will I have the chance? Surely you will be leaving us now that you are so well recovered.''

Jack gave her a limpid look. ''Alas, Miss Shaw, travelling could be very dangerous to one of my en-feebled constitution.''

To Thea's mind, feeble was the very last thing that he looked. Rakish, perhaps. Dangerous, definitely. But feeble—the idea was ridiculous.

''I am sorry that your lordship is not in better health by now,'' she said politely. ''Perhaps you should go inside and rest? Further exercise might prove fatal to one of so weak a disposition.''

"Oh, I believe in exerting myself a little more each day, Miss Shaw," Jack said with a devastating smile, "and I have not yet reached my target for this morning. Speaking of which, is your sister planning further archery practice today? If so, perhaps I might prevail on you to show me the herb garden, where we will be safe?"

Thea gave him a suspicious look, wondering what had engendered in him this new-found interest in gardening. She was certain that it was a pretence, but on the other hand it seemed churlish to refuse him, particularly as Clementine had taken the basket of flowers, and with it any excuse Thea might have had for going back inside.

They crossed the moat by a little wooden footbridge that led straight into the remains of the Oakmantle formal gardens, where Thea had only recently pruned the rosebushes for the coming season. Jack opened the gate at the end of the bridge for her, handing her through. His touch was light and warm and it filled Thea with an acute physical awareness. He was watching her, his gaze steady on her face, and she found she could not look away.

"We collect the rose petals from the bushes here in the summer," Thea said, a little at random, to cover her confusion. "We dry them to scent drawers and chests and…and things. And we grow herbs for eating and for perfume, as well, especially lavender…" She was rambling; she knew she was, and Jack's next words did nothing to calm her.

"So that explains why your bedclothes are scented with lavender," he said softly. His voice dropped. "And you are, too…"

Thea felt a rush of heat under her skin. The lavender scent was all around them, faint but disturbing.

"My lord, you should not say such things."

"Should I not?" Jack's voice had roughened. "I remember from the time I held you…after the wedding. And later…"

Thea moved away, along the path where the line of ragged lavender was starting to show its new spring growth. Her heart was racing, beating so loudly that she was surprised that Jack could not hear it. She could hear his steps behind her on the gravel; he was following her and she had a sudden and ridiculous urge to escape him, to run away. Unfortunately the path she was following led only to the fishpond and to flee she would have to scramble through the shrubbery on the far side. Common sense returned quickly. She was hardly in any danger and would simply walk back the way she had come. On this eminently sensible thought she turned to face Jack. And stopped.

He was a bare three steps away from her and there was something in the way he was standing—something cool, something watchful—that warned her exactly what would happen next. Jack was going to kiss her and she…

Thea felt the last vestige of sensible thought drift away from her as Jack's lips touched hers. He took immediate advantage with a long, exploratory kiss that sent a jolt of pure desire through her body from head to toes. His arms went around her. He tasted of fresh air and something indefinable and far more intoxicating, and his skin smelled of sandalwood. After a moment, Thea found herself raising her arms to encircle his neck and hold him to her.

The kiss was softer and more persuasive than the one in the drawing room, coaxing a response from her rather than demanding one. Yet underneath the gentle surface was something that made Thea shiver. It was both a threat and a promise. He was drawing closer to his goal all the time. And she knew exactly what that goal would be.

It was a long time before Jack let her go, steadying her with a hand on her arm as she stepped back—and came down to earth. Thea frowned, trying to gather her thoughts, which seemed to have scattered like straw in the wind. She looked at Jack. He looked expressionlessly back at her.

"It goes against the grain with me, but do you wish me to apologize for my behaviour, Miss Shaw?"

"No…" Thea had been brought up to be truthful and just at that moment it was a severe trial to her. "It is not a matter of blame—"

Jack's hand tightened on her arm and for a moment she thought he was about to pull her to him again. "A matter of pleasure, then?"

"No!" Thea stepped back abruptly. "That is—yes, but—"

"But no one has kissed you like that before and you are startled at the results?" To Thea's ears Jack sounded odiously complacent even if what he was saying was true. She drew breath to give him a much belated set-down.

"Certainly it is true that I have not been kissed by a rake before! At least not before you kissed me the first time, sir!"

"And did you like it?"

Thea frowned stormily. "Pray stop asking difficult questions, my lord!"

"So you did. Would you like to do it again?"

"No!" Thea backed away. It was the first direct lie that she had told in a very long time and she knew at once that he did not believe her. He caught first one hand and then the other, trapping them both in one of his and bringing them up against his chest.

"Oh, Miss Shaw!" That dazzling blue gaze caught and held hers. "I had formed the opinion that you were always truthful yet now I have forced you into falsehood. It seems I am closer to corrupting innocence than I had realized…"

Thea knew that it was absolutely imperative to break free. She did not move. This time Jack bent his head with agonizing slowness to capture her mouth with his own, the touch of his lips fierce and sweet, their demand explicit. Thea's fingers uncurled to spread against his chest. She could feel the thud of his heart against her hand. The warmth of the sun mingled with her body's heated response and she felt utterly intoxicated. And totally confused. She freed herself from his embrace and felt the reluctance with which Jack let her go. He was breathing hard and his gaze, as it rested on her face, held the same concentrated desire that Thea had seen there before. She caught her breath.

"I am going inside now, my lord. I…I need to think and I cannot do so with you near me!"

"Thinking is a vastly overrated pastime in comparison to some others," Jack drawled. He followed her up the path. "My dear Miss Shaw, is there really any necessity to think at all? Can we not try something else?"

Thea warded him off with her hands. She did not want to speak since just at the moment she had lost all her *savoir faire* and knew she would only make matters worse for herself. She certainly did not want to linger here in the scented garden, where Jack's very presence was too much temptation. Besides, she knew it was all a game to him. He was simply following the dictates of the wager, proving to her just how easy it would be for him to win… The thought hardened her resolve. She would be the greatest fool in Christendom to fall into the arms of a rake who was only looking for a little entertainment.

"Pray excuse me, my lord," she said frostily, turning on her heel. "I have many household duties to attend to."

This time Jack made no move to follow her. Everything that Thea knew about him was conflicting in her head, the good, the bad and the downright wicked. She took four steps away and stopped. There was something she had been meaning to ask him for a long time.

"Lord Merlin," she said slowly, "will you answer something for me?"

Jack made a slight gesture. "If I can."

Thea's cornflower-blue eyes were troubled. "The first day we met—when you offered me the money and told me that principles were for fools—did you really mean that?"

Their gazes held for a moment and Thea had the oddest feeling that she was trembling on the edge of some precipice she did not understand. Then Jack let out his breath on a long sigh.

"Miss Shaw, you have the most damnable way of putting a fellow on the spot!" he said ruefully. "If you will have the truth, it was one of the most foolish things that I have ever said—no, I do not believe that."

Thea's expression lightened and the pretty colour came into her face. "Oh, thank you!" she said.

Jack watched her until her upright figure disappeared around the side of the house, then he drove his hands into his jacket pockets and followed the way that she had gone. He whistled softly under his breath as he walked. Good God, how had that happened? He had been utterly in control, within an ace of winning his wager, yet Miss Theodosia Shaw had almost brought him to his knees with her devastating combination of honesty and innocence. He had no notion how it had happened but he could deny it no longer. He could fight it, perhaps, but the outcome was uncertain. Suddenly he was a rake who felt dangerously close to reform.

He shook his head slightly. If anyone had suggested such a thing to him a few days before he would have laughed them out of court. His parents had been nagging him to marry these five years past and he had always rejected the idea with scorn, preferring the transient enjoyment of a series of *affaires* with women who played by the same rules as he. Yet now his rules appeared to have changed when he had not been paying attention. Jack sighed. If he had learned one thing in life it was not to fight against fate. And he had a feeling that his fate was just about to catch up with him.

Chapter Five

"**S**orry, Thea old thing, but it's dashed difficult!" Bertie avoided Thea's eyes and fidgeted on the rose brocade sofa. "I'd love to help you but I've a previous engagement, don't you know. In—" he closed his eyes briefly "—in Yorkshire! I'll be away above two weeks!"

Thea raised her eyebrows in patent disbelief. Bertie had always been a desperately poor liar and it was clear now that he was spinning her a tale. Now that the difficult matter of the wedding was behind them they had become friends again, but she knew there was something he was hiding from her. She decided to test him a little.

"But, Bertie, Lord Merlin is your cousin! Surely a little family feeling prompts you to offer him hospitality at Wickham…"

"Naturally I should be delighted were I to be at home," Bertie muttered, squirming, "but I've already told you I'm to go away—"

"Still trying to be rid of me, Miss Shaw?" a languid voice drawled from the doorway. Thea jumped. She had not heard Jack come in and now she blushed with vexation that he had overheard her.

She watched Jack stroll over to the carved marble chimney piece and rest one arm negligently along the top. He was standing at the precise angle where he could most easily fix her with that penetrating blue gaze. Thea shifted uncomfortably in her chair, acutely conscious of his scrutiny and aware of the blush that stained her cheeks.

Whilst Bertie and Clementine had been with them over dinner it had been relatively easy to avoid looking at Jack too much, although it was another matter to avoid thinking about him. Thea knew that she had been tiresomely absentminded for the whole meal, aware that Jack was watching her with a mixture of amusement and speculation that was deeply disturbing. When she remembered the kisses they had shared that very afternoon... But here she abruptly dragged her thoughts away. She would not remember them, for that way led inevitably to her downfall. Accustomed to ruling her heart as much as taking care of her home and family, Thea found her inexplicable attraction to Jack Merlin excessively disturbing.

"I am sorry that I cannot oblige you with my absence sooner, Miss Shaw," Jack said smoothly. "Dr. Ryland assures me that it would be foolhardy to travel before the weekend and I am anxious to take his advice. I will, however, make myself scarce just as soon as I am able.''

"Forgot to mention that we are all invited to a ball at Pendle Hall on Friday,'' Bertie said, brightening now that Thea's attention was diverted away from him. "Lady Pendle was most insistent, even when I explained you are still an invalid, Jack! It would crown her house party to be able to boast of your attendance.''

Jack grimaced. "Well, if we must! I suppose it would be bad manners to refuse when the good lady has been sending hothouse flowers over every day to aid my recovery.''

Thea made a business of finishing her cup of tea. In her opinion Lady Pendle was an ill-bred harridan whose motive in cultivating Jack's acquaintance was all too clear. Thea had suffered the Pendles' disdain for several years. The only occasion on which she had attended a ball at Pendle Hall had been marred for her by the patronizing way in which the Pendle sons and daughters had treated her. It had quite taken the pleasure out of her evening and since then she had refused all invitations.

"I shall not be attending,'' she said forthrightly, "and surely neither shall you, Bertie, since you will be away?''

Bertie flushed. "Oh, of course! I shall be in Lancashire—''

"Yorkshire!'' Thea corrected gently. She got to her feet and Bertie politely followed suit. "Good night,

Bertie, and thank you for dining with us tonight. I hope that you enjoy your trip!''

Jack moved to hold the door open for her. ''I am sorry that my cousin could not help you with your problem, Miss Shaw.''

Thea looked up at him. There was a dangerously wicked twinkle in his eye that suggested that he was not sorry at all.

''On the contrary, my lord,'' she said sweetly, ''I am the one commiserating with you. You will get your just deserts at Pendle Hall! I am sure that you will find the Misses Pendle most attentive to you! Either of them would be overjoyed to attach a Marquis.''

Jack gave her a speaking look. ''Thank you, Miss Shaw. Might I not prevail upon you to accompany me then, for protection?''

Thea smiled. ''Do rakes need protection from respectable ladies? I am sure you are well able to take care of yourself!''

Jack caught her hand, drawing her out into the candlelit shadows of the hall. The drawing room door swung shut behind them. ''Do not be so certain of that, Miss Shaw.'' He squared his shoulders. ''All jesting aside, do you really want me to leave Oakmantle?''

Thea flushed. ''I am sorry that you heard me say that, my lord. I had not wished to sound inhospitable—'' She broke off. Here was exactly the situation that she had not wished to explain, for how did she persuade Jack to go whilst keeping a secret her growing feelings for him? She could hardly tell him the truth.

"A matter of propriety, I collect, Miss Shaw?" Jack queried gently. "I realize that my presence here must seem most irregular."

"Yes!" Thea grasped gratefully at the proffered excuse. "For my own part I think the gossips to be idle troublemakers, but…"

"But you would not wish to give them fuel for speculation."

Thea frowned a little. Jack seemed to be making this a little too easy for her. "Well, no, of course…"

"Despite your respectable spinster's reputation, as confirmed by that ridiculous lace cap and the monstrous apron you have taken to wearing."

Thea, aware that he was still holding her hand, tried to snatch it away. Jack held on to it.

"My lord, if you seek only to make fun of me—"

"On the contrary." Jack smiled at her. "I am trying to do the right thing—for once. It is not a matter that has exercised my mind very often before."

"That I can well believe!" Thea said sharply. She gave her hand another experimental tug, to no avail.

"How about a bargain, then, Miss Shaw?" Jack pursued. "I shall leave Oakmantle tomorrow and move to Wickham for a short time—if you will allow me to escort you to the ball on Friday."

Thea frowned. "But if you are leaving Oakmantle

you might as well leave the county altogether, my lord! Why delay?''

She could not read Jack's expression for his face was in shadow. His voice was cool. ''Perhaps I do not wish to leave, Miss Shaw. Come, your answer?''

''And if I refuse to go to the ball, you will refuse to leave Oakmantle?''

''Precisely.''

''How very difficult you can be, my lord! It seems a strange, quixotic idea and I told you before that I do not take kindly to blackmail.''

''Call it persuasion, Miss Shaw, and you may feel more kindly disposed towards me!''

Thea shook her head. ''It seems most irregular, my lord, but I suppose it can do no harm. I accept—for the sake of my reputation…''

''Of course.'' Jack pressed a kiss on her palm and released her. ''Thank you. I will speak to Bertie about making the necessary arrangements.'' He passed her a candle from the stand at the bottom of the stairs.

''Good night then, my lord.''

''A moment, Miss Shaw.''

''Yes?'' Thea's voice was a little husky. She looked into Jack's eyes, realized that he was really very close to her indeed, and moved reluctantly away from him. Jack smiled.

''I thought to mention that if you have not yet come up with a better moneymaking scheme, you could always sell the drawing room sculptures. There are at least two by John Edward Carew that would fetch several thousand pounds in town, although the one with the chipped nose has obviously gone down in value because of the damage.'' He gave her a slight mocking bow and sauntered back to the drawing room door.

''Good night, Miss Shaw.''

Back in the drawing room, Bertie was finishing his port and preparing to leave.

''Have to go and pack for Yorkshire,'' he said gloomily as Jack reappeared, ''though why the devil I had to go and choose such a far-flung place I can't imagine! Must be touched in the attic even to think of getting involved in such a scheme!''

Jack grinned at his cousin. ''My thanks, Bertie! I owe you a favour!''

Bertie's shoulders slumped. ''Pretending to go away just so that you could stay at Oakmantle. Devil take it, Jack, I'm no hand at deception. Thea knows there's something up, you mark my words! Sharp as a needle, that girl!''

Jack laughed. ''There's no deception needed after all, Bertie. Miss Shaw and I have made a bargain. I have promised that I will remove to Wickham on the morrow in return for her agreement to accompany me to the Pendle ball.''

Bertie frowned ferociously. ''What, have I just pledged myself to a trip to Yorkshire all for nothing?''

''You can always cancel your fictitious invitation,''

his cousin said soothingly. "And it is scarcely nothing, Bertie, unless my future happiness counts as nothing to you."

"What exactly does constitute your future happiness, Jack? That's what worries me! Dash it, you had better be aboveboard with this. Don't mind helping you out, but if any harm comes to Thea—"

The laughter died out of Jack's eyes. He met his cousin's gaze soberly. "You can trust me, Bertie. I would do nothing to harm her."

Bertie shifted uncomfortably. "Better not. I'd call you out myself. You may be a damn fine shot, but principles are more important than…"

"Than self-preservation?" Jack laughed. "Acquit me, Bertie! I know my reputation tells against me but I plan to ask Miss Shaw to marry me."

Bertie swallowed convulsively. "Marry! You? Now I know you're in jest!"

"On my honour I swear it's true!" Jack passed his cousin the brandy bottle. "Here, take a glass before you go. You look as though you need a restorative."

Bertie sat down again. "Marry!" he said again. "Of all the mad starts—"

"I know," Jack said apologetically. "A vast comedown for a rake. But I fear I love her. It is inescapable!"

Bertie swallowed half the brandy in one go. "She'll never take you."

Jack went very still. An arrested look came into his eyes. "Why do you say that, Bertie?"

"Because she knows you're a rake!" Bertie pointed out. "She doesn't trust you. What's more," he added incontrovertibly, "she won't marry for money. I should know."

Jack sighed. Since he had just presented Thea with the reason why she need never marry for money, he could not argue.

"I thought women liked to reform a rake," he said ruefully. "Good God, I have spent years avoiding the lures of matrimonially minded maidens in favour of other pursuits and now you're telling me that the only woman I want will not have me? Where is the justice in that?"

Bertie grinned. "About time someone gave you a set-down, Jack," he said without malice. "I reckon you've met your match at last!"

Jack drained his brandy glass. "Now that," he said, "is where we do agree, Bertie. I have indeed."

"Oh, Miss Shaw, you look so beautiful!" Mrs. Skeffington, who had removed her cook's apron to double as ladies' maid for the evening, went quite misty-eyed at the sight of her mistress dressed for the ball. "The Marquis of Merlin is here, madam," she added. "He is waiting in the drawing room."

Thea hesitated before the mirror. It was not concern about her appearance that held her, for she had sought out her only serviceable ball gown and although it was not in the first stare of fashion, it was simple and elegant. No, she knew that what was delaying her was a sudden and cowardly desire to avoid Jack.

In the two days since he had left Oakmantle she had felt quite low in spirits. In fact, she had to admit to herself that she had missed him quite prodigiously. The children had remarked upon it and she knew that they were also feeling quite dejected. They had been difficult and noisy, withdrawn and silent by turn. Ned had got into a temper when she had spoken about him finding a job in London, and had stormed out and disappeared for several hours. Daisy had burst into tears when Thea had told her that Jack was no longer able to tell her a good-night story, and Clara had spent hours playing dirges on the old piano until Thea thought her head would burst and was fit to scream with frustration. They had all missed him, but she had missed him most of all. And now Jack was here, ready to take her to the ball, and she hardly dared to face him.

She picked up her black velvet cloak and her bag and made her way slowly down the staircase. In point of fact, Jack was not in the drawing room as Mrs. Skeffington had indicated; he might have started off there but now he was waiting for her at the bottom of the stairs. He looked up at her as she descended and Thea's heart contracted as his gaze raked her from carefully arranged curls to silk slippers, before returning slowly to her face. He smiled, the old devil-may-care, wicked smile that was so dangerously attractive and Thea feared she might melt into a puddle of longing where she stood. She steeled herself.

"Good evening, Lord Merlin."

Jack inclined his head. "Good evening, Miss Shaw. It is a great pleasure to see you again. You look quite...ravishing."

There was a look in his eye that suggested that ravishment would be high on his list of preferred entertainments for that evening. With a shiver, Thea admitted to herself that the idea held considerable appeal. But this was no good. She reminded herself sternly that she had worked hard to rid Oakmantle of Jack's troublesome presence and it was her own foolish fault if she was now languishing after him like a green girl.

She accepted Jack's proffered arm and went out with him to the carriage.

Pendle Hall was a bare ten-minute journey time away, but Thea had previously given little thought to being in a closed carriage with Jack for that time. After all, ten minutes to a rake was surely plenty of time to effect a seduction. She held her breath, but Jack behaved with impeccable and frustrating courtesy for the whole journey, handing her into and out of the carriage politely, sitting as far away from her as possible and speaking only on totally uncontroversial subjects such as his improved health and the welfare of her brothers and sisters. Thea found it perversely disappointing.

The ballroom at Pendle Hall was already crowded

when they arrived, for Lady Pendle had lost no time in informing all her friends and neighbours of the remarkable coup she had achieved in tempting the Marquis of Merlin to the ball. Jack's welcome was overly warm; Thea's considerably less so. At first she thought that she was imagining the slightly barbed remarks, the exaggerated withdrawing of skirts. Soon she realized she had not. Whilst Jack was forcibly dragged from her side and marched over to dance with the Misses Pendle, Thea found herself besieged.

"It must have been *such* a pleasure to have the Marquis of Merlin as a guest for an entire week, Miss Shaw," Lady Pendle, resplendent in puce velvet, was positively purring with malice. "Such a charming man but such a shocking accident! One scarce knows whether to be more alarmed at your sister's wildness in shooting the poor man in the first place, or at the thought of you entertaining a bachelor at Oakmantle quite unchaperoned!"

Thea took a deep breath. "We were scarcely entertaining the Marquis, Lady Pendle, for he was much too ill to be seeking diversion!"

Another matron pushed forward into the group. "Lord Merlin looks much recovered now, does he not, Miss Shaw? No doubt as a result of your nursing!"

Someone tittered, hiding behind their fan. Thea looked round the sea of faces. Some were avid, some openly disdainful. None was friendly. There was nowhere for her to seek refuge.

"My family and I were happy to be of assistance to the Marquis," she said colourlessly. "We all did what we could to help his recovery."

"And does Lord Merlin intend to stay long in Oxfordshire?" Lady Pendle pursued.

"I am not party to Lord Merlin's plans, ma'am," Thea said. She spoke coldly although she was feeling increasingly heated. "However, I believe he is soon for London."

"No doubt having exhausted the pleasures Oakmantle has to offer," another dowager said meaningfully. "I believe he tires easily—"

"One often does after an illness, ma'am," Thea said. Her temper had quite frayed away. She gathered her skirts up in one hand, about to flee the gossips but with no clear destination in mind. "If you will excuse me—"

"Care to dance, Miss Shaw?" The drawling tones of the Honourable Simon Pendle stopped her in her tracks. He was a well set-up young man who had often looked down his nose at her, but just now Thea grasped him as a lifeline.

"Thank you, Mr. Pendle!"

They moved onto the dance floor and away from the circling harpies. Thea breathed a sigh of relief. It was short-lived, however, as Simon Pendle drew closer to her than the dance steps dictated.

"So how have you got on with Merlin, Miss Shaw? Is he not a splendid fellow? Generous, too, I hear!"

Thea's eyes narrowed. Her nerves already on edge,

she was still willing to believe that she had misread the freedom of his words and his tone—but only just.

"Lord Merlin has certainly been generous to my family, sir," she said coolly.

Pendle guffawed. "No need for false modesty, ma'am! I was hoping you and I might have a little chat later—sort out a few things…" He squeezed her shoulder in a disgustingly familiar manner.

"I do not believe that we have anything to discuss, Mr. Pendle," Thea said frigidly, moving away.

"Oh, come now…" As the dance drew them together again, Simon Pendle deliberately let his hand brush intimately against the side of her breast and Thea recoiled, the colour flaming to her face. "I hear Merlin is to return to Town on the morrow. Then you may be more inclined to talk to me—"

Thea itched to slap him rather than speak to him. She kept her voice low but her tone was arctic.

"You mistake, sir. I have nothing to say to you!"

Pendle leered at her. "Hoity-toity miss! You won't be so quick to refuse when Merlin's money runs out—"

"Servant, Pendle. Miss Shaw, may I beg this dance?" Jack's voice cut smoothly through Simon Pendle's insults and through the angry words clamouring for release in Thea's head. She had not even noticed that the music had ceased, nor that Jack had approached them.

Simon Pendle bowed slightly. For the first time Thea realized that he was more than a little drunk.

"Evening, Merlin. I was just telling your charming *inamorata* here that—"

He broke off, gulping, as Jack stepped intimidatingly close. "I think you mistake, Pendle, as no doubt Miss Shaw has told you already." Jack's voice was dangerous, suggestive of an inclination to take Simon Pendle by the throat and choke the life out of him. "If we were anywhere other than in your parents' ballroom I would show you the error of your ways. As it is—" Jack stepped back "—if I hear you speaking at all for the rest of the evening, I shall call you out!"

He offered his arm to Thea and they moved away.

"That should ensure a little peace for the rest of us," he said dryly. He glanced down at Thea. "Are you quite well, Miss Shaw?"

Thea knew that her hand was shaking and was sure that Jack could feel it, too, for after a moment he pressed her fingers comfortingly with his. She could see the Pendles' guests whispering and gossiping behind their hands. The words burst from her.

"I wish to go home now. At once!"

"You cannot run away." Jack seized her arm in a hard grip. "Do you wish the scandalmongers to say that they drove you out? I did not think you so poor-spirited, Miss Shaw."

Thea's eyes flashed. "It is all very well for you, Lord Merlin! I am just another of your conquests—"

Jack's face was tight with anger, but Thea sensed

it was not directed at her. "Thea, you know that is not true—"

"I know that it is not true, but these people—" Thea gestured wildly "—they will only believe the worst!"

The music struck up again. Before Thea could move away, Jack had pulled her into the dance.

It was a shrewd move. Thea realized at once that it was almost impossible to quarrel whilst performing a minuet, for the stately music and the movement of the dance demanded a show of perfect decorum. It was the slowest and most mannered dance and it was the exact opposite of the wild, ungovernable feelings that were pent up inside her. Yet every time she opened her mouth to launch a blistering attack on Jack the dance steps forced them to part.

"It is all very well for you," she began as they came together, "coming to Oakmantle and causing all this trouble—"

They stepped apart. And together again.

"That is a little unfair," Jack murmured. "You were the one who started it all by planning to marry Bertie. And a more hen-witted scheme could not be imagined."

They moved away, joined hands and circled the other couples.

"Pray do not blame me!" Thea whispered crossly. "You came to Oakmantle to prevent the marriage!"

"Indeed. And a good thing, too. And it was your sister who obliged me to stay here by shooting me..."

Thea ignored this undeniable truth and swept on. "And now you are trying to distract attention when it is *your* behaviour that has been disgraceful—"

They moved apart. And together. Jack grinned down at her.

"I protest! I was an exemplary invalid!"

"So you deny that you offered me *carte blanche?*" Thea hissed. "*And* tried to seduce me?"

They executed a complicated twirl.

"I do not deny your first accusation, but the second?" Jack raised his brows. "That is scarcely fair. I most certainly did *not* attempt to seduce you!"

"Yes you did! You even wagered that you would be successful, but I won *that* bet!"

They stepped apart, turned and linked hands again.

"I admit that I issued a challenge to that effect," Jack conceded, "but I abandoned the idea of the wager after I kissed you in the garden—"

"Hush!" Thea threw a scandalized glance over her shoulder at the other dancers. "Someone will hear you."

Jack shrugged. Thea hurried in to seize the moment.

"Am I then supposed to believe that I only won because you let me, Lord Merlin? And am I also supposed to accept that if you *had* tried to seduce me, I should have noticed the difference in your behaviour?"

"Most definitely you would! And—"

"And?"

Jack raised his eyebrows. There was a twinkle in his eyes that made Thea even crosser. "My dear Miss Shaw, you would have succumbed! I would bet any money!"

"Oh!" Thea stamped her foot, and then tried to pretend it was one of the dance steps as others in the set looked at her curiously. It was infuriating, particularly as he was right. She sighed angrily, caught Jack's eye and the gleam of speculative amusement in it, and almost squeaked with annoyance. "Lord Merlin, you are the most provoking man! I am trying to quarrel with you but you persist in funning me! Yet it is *not* amusing. You are here being feted by these obsequious people whilst I am suffering their censure!"

Jack bowed. "I acknowledge that. It was foolish of me not to anticipate it."

"You have ruined my reputation!" Thea said wildly, feeling her self-control slipping perilously yet seeming powerless to stop it. "Worse, you have wormed your way into the affections of my family, making them unhappy! Now Ned wants to join the army and Harry wants to be a Corinthian just like you when he grows up and…and Daisy wants a new father! You have turned our heads when you should have left well alone!"

She broke off, realizing that her words had struck a sudden chill. She saw the amusement leave Jack's eyes. He still spoke softly, but there was an undertone of something in his voice that froze her and made all her anger shrivel away.

"If you truly believe that I have deliberately upset your family then you are right to reproach me, Miss Shaw. And if you have a concern for your reputation, I suggest you think hard, for you are contributing to your own downfall even now with your intemperate behaviour!"

It was only then that Thea became aware of every eye upon them, every ear flapping for the next snippet of scandal. She could not believe that she had handed it to them on a plate. She wanted the earth to open up and swallow her whole, but worse than her humiliation was the coldness she now saw in Jack's demeanour, the formality with which he offered her his arm to move off the dance floor. Thea knew that he would not abandon her to the gossips but she also knew that he was performing his duty with no sense of pleasure any more. She could not be certain how those undeniably bitter words had spilled out. Yes, she had been worried about her siblings—oh, yes, Jack had turned their heads, it was true, but more importantly he had turned hers. *That* was what had made her so miserable. She had fallen in love with him and she had no one to blame but herself.

Thea closed her eyes briefly and reopened them, hoping that the sea of curious faces might somehow have disappeared, that the clock would be put back, that she could have another chance. The unyielding hardness of Jack's face, the rigidity with which he kept his distance, told another tale. Around her the sea of tittle-tattle rose and fell and she felt like a cork tossed on its surface. Thea was just wondering in despair whether matters could possibly get any worse when the ballroom door swung open.

There was a silence. Then there was a commotion. Thea saw Lord and Lady Pendle detach themselves from the couple they were speaking with and rush forward with undignified haste. She saw Jack turn, and heard him swear under his breath, but before she could even wonder who had arrived so late in the proceedings, and why they were causing such a fuss, the butler cleared his throat to announce portentously, "The Duke and Duchess of Merlin!"

Chapter Six

Thea drew in a sharp breath.

The Duchess was a tall, patrician *grande dame* in pale gold, with an ice-cool countenance. The Duke, who looked startlingly like an older version of Jack, was equally tall and austere.

Beside them, looking shifty and ill at ease, stood Bertie Pershore.

Thea experienced an almost overwhelming urge to turn and run away, but it was too late. The Duke and Duchess were already disentangling themselves from the Pendles' eager overtures and were coming towards them. Thea made an instinctive movement and Jack's hand closed around her arm like a vice, holding her by his side.

"Jack, darling!" To Thea's amazement the Duchess's face broke into a smile of startling sweetness. She came up and kissed her son on the cheek, then turned the full warmth of her smile on Thea, taking both her hands.

"Miss Shaw. Bertie has told us all about you. We are so pleased that you are going to marry Jack!"

"I…" Thea shot Bertie a look of confusion and dire retribution. Her former friend seemed to shrivel beneath her glare. "I am very pleased to make your acquaintance, Your Grace, but I fear—"

She broke off as Jack's hand tightened on her arm almost murderously. He moved smoothly into the gap.

"Pray do not put Miss Shaw to the blush, Mama! We had not announced our betrothal yet."

Thea shot him a glance of mingled horror and confusion. Jack smiled back at her blandly.

"No doubt you were wishing for us to meet your betrothed, Jack, before making a formal announcement!" The Duke of Merlin now stepped forward to shake his son by the hand. Thea felt his gaze on her face, as direct and searching as Jack's own. He smiled at her. "I fear the Duchess is precipitate, my dear Miss Shaw, but it is only because she is so pleased to welcome you into the family!"

"Of course!" The Duchess enveloped Thea in a scented hug. Thea submitted, wilting with shock. "Miss Shaw—Thea—may I call you Thea as you are to be my daughter? I could scarce believe it when Bertie told me. But I am so pleased!" The Duchess turned to Jack with shining eyes. "It is high time you settled down, dear boy, as we have been telling you this age past—"

"Yes, Mama!" Jack said hastily. "Perhaps we could continue this conversation later?"

"By all means," the Duke murmured. He turned to Thea, his eyes twinkling. "Will you grant me a dance, my dear, to grace the Pendles' Ball? They will be *aux anges* to be first with the news and to be able to boast that the Duke led out his future daughter-in-law!"

Thea realized that this was not so much an invitation as a direct order. Jack clearly did, too. He gave her a rueful smile, kissed her fingers in a way that sent Thea's feelings into even more of a spin, and offered his arm to his mother.

"May I offer you some refreshments, Mama? You may then tell me how you come to be here, for I am all agog—"

Thea was desperate to know, as well, but the Duke was waiting. She took his arm gingerly, almost as though she were afraid he would explode on touch. She was convinced that this extraordinary masquerade must come to an end very soon. The Duke covered her fingers very briefly with his own in a gesture that Thea was surprised to find gave her immense reassurance.

"No need to look so terrified, my dear!" the Duke murmured. "I am the gentlest of fellows, despite my reputation!"

Thea laughed a little shakily. "I do not doubt it, Your Grace, but if you were to find that your good nature had been abused by a misunderstanding—"

Merlin's dark blue gaze, so like his son's, fixed upon her. He spoke with emphasis. "But I shall not do so, shall I, my dear Miss Shaw? I am persuaded that you are the ideal wife for my son, and further, I am delighted to see that it is a love match!"

Thea was silent. Indeed, she was not certain what she could say. The Duke of Merlin was clearly too intelligent a man not to have read the situation correctly, but she realized that for reasons of his own he had chosen to interpret it differently. Indeed, the warning in his tone as he led her into the dance told her not to pursue the subject, least of all in public. She would be a fool to do so—the arrival of the Duke and Duchess had transformed her situation from one of scandalous misfortune to blazing triumph. All around her Thea could hear the buzz of censure transformed into pure envy.

"Betrothed to the Marquis of Merlin!... Why did she not say so before... Dear Thea has so much natural delicacy... Indeed, the Duke seems much taken with his future daughter..."

It was true that the Duke did seem most attentive to her, Thea thought, feeling more than a little dazed. His conversation was light but he complimented her sincerely on her dancing and at the end said, just loud enough for the gossips to hear, "Thank you, my dear I suppose I must hand you back to my son now before he starts looking daggers at me! He is to be envied such a charming bride..."

Jack was indeed watching them and his expressio

was quite different from the coldness he had shown
Thea a brief half hour before. His gaze fixed on her
face with an intensity that made her feel strangely
self-conscious. She knew that he was only playing up
to the situation, but it added to her confusion. As the
Duke escorted her from the floor, Jack took her arm
proprietorially in his.

"If you are not too fatigued, my love, will you
grant me one waltz before we retire? Now that our
secret is out, there can be no need to dissemble…"

Thea narrowed her eyes. Jack seemed to have
moved from the formality of addressing her as "Miss
Shaw" to the intimacy of "my love" rather too
swiftly. There was a spark of amusement in his eyes
that suggested he was about to play the situation to
the full, and she itched to give him the set-down he
so richly deserved. But the Duke and Duchess were
smiling indulgently and as she hesitated, Jack slid an
arm about her waist and steered her back onto the
dance floor.

"My lord," she began, as soon as they were out
of earshot.

"Jack," the Marquis murmured, his lips twitching.
"You really must address me by my given name now
that we are betrothed…Thea!"

"We are *not* betrothed." Thea muttered. "I have
no notion how this occurred but I have no wish to be
married to you—"

"Hush!" Jack touched her lips fleetingly with one
finger and the contact silenced her more effectively

than any words could. "Is it your wish to reverse your good fortune? Half an hour ago you were berating me for ruining your reputation. Now you are triumphantly restored and about to throw it all away."

The music struck up and they started to circle the floor. Thea pinned a bright smile on her face, one that she hoped successfully portrayed the happy sentiments of a young lady in love.

"Yes, my lord."

"Jack."

"I perfectly understand that, but the price of such a situation—"

"Is too high?"

Jack's hands moved against her back, drawing her closer to him, and Thea was suddenly and devastatingly aware of him. All coherent thoughts flew straight out of her head. She looked up into Jack's face and felt herself tremble at the look of unabashed sensuality in his eyes.

"Are you sure, Thea?" Jack's breath brushed her cheek, sending the shivers down her spine. His lips just grazed the corner of her mouth. Thea tried to think straight, tried to cut through the web of desire that threatened to envelop her. It was no easy matter.

"Surely this is all a pretence, my lord," she said breathlessly. "You cannot wish for a wife! You are temperamentally unsuited to such an enterprise as marriage."

"I assure you I am becoming more inclined to it by the moment."

Jack's hands slid into the small of her back, holding her hard against his body so that their legs almost tangled. The sensation of the hard length of him pressed against her softness was almost her undoing. Thea gasped.

"Jack!"

"Well, that's an improvement!" There was a note in Jack's voice that threatened to undermine her completely. He was making no secret of the fact that he wanted her. It was in his voice, in his touch.

"You must accept what has happened, Thea," he continued softly. "My parents have trapped us both— so neatly I have to applaud their strategy! They have wanted me to marry for a long time. Finally I have presented them with the opportunity to enforce that wish and I cannot find it in my heart to regret it."

"But surely we are to call off this fictitious betrothal?" Thea searched his face unhappily. It seemed extraordinary to her that Jack might be prepared to go through with it. "Surely you cannot wish to marry me!"

Jack looked down at her and she saw his gaze soften. "Why not? You are delightful and entirely suitable."

"But…" Thea made a despairing gesture, "I know you are putting a good face on this, my lord, but I do not expect that you even like me very much, let alone wish to marry me! After what I said to you earlier—"

Jack's smile faded. "Did you mean it, Thea?"

Thea looked away. His gaze was too penetrating.

It made her feel vulnerable. But even so she was aware that she had treated him badly and owed him an apology.

"No. I am sorry. It is true that you have turned our heads, my lord, but I acquit you any deliberate intent."

"Thank you!" Jack flashed her a grin. "Then we are reconciled...and betrothed—my love."

Thea blushed at the warmth of his tone. She was aware that he had skated very adroitly over her objections, but she could be as stubborn as Clementine when she chose. She frowned. "But—"

Jack's arms tightened about her again. "Thea, if you make one more objection I shall kiss you here and now."

Thea felt a shaky smile start. "Oh, Jack—"

"Well, perhaps I shall kiss you anyway..."

"Pray be serious!" Thea tried to focus her mind. "You have been trapped into this—"

"Yes, and I do not object at all!" Jack's tone became more serious. "Do you?"

Thea looked away from that searching blue gaze. "I do not know." What she did know was that she loved Jack but she was afraid. Afraid that whilst there was an undeniable attraction between them, that was not sufficient to sustain a marriage. Afraid because his society lifestyle was so different from her own that she was not sure she could adapt. Afraid because suddenly she felt that she did not know him well a all. She knew that she loved him, but she did not dare to tell him so.

"I do not know," she repeated softly.

She missed the fleeting expression that crossed Jack's face as he looked down on her bent head, the combination of disappointment and hurt, chased away by determination. His arms loosened about her. The dance was finishing, anyway.

"Come," he said, "I'll take you home now."

When Thea glanced at him his expression was quite blank, but she could tell from his voice that he had withdrawn from her. The excitement, the sensual pleasure, had drained away, leaving her feeling uncertain and cold, and suddenly she was not at all sure what she was going to do.

The Duchess talked for most of the journey back to Oakmantle, directing her conversation to Thea with an excitement that was both touching and disconcerting. Jack, who knew his mother of old, realized that now she had the bit between her teeth she would be as irresistible as a tidal wave. Yet when the Duchess started to speak about wedding dates and trousseau and Thea turned her away with slight answers, Jack felt his heart sink. Here was the confirmation of what Thea had said earlier—she was not at all sure that she wished to marry him.

Jack shifted a little on the carriage seat and maintained his silence, cursing himself for failing to declare his feelings before the Duke and Duchess had arrived. Now that they had been trapped into an engagement, Thea would never believe that he genuinely wished to marry her anyway. The only thing that had prevented his declaration before had been Bertie's assertion that Thea did not trust him. A rake's reputation, Jack thought bitterly, was a damned encumbrance when one wished to make the first honourable proposal of one's life.

She would not marry him for his money. Jack acknowledged that he had known that even before he had told her of the value of her father's sculptures. A smile curved his lips in the darkness. So he would have to persuade her of the genuineness of his feelings. He would have to court her with irreproachable decorum. The problem was that that would take time and he did not feel inclined to patience. And he might even fail to convince her. In which case he would have to seduce her.

Desire shot through him at the very thought. He shifted again, concentrating fiercely on the intellectual side of his predicament rather than the physical. Just how persuadable would Thea prove to be? Surely a bluestocking should be susceptible to an approach through the intellect? Yet she was convinced that he had been obliged to offer for her against his inclinations and once she had an idea she could be very tenacious.

How persuadable did he want her to be, in truth? Jack watched the carriage lights flicker over Thea's bent head and smiled again. If the thought of wooing her was sweet, the thought of seducing her was even sweeter.

"Very sorry, Thea, old thing, but what could I do?" Bertie spread his hands apologetically. He looked like a whipped spaniel. "There was Merlin demanding to know what was going on, and there was I—"

"You were supposed to be in Yorkshire, not London!" Thea abandoned her seat beside him on the garden bench and leaped to her feet. "Really, Bertie, this is absurd! Whatever can you have said to the Duke and Duchess to send them down here with the harebrained notion that Jack wanted to marry me?"

Bertie looked acutely uncomfortable. "Anyone could see the way that matters were tending between you and Jack! Once I had told Merlin a little about you and explained that you had captured Jack's affections he became positively indulgent to me! Never seen the old man like that before!"

Thea glared. "Yes, because you handed him what he wanted on a plate! Oh, Bertie, you know that the Duke has been angling to marry Jack off for these five years past and now you have played right into his hands!"

"Nothing wrong in that," Bertie said virtuously. He ran a finger around his collar where his neckcloth was feeling particularly tight. "Don't see the problem myself. Thought you'd be glad to be rescued from that nest of vipers at Pendle Hall, Thea. Ripping your character to shreds—''

"That is beside the point!'' Thea threw her hands up in the air. "Jack will not release me from this so-called engagement and my future mother-in-law is setting a wedding date—''

"Good thing, too!'' Bertie got to his feet. "Just the thing for you to marry Jack. All your brothers and sisters are delighted—Ned was telling me only yesterday how pleased he was—''

"Well of course he is! Now he has someone to sponsor him through the army!''

Bertie looked at her mildly. "Tell you what, Thea, I'm glad you didn't marry me. You used to be such a sweet-natured girl and now you've turned into a shrew! Perhaps Jack should change his mind before it's too late.''

Thea stopped pacing and stared at him. Bertie's words had somehow hit home. He was right. She could remember a time when few matters had ruffled the smooth calm of her temperament. Certainly she had never been as cross-grained and shrewish as she was now. That had been…three weeks ago. It felt like a lifetime, and it was Jack Merlin who had effected the change by stirring up her life until it could never be the same again. She sat down a little heavily.

"Oh, dear. I have become so very cross about everything, have I not!''

Bertie patted her hand. "Never mind. Perhaps yo

can make up for it, old girl. Especially to Jack, for he does care about you, you know. He told me so.''

To hear that was the final straw. Thea burst into tears. Bertie backed away hastily, a look of horror on his lugubrious features.

''I say, there's no need for that, Thea!''

''Sorry, Bertie!'' Thea sniffed, groping for her handkerchief, grasping after her self-control. She gave a hiccuping sob. ''I shall be better directly.''

She blew her nose hard, trying not to give in to the abject misery that threatened her. She felt wretched. She had quarrelled with Jack from the night of the ball until that very morning, six days later. During that time he had called every day, taken her driving, courted her in exactly the conventional way that her parents would have approved. He had been the epitome of good behaviour, he had gently rebuffed all her attempts to break the engagement and his baffling good humour and steadfast persistence had made Thea want to cry.

Only that morning he had pressed her gently about a wedding date and she had snapped at him that she would not marry him, would never marry him. She had seen an expression cross his face so quickly she had wondered if she had imagined seeing the hurt there, and then he had turned on his heel and gone out. Thea had gone up to her room and cried, without really understanding why, and then she had kept herself very busy until Bertie had arrived. Now, despite herself, another small sob escaped her.

Bertie gave a hunted look around. "Shall I call your sister?" he asked hopefully. "Needs a woman's touch, and all that!"

Thea shook her head. "Everyone is out today. Ned and Harry are playing for the village side at cricket, Skeffie has taken Daisy and Clara to watch, and Clementine is visiting with the Duchess." She brightened a little, scrubbing her eyes. "Do you know, Bertie, the Duchess believes that she might even make Clemmie presentable! Can you believe that? She was talking about giving her a Season next year." She slumped again. "But, of course, if I do not marry Jack…"

Bertie snorted. "Marry or not, you're going a step too far there, Thea! Clementine presentable? I'll wager a monkey against it!"

Thea gave a watery giggle. "Maybe you are right and it is too much to hope for! Oh, Bertie—" she gave him an impulsive hug "—you are the very best of good friends and I am sorry that I have been so horrible to you!"

After Bertie had left, Thea donned an apron over her old blue muslin and walked listlessly to the herb garden. It was a beautiful spring day and the clumps of mint, parsley and thyme were flourishing in the warmth by the old brick garden wall. Thea walked on, past the hyssop and rosemary, until she reached the lavender bed. She took a small knife from the pocket in her apron and cut some new sprigs before going back inside the house.

Oakmantle Hall was very quiet. Thea went softly up the stairs and into her own bedchamber, where she busied herself folding the clean bed linen and storing it away in the armada chest. She folded the sheets, put the sprigs of lavender between them and closed the lid. The scent of lavender was on her fingers, reminding her of that day in the garden, the way that Jack had held her. Perhaps he would not come back now that she had been so horrible to him. Thea blinked the tears back. She seemed to be turning into a watering pot these days and it was most infuriating.

She did not hear the front door open or the tread on the stairs, did not even realize anyone was there until she heard a step in the bedroom doorway and turned to see Jack lounging against the doorpost. He did not speak, simply stood there watching her. There was a look in his eyes that made Thea catch her breath. The words dried on the tip of her tongue.

"Jack."

"Thea?" Jack straightened up and came towards her, moving with what seemed to Thea's unnerved eyes to be the predatory concentration of a cat. Two thoughts occurred to her simultaneously. One was that they had never been completely alone together in the house. The second was that Jack was a rake. And even as she thought it she realized his intention and her heart started to race. She took a step back, crushing one of the sprigs of lavender that had fallen to the floor. The lavender smell entwined itself around them. Jack stepped closer, his eyes darkening as he inhaled the scent.

Thea's words came out in a rush. "Jack, I must speak to you."

Jack barely paused. "We'll talk later."

"But—"

A second more and Thea realized that he was not going to waste his breath arguing with her. Not when he could kiss her. He leaned forward, closing the distance between them slowly, sliding one arm about her gently. His lips barely brushed hers, the merest touch, yet Thea felt the echo of that contact all the way through her body. Her hand came up to rest on his chest and she made one last effort, leaning back a little.

"Jack..." She found she had to clear her throat. "What are you doing?"

The danger and gentleness in his eyes made her feel weaker still.

"I am going to seduce you, Thea." His voice was as husky as hers. "I have courted you with decorum, I have tried to reason with you, but if this is what I have to do to persuade you of my genuine desire to marry you...."

Thea's eyes were huge. "Oh! I am persuaded!"

Jack shook his head. "Too late. If I let you go now you will think of another reason to refuse me. This is the only thing that I can do to claim you for my own..."

To claim you for my own... Thea gave a little gasp

that was lost as his mouth took hers again, this time holding nothing back. The kiss was hot and hungry, spiralling down into desire. Thea felt the passion flood through her like a riptide, huge, powerful, too urgent to resist. She did not even try—at last her mind was telling her that there was no need to hold back, for Jack wanted her for herself alone, not to rescue her reputation nor to help her family but because he wanted to claim her as his, body and soul.

She was trembling as Jack drew her down onto the yielding softness of the bed, and she lay back gratefully for she was not certain that she could stand any longer. The kiss had softened into sweetness now, long and lingering but no less breathless. Finally Jack propped himself up on one elbow, pulled the lace mobcap off her curls and tossed it across the room.

''I have wanted to do that for a long time,'' he murmured. ''And as for this monstrosity of an apron—'' His fingers had found the ties and were tugging hard.

Thea murmured a faint protest and Jack bent his head and kissed her again. And again, until she could scarcely speak.

''Thea...'' When Jack let her go this time, Thea simply looked at him in mute silence. ''I wanted to tell you that when you ran into my arms that day at the church I felt something far stronger for you than I had ever felt for any woman before.''

His fingers were undoing the buttons of her gown

with deft skill. Thea smiled a little as she watched him. "Was that not desire, Jack?" she whispered.

"Perhaps," Jack conceded. "Yes, definitely. But it was not just that…"

He opened her gown and slid his hand inside, baring her small, gently rounded breasts. Thea gasped and arched against him. She was filled with the most sublime ache and when Jack bent his head to her breast and captured one rosy peak in his mouth, she felt a simultaneous rush of exquisite relief and an even deeper need, awoken by the roughness of his cheek against her skin, the teasing of his tongue.

"It was much more than that," Jack continued, his lips against her skin. "My feelings did not take long to deepen into admiration and…love. So you must be gentle with me, sweetheart, for it hasn't happened to me before…"

Thea's heart seemed to do a somersault. "Do you really love me?"

"Yes…" Jack's hands were drifting over her skin in distracting circles, stroking, soothing, making her melt again with love and desire. He leaned over to kiss her long and hard. She could feel her body softening again, aching for him, opening as Jack moved across her, one leg sliding between hers.

"I think you have done this before, though," she murmured.

"It's different…" Jack's words were a breath against her bare skin. He bent his head to her breasts again, teasing her until she dug her fingers into his back in exquisite agony. Her whole body was slipping and sliding down into delicious pleasure. She never wanted it to stop.

Jack sat up reluctantly and tugged off his boots, tossed them aside, and dealt summarily with the rest of his clothes. Neither of them spoke as he rejoined her on the bed and removed the rest of her garments with equal ruthlessness. The touch of his skin against hers made Thea gasp in shock and pleasure. She shivered as he started to kiss her again, long, slow kisses that drugged the senses until she was desperate for him.

Urgency caught them both then, sweet and strong, and Jack shifted again, drawing her to him, parting her thighs, sliding into her gently.

Thea gave a soft gasp and Jack lowered his head, brushing his lips across hers.

"Thea?"

She opened her eyes, dazzling blue, bright with desire. She did not speak, simply raised a hand to tangle in his hair and bring his head down to hers so that she could kiss him again. All the love and triumphant possessiveness fused within him then, and slowly, with infinite gentleness, he made her his.

When Jack awoke the sun had moved across the room and was lying in a bright bar across the tangled bed linens. Thea was kneeling at the end of the bed, craning her neck to see the clock on the mantelpiece, the sunlight turning her hair into a web of bright gold, light and insubstantial like a fairy net. It was a net that had trapped him firmly and would never let him go. Jack examined the thought, the strange but satisfying rightness of it, and felt a smile start to curl his lips. He stretched luxuriously.

At his slight movement, Thea turned her head towards him. She was in shadow, every curve outlined in black like a silhouette. Jack felt his body stir. He told himself that he had a lifetime in which to watch Thea, to memorize her face, to explore all those tantalizing lines and curves. However, when she almost lost her balance on the tangled bedclothes and leaned over the foot of the bed to steady herself, the need suddenly seemed urgent.

Jack moved swiftly, catching Thea around the waist and tumbling her back down beside him. She lay still looking up at him, her eyes widening as his desire communicated itself to her. Jack brushed the hair away from her face, bending to kiss her.

"I am thinking that whilst I have made a most humbling declaration of love to you, sweetheart, you have not actually told me that you love me…"

Thea looked at him. Her face was flushed pink, her lips parted. "Oh… I thought that you knew. Yes, of course I do…"

Jack kissed her softly again, his lips clinging to hers. She felt sweet and warm and wonderfully yielding.

"In that case I must go and get a special licence At once. There is not a moment to lose."

He felt Thea shift beneath him. Her hands caressed him tentatively and he drew in a sharp breath.

"Jack—" it was a whisper "—can it not wait a little?"

"Well..." He moved inside her again, gently, tantalizingly. Thea gasped. He bent his head to her breast. "Perhaps it can wait just a little longer..."

Whereas he knew that he could not. As he reached for her and she responded in full measure, all Jack's good resolutions fled. He had meant to be tender, to introduce her to the pleasures of making love gradually and with consideration, but her natural sensuality swept all of that aside. This was a wild lovemaking with none of the gentleness of their previous encounter and at the end they were both dazzled, sated with pleasure. Jack wrapped his arms about Thea as they slowly drifted down to earth.

"The children will be back soon," she murmured against his shoulder.

Jack made a sound of sleepy contentment.

"We must get up." Thea wriggled out of his embrace and groped around for her clothes, which seemed to be scattered to the four corners of the room. "Daisy will want her story, and Clara will want to play for you and the boys will want some more cricket coaching if the village team lost—"

Jack rolled over and looked at her. His midnight-blue gaze raked her lazily from head to foot. "And what do you want from me, my love?"

"Oh, just to marry you," Thea said airily. "That

will suffice!'' She looked at him and smiled. ''I know those sculptures are worth a fortune but I could not bear to sell them for sentimental reasons! My father was prodigious fond of them! So I am sorry, Jack...'' She bent over to kiss him, ''I have to marry you for your money! It is the only solution!''

* * * * *

Modern Romance™
...seduction and
passion guaranteed

Tender Romance™
...love affairs that
last a lifetime

Sensual Romance™
...sassy, sexy and
seductive

Blaze™
...sultry days and
steamy nights

Medical Romance™
...medical drama on
the pulse

Historical Romance™
...rich, vivid and
passionate

27 new titles every month.

*With all kinds of Romance for
every kind of mood...*

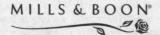

MILLS & BOON®

DON'T MISS...

VOLUME FIVE

On sale 1st November 2002